TROUBLE NO MORE

TROUBLE NO MORE

Crime Fiction Inspired by Southern Rock and the Blues

EDITED BY
MARK WESTMORELAND

DOWN & OUT BOOKS

Down & Out Books
3959 Van Dyke Road, Suite 265
Lutz, FL 33558
DownAndOutBooks.com

Cover design by Zach McCain

ISBN: 1-64396-230-2
ISBN-13: 978-1-64396-230-6

TABLE OF CONTENTS

SET ONE: THE MOST PAINFUL ACTS

"As they say in the Bible, that you're supposed to rejoice
when people die and mourn when they're born,
because it's one of the most painful acts
you go through in life, is being born, and dying."
—Gregg Allman

STATESBORO BLUES
With Respect to Blind Willie McTell
Brian Panowich

Before.

Well, listen here a second and I'll tell you what. To the best of my recollection, anyway.

Man, when the taste of your own blood becomes so familiar, so nostalgic even, that a mouthful of wet copper begins to act as a trigger for memories of the most important landmarks in your life, my brother, it is time to seriously reevaluate the road you've been heading down.

I'll start with the night I met Kaycee Jane.

I was twenty years old. Just a pup in the middle of my sophomore year at Georgia Southern, and as it would turn out, spending our Thursday nights at Blind Willie's—a dank little shithole bar just walking distance from campus—was a regular thing for the both of us, me and her, but I never caught so much as a glimpse of Kaycee Jane before that night. I don't for the life of me know how she kept slipping by me, Thursday after Thursday. I guess I drank too much even back then. I guess, hell—that's not entirely honest. There's no guessing involved. I'd been prone to blackout drinking ever since I'd discovered my Deddy's stash of Beam back in high school. But that ain't the point. See, that night I must've been sippin' it slow because once *she* came into my line of sight, *she* became all I saw. Like in the movies, when the background goes all fuzzy and out of focus except for the girl.

Wait, that's not entirely true, either. There was nothing fuzzy or out of focus about that sledgehammer that come swinging at my head about thirty seconds later. And thank holy Christ, too, because if that five-fingered bowling ball of meat and bone had connected with my noodle, that would've been all she wrote for your boy. It would've all been over before it started.

No Kaycee Jane.

No memory.

Shit, no me either, for all I know. That fucker was massive.

But as luck would have it, that ain't what happened. Like I said, I must've been sippin' it slow that night because I just managed to sidestep that sucker punch and found my footing without even spilling my drink. Now, I ain't fool enough to lie and say I took ol' boy down all quick-like like Swayze in *Roadhouse*. It wasn't like that at all. It took some work. More work than I thought I was capable of dishing out, but this wasn't about no money owed or two dudes arguing over baseball. This here ruckus was about a girl—*the* girl. It took a while, and that fight lasted all the way through a crowd of shouting heathens egging us on until we finally busted through the front door and kept to beatin' on each other outside. A circle of drunk frat-holes surrounded us, all hootin' and hollerin' until just when I thought I'd done given it all I could give, that big boy gave me an in, and I landed the perfect swing at the perfect time. Needless to say, that meathead cowboy Kaycee Jane came with that night finally went down. And, damn, son, when I say he went down, he went down hard—like a fresh-cut redwood. I spun that joker around until he took a picture-perfect faceplant into the shale-covered parking lot that would've made my Deddy proud. I'd like to tell y'all he didn't get but a couple licks in, but that fella did a job on me that night that turned my face into what resembled after-pictures of DeNiro via *Raging Bull*. And you wanna know something? I truly don't even remember how the scuffle started, but I'm sure it was my mouth. I'm almost positive I said something *way* out of line. But who could blame me? I couldn't help it. I saw her. And that's all it took for my jaws to start flappin'. See, I *saw* her, and I knew inside of that split second that I'd never be able to *unsee* her. So, at the end of that particular Thursday night, I might have sprained my left pinkie all to hell and lost two teeth, but the girl of my dreams picked me up off the ground, drove me home, and she never left.

I'd call that a fair trade.

But anyway, back to what I was saying before all that. The first time my wife-to-be kissed me, there was blood in my mouth. Just like right now.

Now.

I ran my tongue over the broken stumps and swollen gums where my fake front teeth used to be. My Deddy would be spinning pinwheels in his grave if he knew, after all the money he spent to fix my choppers that first time back in college, that they were now all broke to shit again on the floor of this rank-ass basement. I think it's a basement anyway. I can't see for nothing due to the pepper spray they hit me with, but I do know they hauled me down some stairs. Yeah, there were two doors and some stairs. Then they just dropped me here—right before they kicked my teeth in.

I could take pain. I'd gotten used to it, but I'm sure I blacked out for a second. I saw my wife in the darkness. If I could get to her. If I could get to Kaycee Jane, she would patch me up, no questions asked. She'd tell me I was going to be okay. She always said stuff like that straight to my face without batting an eye, blanket declarations of guaranteed happy endings that she insisted were right around the corner. She'd swear to it, bless her heart. She always held tight to some rock-solid belief that there was still good in the world, no matter how bad I made things or how sideways the situation always went. Sometimes I even came close to believing it myself.

Close, but never all the way down the rabbit hole.

Most of the time I just mumbled something moronic and walked away all resentful of her for all that damn optimism. How stupid is that, right? Okay, now you're beginning to get a picture of the kind of asshole I turned out to be.

Kaycee Jane followed me to Nashville from Statesboro after graduation. She just dropped everything she had planned—everything her parents had planned—her whole goddamn life—to follow me to Music City. I couldn't believe it. How did I get so lucky? Girls like her don't gamble their carefully preordained futures on guys like me. Girls like Kaycee Jane don't play roulette, and if they do, they damn sure don't bet it all on twenty-one black, but that's what this one did. She was without a doubt my biggest fan, and from day one after that showdown at Blind Willie's, she became my sole partner in my ridiculous crusade to turn an East Georgia hick and his pawn shop Epiphone guitar into the next big heartbreaker on Music Row. Looking back on it all, I'm pretty sure the only heart I ever broke was hers—over and over and over again. I know as sure as I can taste that jar of pennies in my mouth again, she would have left me years before she finally did if it wasn't for Gracie.

Ah, Gracie.

Even lying here on a cold cement floor in the middle of who-the-fuck-knows-where, with my mouth on fire and my eyes welded shut, the thought of that little kid puts a smile on my face. It hurt to smile, but I managed. That little girl is the one thing I did right in twenty-eight years of doing wrong. The one thing untainted by her old man. She's the reason I'm back here in Nashville—the reason I left my safety net back in Statesboro. Kaycee Jane made the rules and I don't blame her one bit. I get to see Gracie twice a year. Her birthday, which I missed—again. And Father's Day—tomorrow. Kaycee Jane don't even owe me that much, but to this day she still thinks maybe things will change—her infernal optimism. Maybe she's right. Maybe they will.

Who am I kidding? Have y'all been listening?

Last year, Kaycee Jane still wasn't ready to let me know where she and Gracie were living, so she had me meet them at a doughnut shop in Franklin. Daylight Doughnuts or some shit like that. She said Gracie loved the place. I had to take her word for it because I couldn't count three things my own daughter loved without guessing. I was never around to find out. But on that day, our last Father's Day, for almost an hour, I hung out with that six-year-old little girl, eating donuts and crullers, with milk for the kiddo and coffee for Dad, while her mom, wrapped in a short light-blue sundress that owned every passer-by, waited outside sipping her flower-power tea at one of the shop's outdoor tables.

Father's Day, my one day with Gracie, my one memory unspoiled by the blood-in-mouth curse—until now. Now this snatch-and-grab debacle would be my new go-to Father's Day memory.

I heard the door being unlocked and opened at the top of the stairs to my right. I still couldn't see a thing but could tell when the lights cut on through the pink flesh of my bloated eyelids. After the men—I counted three, maybe four—surrounded me, the first guy down the stairs started to speak. I knew right then exactly what all this shit was about.

"Well, fuck me running, if it ain't Danny-Dan the music man."

The voice belonged to an inbred fuck-stick named RT. And, by the way, those aren't initials that actually stand for something either. That's his entire name, R and T, just those two letters. His backwoods hillbilly parents just thought it sounded cool. And, get this, they figured that one day he could just fill in the blanks if he wanted to—when he growed up and all. He told me all about it one time over a few beers at the Exit/Inn. I mean, what in holy hell? Who brags about stuff like that? I guess the same kind of guy that says shit like "fuck me running" or would call me "Danny-Dan the music man." RT was a short, neckless ball of muscle. He came to Nashville by way of Mississippi for the same reason everyone else comes to this city. But it only took him about three months to find out no one wants to offer a recording contract to a short, bald, meathead country singer with a homoerotic fixation on Elvis. Coupled with the fact that he couldn't sing a lick, he opted to put those massive guns of his to good use as an enforcer for a big fish named Powell. Leroy Powell. I know all this because I worked for that big fish, too, doing the same kinda thing. It's also worth mentioning that I also kinda stole something from Powell before I quit the scene and rolled back home to Georgia. I'm guessing he wants it back. And I'm also guessing that's why I'm down here.

"Goddamn, RT, was all this necessary? It's going to cost a fortune to fix these teeth—again." I rolled over to face where I thought he might be standing and gestured from behind my back with my bound wrists. I hoped he wasn't the one who jumped me and brought me here, and he might take a little mercy on an old acquaintance—at least cut my hands free from the pinching zip ties. RT squatted down next to my head and rolled me over onto my back, pinning my arms between the floor and me. I reckon old acquaintances be damned.

He giggled a little before he spoke. "You know, Powell about shit himself when he heard you were in back in town. Hell, Danny-boy, I couldn't believe it either. You're one dumb son of bitch, man. You know that, right?"

I spit some blood across my cheek. "Look, RT, I know what this is about. I still have it. I brought it with me. It's back at the motel. I was meaning to give it back, anyway. I never felt right about taking it in the first place. Just untie me and we can go over there and get it, or just bring me to Leroy and we can work all this out."

"No need, Danny-boy. The man's on his way here right now. He told me to keep you uncomfortable but alive. He wants to talk to you hisself."

"C'mon RT. It's just a Telecaster. And it's a reissue at that. It's not like it belonged to Tom Petty or Springsteen. I'm trying to make good here—"

RT kicked me in the short ribs with enough force to slide my entire body a good twelve or so inches across the floor. The pain shot through my abdomen like rough-cut lengths of rebar. I might have blacked out again but only for a second—no Kaycee Jane this time. Just a hit to the kidney that ensured that even if I made it out of this room alive, I'd be pissing blood for a month. RT chuckled again. All the other pricks standing with him did, too. "Listen, Dan, I don't know anything about your troubles with Powell, and to be honest, I don't give a pinch of dried horse shit, either. I just do what I'm told. The man told me to keep you uncomfortable, and here you are talking to me all familiar, like you was...I don't know...comfortable? So, I had to hurt you some. So, do you want to keep chatting me up? Are you still feeling comfortable?"

I spit more blood on the floor but most of it just got in my beard or drizzled down my neck.

"Good answer, Dan. Now, you stay uncomfortable a little while longer, and if you need help maintaining that condition, you just holler and me and the fellas will be happy to come on back down and remedy that shit."

That's all I heard before RT and his crew took to the creaky wooden stairs and headed back up. I waited for the click, and the lights went out.

"Jesus," I thought out loud. "These people are gonna kill me over a thousand-dollar guitar."

I was never going to see Kaycee Jane again, or Gracie, because of a stupid decision I made on a whim to stick Leroy's git-fiddle into my case instead of my own beat-up Epiphone on the night I left Nashville? I mean, damn, after all the horrible things I've done, I'm going to die of terminal stupid. I almost laughed. Shit, man, I figured Powell wouldn't even miss the damn thing. It's not like he didn't have a warehouse full of guitars worth a whole hell of a lot more. And—he couldn't even play worth a shit. I think I did manage to laugh a little at that.

I wiggled my wrists and strained to break the zip tie, but I only made it worse. I was beginning to get some sight back in my left eye, and I could see some thanks to the rim of light coming from around the doorframe at the top of the stairs. I flipped my head franticly from side to side trying to find something I could wedge between my bound feet to rip them free. If I could stand up, I had a shot at getting out of here. Nothing. No luck. Of course not, why would my luck change now? The room was empty except for an old washer and dryer in the far corner to my right and a dusty overturned mop bucket. For a second, I thought maybe I could use the metal casters on the bucket to somehow cut through the binding on my feet, so I started to inch my way toward it. Suddenly it all struck me funny again and I croaked out another laugh. "Hey, Kaycee Jane," I whispered. "I could use a little of your optimism here. If I manage to free myself, with a mop bucket no less, and then somehow make it up those noisy stairs, with one good eye, and then out of a basement through the only door there is—a door that leads directly into a room full of men that already beat me, blinded me, and kicked my teeth in, I swear, baby, I will never complain about your brightside thinking again. I promise." In fact, I swore to her that I'd never complain about anything again. I'd make things right with Powell. I'd make things right with Gracie—with Kaycee Jane. I'd be the man I was the night I first tasted blood in my mouth for her.

"Right," I whispered as I inch-wormed across the cold floor. Maybe I hadn't been listening either.

By the time I reached the bucket, I heard the click of the lock upstairs and light flooded the room.

"Daniel, my brother," Leroy Powell sang from the top of the stairs. He always sang that greeting like the line from the Elton John song of the same name. I always hated that song. Powell knew that as he sashayed down the stairs, pushing his long, thinning hair back over his shoulders with both hands. He looked like he hadn't taken a pair of scissors to that hair or a razor to his face once in the three years I'd been gone. He looked like Jesus would, if Jesus opted to dress like a Flying Burrito Brother. His suede coat had long tassels dangling from the chest and arms that blended seamlessly into his hair. I reckon I was still a touch delirious from the thought of my "escape plan," so I couldn't help but shake my head a little at the thought of how much this guy put into looking like he was a long-lost member of The Black Crowes.

What a douche.

I could see a little better and watched RT and the rest of his crew as they followed Powell down the stairs until they were all standing in a circle around me. Powell lit one of those skinny bitch clove cigarettes with a Zippo, clicked it shut, and then squatted down to face me.

"I can't believe you came back here, Dan." He blew a cloud of that stank-ass smoke directly into my face as he spoke. "But I guess with the wife and kid here, there was always a chance of you showing back up. I just figured you were smarter than that. These guys here"—Powell gestured with his sissy cigarette around the room at RT and all the other monkeys—"they're a bunch of numbnuts. But you, D? You were always the smart one." He took another long drag and blew it out slow. "I guess that's why you did what you did, huh? You thought you were smarter than me, right? You thought you was better than me, Dan? Was that it?"

More blood wheezed onto my beard. This shit wasn't funny anymore. "C'mon Powell, what are you going on about? What's the big deal? You could've got another one anytime. Those things are a dime a dozen."

Powell put his cigarette out on my neck. I shrieked and pulled back, but two of the monkeys jumped down to hold me in place as my skin sizzled. Powell held that clove against my neck until the cherry burned out while he talked. "Not like her, Dan. She was one in a million, you son of a bitch. One in a million and you stole her, right out from under my nose. Made me look like a damn fool, and so now, Danny-boy, you're gonna pay the piper." Powell tossed the burned-out clove on the floor and stood up. Another one of his boys handed him a baseball bat—my baseball bat. See, back at GSU, I played third base for the Eagles. That's how I got into college in the first place, playing baseball, until a few months after I met Kaycee Jane and blew out my knee. I traded in the bat for a guitar. I had chops. That's when I decided to come to Nashville—to be a star. Of course, when music didn't pan out like I wanted, instead of packing it up and going home like Kaycee Jane begged me to do, I fell in with Powell. The money was good, and I had a new daughter to support. I couldn't just leave with my tail between my legs. What could go wrong, right? That bat was my calling card when I did collections. I wasn't going to be able to beat men half to death with a guitar, so the bat was the logical choice. I knew how to handle it. I also knew what it was capable of doing to a person's body. I became acutely aware of that fact while I was lying on my back, watching Powell caress the damn thing like a woman's thigh.

"Please, Leroy," I begged. "Don't do this. I've got it back at my motel room. I was just telling RT that. It's still in the same shape it was in when I took it. I swear it, man. I barely even played her. Just take it back and let me go. I'm sorry, man. Please. I got a little girl."

Powell stopped stroking the bat and cocked his head at me. He narrowed his eyes and squatted back down. "What's back at your motel room, Dan?"

"The Tele, man, the Tele. I'm sorry I took it. You don't have to do this."

Confusion played like soft static over Powell's face. He looked over at RT and then back at me. "What Tele?"

Now, at this point, I had to admit, I was confused. Everything I said next came out like a question. "The '52 Telecaster? The blonde reissue? The one I stole from you three years ago?"

Powell's expression didn't change. He still looked as confused as I felt, so I kept rambling. "I don't know why I did it, Leroy.

You were always good to me, man. I just figured since you had so many, you wouldn't even care if it was gone. I was wrong, man, so wrong. And I'm sorry. Let me make it right."

Powell's blank expression slowly eased into a smile, and then he started to chuckle a little before finally bursting into a full belly laugh that infected everyone in the room—me included. The whole room erupted with uncomfortable laughter. *Shit,* I thought, *maybe this had all been a huge mistake.* When Powell started twirling the bat in a figure eight above my head, all the laughter faded.

"I always wondered what happened to that thing," he said. "I figured one of those pretty-boy dipshits from the label always slabbin' at my place to earn street cred stole it." He stared at the bat as it swirled in the air. "Man, I wrote that thing off forever ago. I got me a real '52 now. It used to belong to one of them dudes from..."—Powell stopped twirling the length of wood for a moment and snapped his fingers at one of his men—"...who used to own the '52?"

"Lee Freeman," the man answered.

"Right, right," Powell said, but the name still didn't ring a bell. He laid the bat across his shoulders, behind his neck. "Who'd he play for again?"

"Strawberry Alarm Clock," the same man answered.

"That's right, Strawberry fuckin' Alarm Clock. 'Incense and Peppermints.' You remember them, Dan, don't ya?"

I inched up onto my shoulder the best I could. I felt a little inflated with some newfound hope. "If this ain't about the Tele, then what is this all this about, Leroy? This has to be a mistake."

He swung the bat down off his shoulders and nestled it firm against my cheekbone like a golfer teeing up a shot. The banter was clearly over, and he poured as much bile and venom as he could into one word.

"Raylene."

"Raylene?" I repeated, confused as ever.

Powell pressed the bat down even harder on my cheek,

mashing my face into the cold stone floor. "Don't you say her name, you thievin' piece of shit." I couldn't talk, but he could. "I know all about you two, Danny-boy. She came clean. Told me everything." He raised his voice. "I gave you a job, boy, a home. I found you gigs, I paid off your bookies, and that's how you do me? She was my wife, motherfucker. She was the only thing in my kingdom that was off limits, and you had to have her too, didn't you?" His eyes went full dark.

It took a few seconds for the insanity of what Powell was saying to sink in, but when it finally did, my brain started to scramble to get out the words. "No, no, Leroy, you got it all wrong. Jesus, man, I never touched your wife." And that was the god's honest truth. I never touched the man's wife. I was a shitty husband, sure, but I never cheated on Kaycee Jane—ever—not once. I had at least that much to be proud of. I'd never laid a hand on any other woman, much less Raylene—but, goddamn, if I knew who did. My good eye scanned the room until I found the right set of eyes looking back—surprised eyes, filled with the sudden fear of the coming revelation. I locked on those eyes. I struggled to get the words out. "Jesus, Leroy, you got the wrong guy. It wasn't me. It was—"

RT hammered a steel-tipped cowboy boot into my guts for a second time. It knocked the wind out of me, and I wretched up more blood onto the floor.

"Just kill this piece of shit, boss. After what he did to you? Making a fool of you and all? Now he's gonna lay there and call your woman a liar?"

I couldn't talk. I couldn't breathe. I couldn't—it didn't matter.

"Yeah," Powell said, "damn all that." And he swung.

Soon After.

Now, I ain't quite sure that time just how long I was out, but it had to be a while because when I came to, I was alone in the basement again. My whole skull was throbbing like I was being held underwater, but as I came around, I started to think straight. There wasn't any serious damage done so's that I could tell. And well, I couldn't believe it. I guess you gotta have some ass behind the swing if you want to inflict the kind of pain I used to dole out with that Louisville. Maybe that's what happens when you smoke those sissy-ass clove cigarettes. And Powell was a bony prick, besides. I moved my head from side to side. No blurred vision. And I could see through both eyes. I had to have been out for a hot minute for all the swelling to go down. It didn't even feel like he'd broken any bones. Wait, maybe he didn't want to. Maybe he took it easy because he knew I wasn't lying. He did call me the smart one, right? Maybe he's upstairs dealing with RT right now. I always suspected that shiny-headed dirtbag of balling the boss's old lady, I just never called him out on it. It was never my business. I pushed myself up to a seated position and started rubbing my sore wrists before it even dawned on me that I'd been cut loose. The zip ties were snipped off and lying on the floor next to me. I felt off. Either them boys left me here for dead, or they were letting me go. No matter, there wasn't no way in hell I was sticking around to find out. I was on my newly freed feet and up those stairs in seconds. I paused at the door and gave the knob a full ten count as I turned it. I'd be dipped in shit, the damn thing was unlocked. Kaycee Jane, baby, you did it. My ship had arrived. I opened the door just as slow and silent as I turned the knob, inching it just wide enough to slide my body though, and crept like a damn burglar with my back pressed to the wall all the way through an empty kitchen, then down an empty hall, until I came to an empty living room where, I'll be damned, my watch, my wallet, and my cell phone were all laid out on a makeshift table made out of cinderblocks and a rotten sheet of plywood. I about shit and fell back in it when I saw the few hundred bucks I had in cash was still in my billfold. I couldn't fuckin' believe my luck. I blew kisses toward the sky and stuffed my wallet into my pocket before I snuck a peek out the yellowed glass of the front room window. Not a damn car in sight, just an empty driveway. I blew out a long exhale, snatched up my phone, and called an Uber. As it turned out, the squat house ol' RT and his butt-buddies had brought me to was right outside Franklin, only a few miles away from Gracie's doughnut shop. My driver would be there in six minutes, and despite my mouth and sore ribs, it was shaping up to be a beautiful day. The sun was high noon in a bright blue Tennessee sky and I, Dan the fucking Man, was going to be early to see my family for a change. I called Kaycee Jane next to let her know I was in town and only a few minutes away. She might've even sounded happy to hear from me, but that was most likely me projecting my good fortune. I can say she didn't sound filled with dread like normal, so hey, that was progress. I had that goofy bastard Uber driver with the manbun drop me a block away from the doughnut shop so Kaycee Jane wouldn't see my mangled mouth and freak out. I even tipped the driver a few extra bucks in cash for keeping his trap shut about what happened to me when he saw me. I mean, my face was The Wreck of The Hesperus, so I wanted to ease my girls into it from a distance. That's why when I turned the corner on Metcalfe Ave. and saw her, I just stopped, leaned back on the brick, and drank her in for a minute. She really was something to see. Kaycee Jane was standing outside the doughnut shop, leaning against a newspaper dispenser, half reading, half skimming through a copy of the Nashville Scene. She was wearing that same short powder-blue sundress that rivaled the sky. The sunlight tangled in her springy blonde curls, causing her hair to glow like it might catch fire at any moment. She hadn't aged a day since I seen her last, despite what I had put her through. Hell, she still looked exactly like she did all those years ago in school. Every curve, every line of her untouched, just like the girl I lost my teeth over the first time we met. I rubbed my tongue instinctively over the stumps in my mouth and tasted the blood.

It tasted like home.

I came off the wall and slowly crossed the street toward her.

I tried to smile, careful to keep my lips pressed tightly together to cover the gnarled gap where my fronts should've been. When she saw me, she smiled back, warm and perfect. She folded the paper and tucked it under her arm and straightened herself out. "You look like shit," she said. As if it were normal to greet me that way, and well, it kinda was.

"I know," I said. "I sorta ran into a thing when I got here."

"Of course you did."

"But you, KJ, you look amazing."

"I know," she said, still smiling.

"Gracie inside?"

She turned and pointed through the storefront window to a sandy blonde little girl waiting patiently in line in front of the pastry case, holding what looked like it might be a Father's Day card. "I guess I better get in there, then."

"I guess you should."

"Will you join us?"

"Maybe later," she said. "But this is just for you."

I started to push the door open and go in but paused and looked at my wife. I mean, I really looked at her. "I love you, Kaycee Jane. I've always loved you."

She put her hand on my cheek and smiled even wider. "I know that, too, Dan."

I pushed the door open the rest of the way, and a bell rang above me alerting the folks inside that someone new had come in. Gracie turned to see me and ran toward me, grinning ear to ear.

"Daddy!" she yelled. She didn't seem to care one bit about my face. She jumped into my arms, and I held her like it was the last time I would.

Later.

"This the place?" Officer Bowers said to his partner as he wheeled the cruiser into the driveway of one of the several condemned flophouses lining the shit end of East Nashville.

"I guess so," Bowers' partner, Meadows, said. "It's hard to tell the way all these places are stacked up on each other. Nothing is numbered."

"Who called it in?"

"Couple of kids. Most likely bullshit."

"Well, let's take a look anyway."

Officers Bowers and Meadows walked up the drive of the decades-old house—fallen into disrepair before either of them were born—and circled the premises. Bowers entered through the front, Meadows moved around through to the back.

"Davidson County Police," Bowers said once inside, gesturing for Meadows to move toward the basement door in the kitchen. "Anyone here?"

No response.

Meadows cupped his nose. "You smell that?"

"Yeah, whatever's down there is pretty ripe."

Bowers eased the door open and Meadows took to the stairs. He was the first to see the body. Whoever it was, or had been, was bound at his hands and feet with zip ties, and by the rancid smell, the poor bastard had been dead for quite a while. "Obvious Forty-five." Meadows yelled up to his partner. "Call it in." He checked the body for a wallet and found a Georgia State ID.

DANIEL ADAM GLENN
DOB: 03/13/1979
22 BLUE JACK ROAD
STATESBORO GA 30460

"Hey, Steve, I think I know this guy."

"You recognize him?"

Meadows looked at what was left of the man's head. It looked like a hollowed-out pumpkin painted red and filled with coffee grounds. He turned and saw the baseball bat on the floor. The same red. The same coffee grounds. "Nah, nobody will ever recognize this guy again, but the picture on his ID and the name. I think I saw him play The Bluebird a few times."

"Any good?" Bowers asked.

"Yeah. Yeah, he was. He had heart. I don't remember the songs, but I do remember he played a slide guitar like a madman. I'm talking Duane Allman good."

"Well, that's a damn shame. We could use a little more of that around this town. Instead of all this drum machine bro-country shit."

"Yeah," Meadows said. "You could say that again," speaking mostly to himself than his partner. He slipped the ID back into the wallet and pulled out a worn and faded picture of an attractive woman with curly blonde hair holding the most adorable little girl. The Davidson County Policeman found himself caught off guard by the photo. He found himself not thinking about the tragedy at his feet but felt a twinge of hope that the child in that little wallet picture at least got the chance to hear her daddy play slide.

TROUBLE NO MORE

Mark Westmoreland

Meatloaf Moody kicked my trailer door off its hinges and barged into the living room. The mullet-wearing peckerwood aimed a pistol all around until it found my chest, and he focused it there. It wasn't the first time I'd had a gun aimed at me, and my hands went up out of instinct. He snarled like a dog eye-fucking a piece of ground beef, and I wondered just how these situations came to be. Not that it mattered one way or another because sometimes shit just happens. Trouble always finds the trouble-makers.

Moody fired a shot that went wild. I turned to my right and saw a bullet hole clear through the signature of my autographed picture of Herschel Walker that Mama got for me. It pissed me off more than the threat of dying, and when I turned back to Moody to let him know, he laid flat on his face. Jessa stood over him in nothing but the skin God gave her and cracked the back of his skull with a Louisville Slugger. Moody's head was busted open like a dollar store pinata and he bled all over the carpet. There wasn't no way I'd get my security deposit back for this one.

Jessa dropped her bat once it was obvious Moody's brains were scrambled. He groaned and pushed up on an elbow and held himself there for a second. I couldn't believe he was still alive after having his noggin knocked out of the ballpark and kicked his pistol across the floor just in case he could still see straight enough to shoot.

I stepped over him to head for the kitchen and grab something to clean up the floor, but Jessa blocked my way. She planted her feet firmly in the carpet and dug her toes into it. The muscles in her thick thighs flexed and her hands rested on her hips. Her chest rose and fell with every hard breath and she stared me down with a razorblade glare. I knew an argument was coming I didn't want to be involved in, because the only time I got that look is when I drank too much, didn't do what Jessa asked, said something she didn't appreciate, or any number of other things that might set her off. They were numerous and hard to keep count of.

"What the hell you got into, Mack?"

This argument would be worse than I reckoned because she never called me by my name. It was always "sweetie" or "sweetheart" or some variation of sweetness.

"I ain't got into shit," I said. "I don't know why that's what you automatically assume."

"You tell me what I'm supposed to think when somebody kicks the door down and starts shooting up the damn place?"

"Jessa, when would I have time to start anything up? I ain't hardly left the house since you moved in."

"Then is it something your brother's into? Who knows what kinda trouble he's been causing."

"I ain't talked to my brother in six months. Not since he's been working for Peanut."

"Mack." She threw my name at me like a boxer throwing a quick jab. "Don't lie to me. I told you never to lie to me."

"Goddammit, does it sound like I'm lying? I got no idea what possessed Moody to bust down the door like I owe him money or something." I waved over at Meatloaf, and he'd pushed himself onto his chunky ass and glanced around the room with a faraway glaze. "Why don't you ask him what he's doing here? He can probably tell you better than me."

Jessa grit her teeth, and it made the muscles in her neck and shoulders tense. She hated it when I deflected blame in an argument, but in this particular instance, there wasn't no blame for me to accept. The only person that could acknowledge that I told the truth was Moody, but there wasn't no telling what he'd be liable to say and Jessa'd already knocked him half stupid. This whole thing was like navigating a minefield without knowing where the explosives were buried.

Jessa's features sharpened until a man standing just outside the door spoke and she softened up.

"How's my baby girl doing today?" He was a slight man but commanded all the attention in the room. A torpedo-shaped cigar danced on the edge of his lips and the rest of his mouth curled into a Chesire smile. His presence made Jessa wilt, and I could tell for the first time she was ashamed of being naked. He looked her over without a hint of lust and kept his eyes away from her privates. He said, "Boy, you sure have growed up."

Jessa turned her body at an angle, and all that ferocity she'd built up on account of me was no longer present. She acted childlike and her voice became a feather wisp. "What're you doing here, deddy?"

The man took the cigar from his mouth and used the back of his hand to wipe a string of spit from his chin. He smiled with his whole mouth now and showed off his pearly whites. He took his eyes off Jessa and moved them over to me. It was a short distance to travel, but he took his time doing it, and once he set them on me, he said, "I'm here to meet your new beau."

He put his hand out to me and introduced himself. "Milton Winchester Cash. All my friends call me Win because that's what I do. But you can call me sir on account of you dating my daughter. If you ain't figured it out yet, I'm Jessa's deddy."

I took Win's hand, gave him my best grip. He did the same in return, and I said, "I've already met Jessa's deddy, and he ain't the kinda asshole that busts into somebody's home and tries killing 'em."

Win took his hand from mine and looked down at Moody. That smile never left his face but there was a coldness in his eyes. He looked back at me and that expression gave me chills. He said, "No, boy, you met Jessa's jelly-spined stepfather. We ain't nothing too alike. He ain't got no say in whether or not you'll court my daughter. That right there is up to me."

He put a finger to his chest then returned the cigar to his mouth. My instincts told me to shove that smoke tube down his throat and choke him on it, but I waited to be told this was all a joke. When that didn't happen, I said, "Maybe that decision oughta be left up to Jessa."

Win didn't give that statement time to settle before he shook his head and said, "Now I'm sure my daughter is capable of making some fine decisions but settling down with a man should always have some say from the father. We have a special gift of knowing somebody's character, and I don't have a good impression of you so far, boy. It should've been you that stopped Moody from invading this home, but it was my daughter. How can I even trust you to keep my baby girl safe?"

Before I could answer the question, Win opened his blazer, flashed a pistol in a shoulder holster, and said to Jessa, "Go put some clothes on, baby girl. We're all going for a ride."

I sat shotgun with Win while Jessa sat in the backseat of the extended cab pickup with Moody. Moody held a towel to the back of his head to keep from bleeding on the upholstery. Win told him if that happened, he'd scalp that mullet right off the top of his head. Jessa hadn't spoken a word since we'd left my trailer. She'd gone into a shell and wouldn't hardly look at me.

Win drove us out of Tugalo County into Blackwood, Georgia, deep into the foothills of the Blue Ridge Mountains. He drove like he'd never been behind the wheel of a truck before and made me wish I'd used Moody's gun to talk my way out of this ride. It'd been locked in the middle console because Win said he didn't trust none of us to carry it.

After a while he reached over and turned the volume down

on Gregg Allman's whiskey-seared vocals. Then he took his cigar from the ashtray, bit down on the end of it, and spoke. "Tell me what my baby girl there told you 'bout me."

I stole a glance to the backseat, and Jessa's legs were pulled into her chest. She hugged her arms tight around her knees and kept her eyes down. Win smiled at me when I looked over at him, and I said, "She ain't never even told me you existed."

If that bothered Win at all, he didn't show a crack. His smile never left his face and he sucked the flavor right out of his cigar. "Now that's unfortunate," he said. "You've got a lot of catching up to do and ain't got much time to do it. We're going to have to make this quick."

Before he could get started, I asked, "Why do I even care who you are?"

That question either didn't register with Win or he just plain ignored it. He propped a hand over the steering wheel, leaned into the console, and got closer to me. He spoke low like he was telling me a secret. "In case you ain't figured it out, Jessa's mama doesn't like me very much."

"I bet I can figure out why."

"Don't be a smartass, boy. You're already on my bad side." He shifted around, propped an elbow on the armrest of the door, took his eyes off the road, and looked at me. "When I first got together with her mama, we were so in love. That woman thought I'd hung the moon and set the sun on fire. I was always an open book with her about my life, but she didn't care what I did. Not as long as I took care of her and the babies she gave me."

I pointed at the road to let Win know he needed to watch where he was going and said, "Maybe she was too scared to care what it was you did."

"That's bullshit." Win slapped the steering wheel, and for the first time, that cool front he'd presented dissipated. "All that woman cares about is money, and I made a whole bunch of it. She was always too busy spending it to take the time to be scared. I could've given her plenty of reasons to fear me but I never did. I loved that woman like she loved me."

Win took his cigar from his mouth and smashed it into the ashtray. He'd gnawed the end of it down to a nub and didn't touch it again. We sat in an electric silence until Win found his composure. "Her mama don't like me because I went to prison. Even though I'd always told her it came with the lifestyle, and hid away enough money that she didn't have to worry for shit, she wouldn't wait for me. Wouldn't even let me watch my kids grow up from behind bars. Said she needed to think about what kinda worldview they'd have. Next thing I know, she was seeing that herniated asshole you called Jessa's deddy. But he won't be called that no more. 'Cause I'm back and I plan on making up for lost time."

I turned back to Jessa; her whole body was rigid. Her eyes glowed from withheld anger, and her nails dug deep into her skin. This man wouldn't never be a deddy to her no matter how bad he wanted it. I could tell that without Jessa even saying so. There was bad blood here, and we needed to get out of this situation before any of it was spilled.

Win leaned back across the console, watched me from the corner of his eye, and said, "It was them Bohannons you work for that got me sent off to prison."

I kept my eyes on Jessa and said, "I don't work for no damn Bohannons."

"That so?" Win sat straight up in his seat and spoke like this was a revelation. "'Cause that ain't the word I heard."

"Whatever you heard ain't got a damn bit of truth to it."

"That's good then." Win reached across the cab and slapped me on the shoulder. "'Cause if it was true, we wouldn't even be having this conversation right now."

"What's this conversation we're even having here? All you've done is reminisce over a woman that don't want nothing to do with you and scare a daughter that doesn't even know who you are."

"That ain't my goddamn fault." Win stabbed the steering wheel with the point of his finger. "I'd carved out a little enterprise of my own. It didn't interfere one bit with what the Bohannons did. I didn't want nothing to do with drugs or running guns. All I did was put on cock fights and started branching out into dogs when they tried cutting into my pie. That wasn't some shit I'd tolerate and I let 'em know it. Told 'em they could supply the drugs and entertainment but the fights were mine. There wasn't no way they were getting a percentage of that. Thought we'd have a deal, but the next thing I know I'm being thrown before a judge and being sent off to prison for ten years. Dog fighting don't even get you ten years. It might get you two, but they hit me with everything they could think of."

Win paused long enough for me to interrupt. "You still ain't told me what this conversation is we're supposed to be having."

He turned to me with a million-dollar smile, said, "I'm getting back in the game, boy, but this time I'm fighting men, and you're going up against my prizefighter. Don't think I don't know your reputation. You would've been the state wrestling champ two years running if it wasn't for my son pinning you in the semifinals."

This time I leaned across the console and got in Win's face. He didn't flinch, and I could taste the tobacco on his breath. "Go fuck yourself," I said. "I ain't fighting nobody for you."

Win leaned even closer to me, and I'm sure we looked like a pair of pit bulls raring to fight. He said, "That's unfortunate then, because that must mean you don't love my daughter like she deserves to be loved."

"I love her so much I ain't beat the shit outta you yet."

Win cackled right in my face and Moody joined in. I'd forgotten all about him being back there, but the ogre-sized redneck was doubled over in his seat, slapping his knee. The anger that'd emanated from Jessa just a few minutes before was now replaced by worry, and she mouthed something at me even though she knew I couldn't read lips for shit.

"Boy"—Win stretched that word out to its fringes while he wiped tears from his eyes—"'Least you got that fighting spirit somebody needs to get in my pit. That's what I'm calling it. The Pit. And if you can get into The Pit and come out victorious, I'll make a deal with you that I won't give y'all trouble no more."

Win led us to a barn on the backside of his property. He sipped a glass of sweet tea and twirled an unlit cigar between his fingers while he walked. A couple of men guarded the barn doors and moved out of the way when he approached. They barely took the time to notice me because their eyes went straight to Jessa.

Win saw this and said, "Get one good look because that's my daughter there and if I find out y'all even thought something inappropriate about her, I'll slice your ball sacks off and feed 'em to you."

The men turned their eyes away from Jessa and put them back on me. I'm sure under the right circumstances I would've felt intimidated, but I'd gotten hotter than an infected yellow jacket sting. It's always been a struggle of mine not to be afraid of someone that could blow a breathalyzer score higher than their I.Q. I doubted these two dummies would even register on the scale if they combined their brainpower and probably didn't do any thinking of their own. Win did that for them, and that didn't scare me one bit. He wasn't going to let them hurt me before I got into The Pit. After I won, it might be a different story, but I went ahead and returned the dirty look they gave me.

Win appreciated the showdown as it unfolded. He made a bet with Moody about who would break the stare first and then lit up his cigar. He puffed on it until it was chugging like a freight train and then blew a fat cloud of smoke into his guards' eyes. They both coughed and hacked and couldn't look at me no more.

Win put his hand out to Moody, and Moody said, "That was cheating."

Win smiled around his cigar. "It ain't cheating when you

make the rules."

Moody rolled that around his brain and couldn't think of a counter-argument. "Take it out of my pay."

"I don't wanna hear no shit when I do it then." Win turned to his guards, said, "Open these doors and let my guests inside."

The barn doors were too big for one man to open by himself, but the guards heaved until there was enough space for us to walk through. Win put an arm out to Jessa, and she took a step behind me. His face screwed up and he said, "Baby girl, I know it's been years since you seen me, but I ain't gave you no reason to be so scared of me."

Truth be told, I'd never seen Jessa act this way before and that put a real fear inside of me. She could be smart-mouthed and hard-headed at the worst possible times but that wasn't the girl standing behind me now. She'd become soft-spoken and fragile but stood her ground over this, and I stood a little taller for her.

Win rolled his cigar between his fingers and sipped his sweet tea. His bottom lip quivered and he couldn't keep from shifting his weight from one foot to the other. He took a big puff from his cigar just before it burned out. "Why don't you lead us inside then? 'Least that way a lady will be going first."

Jessa grabbed the back of my shirt and I could feel the tension in her grip. She held onto it until she stepped around me and walked inside the barn. Win cut me off so I couldn't follow her, and Moody shoulder-bumped me forward as he took up the back of the line. The barn doors were pushed shut and a dimness settled all around us except for at the very center of the building. Floodlights were mounted all around the hayloft, shining down on Win's pit.

There wasn't nothing fancy about the fight pit, and I figured that was part of the draw. Four-by-fours were planted in a big circle and wrapped in chicken wire to fence the fighters in. There was a makeshift door that men could come and go by, and Win even had a guard manning it. The pit was surrounded by a rickety set of bleachers, and a handful of men filled them. Win squeezed his way through the fight pit's door, walked to the center of it, and put his arms out to his audience.

"Welcome to Win's Barnyard Brawl," he announced. "Today's fight is a special event and y'all're here by private invitation. There ain't rules or time limit. Just last man standing. Set your bets high because that young man over there is fighting for the love of my daughter."

Jessa grabbed my arm, dug her nails into the skin, and got close so she could speak in my ear. "We don't need to be here, Mack. I don't know why we've followed my deddy this far but let's get outta here. He can't stop us."

"Look around you, Jessa."

She did a slow take around the barn and saw the men that'd filled in behind us. They posted up at the only exits there were and would make sure we couldn't leave.

Win walked up to us, puffing his cigar in my face, put his hand on my shoulder, and asked, "You ready to fight, boy?"

Before I could answer, Moody shoved me toward the pit, and the guard at the door pushed me inside. I fell over, hit hard on the red clay floor, and looked up at the guard. He towered from where I laid and was built like a refrigerator but that didn't stop Jessa from coming at him. She kicked and clawed and yelled for her deddy to stop this foolishness. Moody scooped her up like a toddler throwing a tantrum and Win just laughed.

He said, "Let's go have a seat and enjoy the festivities."

They went over to a bleacher of their own, and Moody pinned Jessa in place when they sat. Win stood beside them and snarled like a wildcat ready to pounce on its prey. He addressed the crowd. "I know why y'all're here today. Y'all wanna see if my boy is as vicious as they say. I can tell y'all every word y'all've heard is true, but I won't make y'all wait to find out. Come on out, son."

"Son" wasn't some pet name Win'd given to a random fighter. A stall door opened and Jessa's older brother came out. He was dressed in cut-off denim shorts and steel toe boots, and his fists were wrapped in tape. The sight of Justin got another rise out of Jessa, but he ignored her on the way to The Pit. Win sat down beside his daughter and patted her knee like that would make it all better.

Justin stepped through the pit door, met me at the center, and faced me down. We'd wrestled off and on throughout high school and he'd kept me from wrestling for a state title my junior year, but that'd been a decade before. He was still built like he wrestled full-time, and he eyed me like I'd made a dirty joke about his mama. I couldn't tell where that animosity came from because we'd shot the shit over a couple of beers a few weeks before. There wasn't no sense in reminding him of that because he planned on walking a mudhole right through me.

Win gave his private audience time to take this scene in and place a few bets, and then he approached the fence. He spoke loud enough for everyone to hear. "Y'all shake hands and fight."

My deddy never raised me to be friendly about ass whoopings, and when Justin put his hand out for me to take, I snapped an elbow across his face. His head snapped sideways and his nose bent crooked. Blood swirled and he stumbled back a couple of steps. I threw the hardest punches I could wind up and tuned out Jessa's screaming. Justin was on his heels when he bounced off the chicken wire and I wrestled him to the ground. He mashed my face into the red Georgia clay and kept me from getting on top of him. I grinded an elbow into his eye socket, and he smashed my throat with his forearm. It made it so I couldn't breathe, and when I dropped my guard, he hammered his forehead into the bridge of my nose. My vision was all flashbangs and fireworks, and I tried rolling away from Justin but was too disoriented to move and rolled right into his feet. He planted the heel of his boot in the center of my back and then punted me in the belly with that steel toe. All the air in my body came out in a rush and I dry heaved in the mud. Justin grabbed me by a handful of hair and dragged me to my knees. He stood with his legs spread wide open, and I punched him in the balls.

I've hit some men pretty hard in my life but never hard enough that it killed them on the inside, but that's what happened to Justin. His eyes rolled back into his head and his soul departed for another world. He willed his body to keep upright, and I punched him in the nutsack again. Win stood at the fence and hollered, but it all sounded like white noise to me. I followed Justin as he fell back and pounded his nose into a piece of flattened roadkill. When he hit the ground, I was on top of him and bombed him with one blow after another until Moody pulled me away.

Win stood over his son, and a graveness shadowed him. All the men that'd come by special invitation cleared the bleachers, and Jessa ran to me. She dropped in my lap and hugged me tight around the neck. Win watched his audience file out the exit and waved his men out after them. He motioned Moody over and said something I couldn't make out. Moody left the pit for one of the stalls, and Win approached us.

He'd shoved his hands in his pockets and spoke with a touch of somberness. "That just cost me 'bout five or six grand right there. Didn't even place a bet on the boy. People just wanna see him fight. Word's gone spread about that and it'll be hell rebuilding his image."

I dropped my voice low like Win's and mocked him. "That's unfortunate."

That brought a smirk to his face, and he said, "You know, boy, we could make a killing working together. People'll pay top dollar to see you fight after they hear what happened today."

I pushed to my feet and dusted myself off to think about the number of different ways I could tell Win to fuck himself, but I didn't need to. Jessa did that for me.

She stepped right up in her deddy's face, her fists tightly balled at her side. If she planned on knocking the spit out of him, she didn't have to worry about me holding her back, but she kept her composure. Her voice remained steady as she spoke, and this time it was Win's turn to wilt.

"Deddy, I hope this was all worth it to you, because I'd rather die than ever have to see you again. Mack ain't fighting for you and there's no amount of money you could offer to get him to say yes. Your money is as unwanted as you are."

Win turned away from his daughter and spit in the mud. He put his hands on his hips, and when he turned back to us, there was a murderous glint in his eyes. "I was afraid you'd say that. It's unfortunate, but I done made y'all a deal. If Mack fought in this pit, I said I wouldn't bother y'all no more. And I ain't. But there's one more thing—if y'all want outta here, y'all gotta take out my trash."

Moody kicked the stall door open and shoved a man into the mud. His hands and feet were tied, and duct tape kept him from yelling. He'd been beat up and mistreated and flinched when Moody came near him. The sight made Win grow in stature and he bounced on the balls of his feet. Moody peeled back the chicken wire door and tossed the man inside.

I looked down into his face and said, "What the fuck is this?"

Jessa recognized the man next and dropped to her knees. She lost the composure she'd built up, and the steadiness left her voice. Fear settled in and it crackled when she spoke. "My God, deddy, are you all right?"

This time the man she called deddy was actually the one who raised her. She ran her hands over his swollen eyes and broken nose and tried peeling the tape from his mouth, but her hands shook too hard. Win watched the way she gave her real deddy comfort and affection, and that murderous glint turned to a sparkle. He nodded to Moody, who took Jessa by the shoulders and pulled her to her feet. Win blocked her way when she tried going back to her dad, and Moody stopped me when I tried going after Win.

Win said, "I was going to save this last test for your beau over there, but I think it's better suited for you. Besides that, I don't trust him with no gun."

Win pulled up his pants leg, reached down to an ankle holster, and drew a .38 Special. He took Jessa by the wrist, shoved the pistol in her hand, and stepped behind her. He put his mouth next to her ear and said, "There's one bullet in that gun's chamber, and I want you to put it right between that asshole's eyes. He stole your mama away from me and ruined our family. I could've been the deddy that told you 'happy birthday' and tucked you in at night. Do this for me, baby girl. Help me get my life back."

Jessa's whole body shook under her deddy's touch, and her chest heaved as she cried. The sound of it echoed around the barn, and her stepdad cried right along with her. He'd shimmied over to her and put his broken fingers on her foot. Whether it was to comfort Jessa or to beg for his life, Win didn't appreciate it. He stepped around his daughter and stomped on her step-daddy's fingers until he took his hand away.

Moody held me in a tight bear hug, and I hurt too much to put up a fight. My head was woozy and my insides didn't feel right. I tried speaking but Win spoke right over me.

"Shoot this man, Jessa. Shoot him for your deddy. Shoot him for the man that gave you life and thought about you every second he was behind bars."

Win waited for his daughter to pull the trigger, but she couldn't lift the gun from her side. That murderous spark that danced in his eyes a little bit before was a raging bonfire now. He looked down on the man that'd taken his place in his family's life and then looked at Jessa.

"You're just like your whore mama. You hear me, girl? All you care about is yourself. Just goddamn greedy. You wouldn't've turned out that way if your mama let me have anything to do with you. I'd've made sure of it." Win nodded to add emphasis to the words and then pulled open his blazer. "If you can't do this for your deddy, then I damn sure will. I've been thinking about it every day since your mama came to tell me she was leaving. This won't bother me one bit."

Win drew the pistol from his shoulder holster, and Moody crushed me as I tried to get away from him. Jessa watched her deddy point his gun at the man that raised her like she was his own, and that .38 Special left her side. She aimed the barrel at the man that'd given her life and pulled the trigger on some real Cash family drama.

AIN'T WASTIN' TIME NO MORE

Joey R. Poole

"It's not even stealing," Lane said for at least the fifth time that day. "Because it's shit that's already been stolen. You steal something from a thief, don't make you a thief. Makes you...I don't know, something else."

"An agent of karma," said his nephew Teddy, who nearly everyone called Little Teddy even though he was a grown-ass man and his father Big Teddy had been dead for fifteen years.

Lane thought about that for a moment, turning the words over in his mind. "Agent of karma," he said. "Shit like that right there, that's why you need to be in school instead of wastin' your time working for me cutting grass and planting bushes. Shoulda whooped your ass when you quit tech is what I shoulda done. One professor turns out to be a dickhead, and you up and quit the whole fuckin' thing. Gonna have to put up with a lot of dickheads in your life."

"Putting up with one right now," Teddy said.

"You know that's right."

"And it might not be stealing, but it's definitely some crackhead shit. Copper wire? Yeah, that's some crackhead shit right there."

"Actually," Lane said, "it's *meth*-heads mostly nowadays, at least around here. But this ain't like that. Meth-heads, those motherfuckers is like roaches. Run in, steal a little bit of wire, sell that shit fast as they can to get a couple dollars. This here would be a goddamn *heist*. This guy, he's got a fuckin pile of copper in there. The meth-heads sell it to him because they done stole so much off construction sites and abandoned houses and shit they probably on some kind of FBI watch list, can't find nowhere legit to sell it. And he just hordes it, waits 'til the market's high or whatever, like he's a stock dealer or some shit."

"Sounds like prison time is what it sounds like," Teddy said. "Sounds like getting shot. Sounds like you trying to talk yourself into something stupid."

"Ain't like that. Told you, this guy, he knows what he's talking about. And this is a lot of fuckin' money. It's invest-in-the-future money. Driving-around-on-zero-turn-mowers-instead-of-these-busted-ass-sumbitches-I-got-now money. You-ain't-got-no-excuse-not-to-go-back-to-school money."

"How you know all this anyway?" Teddy asked.

"Told you already, but you staring at that phone all day and you don't listen. I know a guy. Got some inside information."

Teddy was about to say something, but his phone buzzed again. He was hoping it was Mandy because he didn't know how she was going to take what he'd texted her earlier, but it was just the power company telling him they were about to shut off his lights if he didn't give them half his next paycheck.

Lane took off his Braves cap and rubbed his head, which he'd just shaved bald after finally giving up on having hair. He'd gone without the hat for most of the day while he and Teddy had been cutting grass, trying to get the formerly haired parts of his head burned the same weathered red as the rest of his face. It hadn't worked; he still looked like a chemo patient. Finally he stood up and rested his hands on the railing of the deck he'd built on the back of the doublewide and surveyed the yard like he was looking out over a much grander kingdom. "So anyway," he began.

"I don't want to talk about that no more," Teddy said. "Been talking about it all day."

"Wasn't going to say anything more about it," Lane said. "I was just...I mean, you alright? You ain't said a dozen words all day. And I don't need no psychic help like Sister Rose out on Highway 52 to tell me why. Haven't seen that little girl you used to be so crazy about around here in a minute, so something's definitely goin' on with that."

"Yeah. You could say that," Teddy said. "But it's alright." But it wasn't alright, he thought. It was a lot of things, but alright wasn't one of them.

"Just sayin'. Seems like you got something on your mind. You wanna talk about it, let me know. Otherwise I'ma shut up about it." Teddy thought Lane was about to launch into his spiel about how he'd promised Big Teddy that he'd always take care of his son, and how he was sure Big Teddy had heard him even though he was laid up in a coma after sliding his motorcycle into a peach truck on the way to Little Teddy's fifth birthday party. But Lane had mostly left all that unsaid since he'd quit drinking a few years back, and he just asked if Teddy wanted to come inside and eat.

"Nah," Teddy said. "I'm good. 'Bout to head out."

"Alright, bo," Lane said, sounding a little bit hurt. "Ain't too much work tomorrow. Just two houses. Just grass, no bushes or anything. Probably start late. I'll pick you up maybe ten o'clock."

Before he drove away, Teddy checked his phone one more time even though it hadn't buzzed, just to make sure. There was nothing. He pulled out of Lane's yard and onto the highway, his mind churning with all the things he should've said and all the things he should've left unsaid.

"It's a different way to look at your yard," Lane's buddy Myron said two days later as Teddy and Lane stood in his overgrown backyard. He sounded defeated; he'd already lost this argument in court with his neighbors and was rehashing his side of it for Lane and Teddy. "A different way of thinking about what a yard can *be*. People been brainwashed to think a lawn is natural. But, thing is, when you put in a lawn, you *take out* everything natural and just carpet it over with a goddamn monoculture of one plant that's designed to choke out everything else and provide no food whatsoever for your pollinators, no habitat for wildlife, nothing. And on top of that, they got you buying weed killers and shit that's contributing to the insect apocalypse, dumping that shit right on your yard."

"Preach, bo," Lane said, giving Teddy a side-eye that read *told you this motherfucker was a trip*. For a moment it seemed that Myron was done, but he caught a second wind and launched into another diatribe, finding a little fire instead of just despair with this one.

"See them blue flowers over there in the low part of the backyard? That's spiderwort. *Tradescantia Ohioensis*. Bees pollinate the shit out of it. It's native, too, evolved to live in that soil right fuckin' there. I spent all last year pulling invasive species and vines with roots big around as my arm outta that spot, found some spiderwort in there, and cultivated it along. So, yeah, y'all just mow that shit right down. Pokeberry back there? Caterpillars love that shit. Birds need caterpillars to eat. But fuck birds and caterpillars, I guess. Fuck honeysuckle, too. It smells like God's pussy and it's beautiful and bees love it, but they don't sell that shit at Lowe's, so mow it down too. Just clear-cut the whole lot, come back next week and lay me down some sod, make the whole goddamn thing flat and dead as a fuckin' golf course. Then put me a sign in the front yard with a big hand flipping the bird and it says 'Fuck you, neighborhood! Fuck you, homeowner's association! Fuck you, all you Trump-y fuckin' pricks.'" He grew louder for the last bit, waving his arms in religious frenzy, shooting double birds all around at the whole neighborhood and maybe even the world.

"Oh Lord. He done got political, now," Lane said. "Might be here for a while. This guy, you get him started on that politics, I'm telling you…"

"Just saying, these HOA people, these are the same motherfuckers that…"

"I know. Hell, I cut half they grass. They some assholes, alright," Lane said, cutting him off. "But what you say we let Little Teddy get started on your jungle back there and let's go inside and talk about what we was gonna talk about."

Myron conceded and Teddy fired up the mower and spent most of the morning decimating the budding wilderness of Myron's backyard, grasshoppers soaring away from him in terror, an army of skinks and a couple of rabbits fleeing the tyranny of his riding mower. Bees buzzed confusedly around him, and he imagined them more sad than angry, steeling himself for stings that never came. A pair of mockingbirds who'd had a nest in the flattened honeysuckle thicket attacked him, pecking at the bill of his cap until finally they gave up and sat atop the privacy fence to glare at him with hatred in their hearts but not one ounce of fear.

It was terrible what he was doing. But it was, arguably, the right thing too. Going natural was admirable. But the nearly impenetrable tangle of Myron's backyard was something else entirely—created, Teddy suspected, as much from neglect as it was by design. Still, he hated doing it.

It was the same with what Mandy wanted to do. She'd been absolutely right when she told him it was ridiculous to keep the baby. She had another year of nursing school. He cut grass for his uncle. They didn't have a safety net because his parents were dead, hers Jehovah's Witnesses. They weren't the kind of people whose lives could absorb fuckups as big as the one they'd made, and it wasn't like they'd been getting along lately anyway. It was a mess. And it was her body, her choice, not his.

He couldn't argue with any of that. But it still seemed like a terrible thing, even if it was for the best. And he knew that things would be different if he hadn't had his head up his ass for so long, hadn't wasted so much of his life already. If he hadn't flamed out at Tech, he'd have transferred to Clemson, would've graduated last year, maybe would've been an engineer. Would've been *something* at least, somebody who could keep his lights on and make a home for a baby that hadn't asked to be born but was on the way nonetheless.

She'd made it clear that she wasn't in the mood for talking, so everything he'd said to her about it had been via text. The last thing he'd texted her two days ago was:

> K. Don't have it now but can bring you the $300 Friday if that's what you want.
> I know things are fucked up but would u ever think about us keeping it/him/her?

She hadn't replied, and by now he guessed he knew the answer. But when he'd finished with Myron's backyard and took a break to drink a Mello Yello from the cooler in the back of Lane's truck, he saw a text from her:

> IDK. Maybe. If things were different. If I could stay in school. If we had enough $$. But theres no way. Please come Friday dont just send the $$ you can stay the night in Columbia.

Just then, Lane came out of the back door. "Damn, you done finished?" he asked. "What you say we get us some cheeseburgers? I wanna show you something."

There was one little detail about his plan Lane had left out—it wasn't just about the money, it was personal. Mitchell Vance, the supposed copper magnate, had stolen Lane's wife around the same time his brother, Big Teddy, slid his motorcycle into a peach truck and went into a coma until they'd unplugged him. Lane had never been able to bring himself to hate Anna, so the feelings that could've flowed in her direction doubled back on Vance, stewing him crazy when he couldn't leave his mind alone, even now, fifteen years later.

The plan was born when Lane discovered that Myron, the only one of his old drinking buddies he still hung around with long after he'd quit drinking, hated Vance almost as much as he did. Myron's reasons were decidedly vaguer than Lane's—he'd known Vance since high school and had always figured him for a spoiled rich kid and all-around asshole, plus there was something creepy about the guy he could never quite put his finger on. Nebulous as his ire for Vance was, it nonetheless drove him to build a tiny flaw into the alarm system he installed and managed on Vance's property, which included a beautiful home with a pool and a sprawling lot studded with stately, ancient oaks and classic Mustangs in various states of refurbishment. At the back of the lot was a warehouse-sized garage where Vance allegedly kept his horde of stolen copper, which Lane had learned about years ago from another old drinking buddy who claimed to know someone who'd seen it.

When Myron installed Vance's security system, he did something he'd never done with any other client: he'd left a tiny chink in its invisible armor. He wasn't a criminal and had never intended to use it. He just liked knowing it was there. He'd never told anyone about it until one night he'd accidentally had eight beers and a shot at the bar and called Lane, the only person he knew who was bound to be sober, to give him a ride. Somehow they'd gotten to talking about what an asshole Vance was, and Myron bragged that if anybody wanted to take the guy down a notch, he knew exactly how.

Taking Vance down a notch was something that Lane wanted to do so badly that once it got inside his mind, he could never turn it loose. He rationalized it to himself for three months, putting himself to sleep at night thinking about slipping into Vance's shed like, well, like a thief in the night. He'd done it in his mind so many times, worked out all the variables to the point it seemed foolproof. Otherwise he never would've involved Little Teddy.

***

"That's it right there," Lane said, unwrapping a Rush's cheeseburger and gesturing toward the side of the highway as he drove. "I'll turn around up here and drive you back by it slow so you can see it."

Teddy did indeed see it on the second pass. There was a high chain-link fence hidden by the trees alongside the highway, just the hint of a building beyond it in the shadows.

"That's the back of his lot. That building you saw, right there, is where he keeps the copper. Myron rigged it up where the window on the back of that garage is off the security grid. All we gotta do is clip through that fence with some wire snips—ain't no electricity or alarms or nothing on the fence—get in that window, and clean his ass out. Nobody lives back here, just soybean fields and trees and shit, and we can pull off the road and hide the truck under some trees, cut the lights, and won't nobody see us."

He was quiet for a moment, chewing his cheeseburger, steering with a wrist laid casually over the top of the wheel. Then he said, "I know you ain't interested. You got too much sense for stuff like that. Just wanted to show you is all."

"How much money you talking about here?" Teddy asked.

Lane grinned. "Lotta money. And, thing about it is, ain't no way to get caught."

"How much?"

"Oh, man, I don't know exactly how much he's got in there, but..."

"Guesstimate it. Don't overshoot it. I want a number, a realistic number."

Lane gave him a number. It was higher than Teddy figured, even adjusting for bullshit.

"Alright," Teddy said. "When can we do it?"

"Shit, bo," Lane said. "Tonight. Gonna be cloudy and half-ass raining and dark. It's perfect."

"You think I might get a little advance on it with Friday's paycheck?"

"Yeah, we can probably do something like that. But what you need money for in such a hurry?"

Teddy told him everything—the stupid fight they'd had, the baby on the way, how he thought maybe they could try to work things out and keep the baby.

"Damn, bo," Lane said. "I thought you was gonna tell me you found out she was screwing some college dude or something. I wasn't ready for all that." He was somber for a moment, then he started beaming. "What you think my grampa name oughta be? I'm not feeling *PawPaw* or some shit like that."

He went on for a good while, dispensing what scant fatherly advice he had, opining on whether Teddy ought to just go ahead and marry her or not. The tone was jubilant, but then he fell silent for a moment. "Damn, Teddy," he said finally. "Your life about to change."

They sat in the cab of the truck for a moment after Lane killed the lights, letting their eyes adjust to the darkness. "Started to smoke me a joint before we came out here," Lane said. "But I'm glad I didn't do that."

He was quiet long enough that Teddy was beginning to think he'd changed his mind. "We gonna do this or what?" Teddy asked.

"Yeah. Just sitting here thinking about it, visualize how it's gonna go down in my head, making sure we done thought of everything. Like the tag. Taking the tag off the truck in case somebody happens to drive by and see it, that was a good idea you had. Just like this here is a good idea." He reached into the cargo pocket of his shorts and pulled out his .45. It was blacker than the dark, glinting just a little in what little light there was.

"Fuck is that for?" Teddy asked.

"Just, you know, in case."

"In case what?"

"In case, I don't know...maybe they got a big mean-ass dog

in there."

"I thought Myron said there wasn't no dog."

"Said he hadn't *seen* a dog. Maybe they got a big mean-ass dog stays in the house all day and patrols the property at night."

"Better not be a dog. I didn't sign up for killing no dog."

"I love dogs. Ain't never shot a dog in my life if you don't count putting JoJo down after he got hit by a car. But if there's a big-ass Doberman or some shit in there 'bout to eat you, I'ma fuck his ass up. But won't be no dog. Still, just in case..." he clicked the safety on and slipped the pistol back into his cargo pocket.

"Alright," Teddy said. "Let's stop dickin' around and do it, then."

"Yep," Lane said, beginning to drum softly, nimbly on the windshield and sing, "'cause meanwhile, Teddy, he ain't wastin' time no more..." He broke off singing. "You know that song, right? Yeah, you do, because I raised you right. Well, your mama raised you. But I was there."

"You sitting here wasting time while you singing a song about *not* wasting time," Teddy said.

"Alright. I'm just being stupid because I'm nervous. I mean, this thing's gonna be easy, no worries. But, I mean, I ain't trying to drag you into some bullshit, Teddy. If something goes wrong, you get your ass outta there and don't worry about me."

"Okay," Teddy said, getting out of the cab and shutting the door as quietly as he could.

The first stage of the plan went fine. Using two pairs of wire snips, they cut a large section of the chain-link security fence to fold open a door roomy enough to walk through without stooping over. The back of the garage was only a few yards from the fence, the lone back window that Myron had told them about set off in the right-hand corner. They'd even remembered to bring a few cement blocks to stand on to make getting in the window easy.

With a towel wrapped around his fist, Lane knocked out the

bottom windowpane. The initial crack and the ensuing tinkle of glass on the floor inside no louder than the throbbing of the cicadas and tree frogs all around them in the dark. He reached in and unlocked the window, and they slipped inside. They landed in some sort of back office, just as Myron had said. There was a desk, a couple of old calendars with half-naked women posing on classic muscle cars, a plastic tree in the corner. Everything was exactly as Myron had described it to Lane.

"Alright," Lane whispered. He closed his eyes and pictured Myron's layout. "Out that door right there is the garage. It's huge. Over on this side, there's like a little showroom thing set up where he keeps a few of them Mustangs he collects, the best ones. Over to the left, there's a buncha junk—more cars, engine parts, them little go-karts, all kindsa shit. Up against the side wall is one of them big containers like you use for the trash when you tearing down a house. That's gotta be where he keeps the copper."

"You saying nobody's ever seen it?" Teddy asked, pinching the bridge of his nose and wrinkling his forehead. "Fuck are we doing here?" he said, mostly to himself.

"Calm down. Worst thing can happen is we get over there and there's no wire or anything in there. Then we just slip back out the window and be gone. Ain't no alarms sounding, no automatic lights. We wearing gloves, so ain't no fingerprints. But, trust me, this dude is shady as fuck. He drives them little go-karts around at parades, wearing them weird hats and taking up money for terminally ill kids and all that, but he's a fuckin' crook. You don't have this kind of money if you ain't some kind of crook. There's a goddamn pile of copper sitting in that bin."

Lane eased the office door open and snuck out. To get to the bin on the junkier other side of the building, they had to walk through the showroom. Two late-sixties Mustang convertibles, one candy apple red and the other blue, sat on a buffed concrete floor, shining in what little light there was. They made it to the other side of the building, picking their way through the remains of other Mustangs in various stages of repair, one fastback set up on a lift with its engine suspended from chains just above.

In the front corner sat the boxcar-sized metal bin they sought. They were just about to peek inside when one of the garage bay doors, the furthest one in front of the showroom, began to rise open with a grinding, motorized whirr. The bottom dropped out of Teddy's guts. Lane killed the flashlight he'd just turned on, and they crouched behind the bin, jammed between it and the corrugated metal side wall in the dark, listening in muted horror while the door went back down. There were a couple of voices, cartoonish and happy but indecipherable, oddly muffled and weirdly pitched. Teddy peeked out from around the corner of the bin just as a couple of spotlights flipped on, shining down on the two Mustang convertibles on the polished showroom floor on the other side of the building.

What he saw in those spotlights took a moment to sink in because he had no template for it in his brain. A man-sized chipmunk, or rather someone in a mascot-style furry chipmunk suit, knelt in front of one of the cars, its red cartoon nose buried between the legs of a somewhat sleeker furry fox who writhed in pleasure on the hood, the expression on its costume head never changing despite the apparent ecstasy of its gyrations. A purple bear leaned on the fender, watching the show and pawing at its crotch while a bunny rabbit hovered nearby, recording it all on a phone.

While he watched, still trying to make sense of the scene, the fox pushed the chipmunk's head away and spoke in a petulant cartoon voice. Teddy couldn't make out what the fox said, but it must've been nasty because the rabbit brought its hand to its face and looked around in scandalized silence, a bucktoothed grin frozen on its face. The rabbit may have been shocked, but the bear knew just what to do, waddling in between the fox's legs and humping away, slowly at first and building to a frenzy, stopping once or twice to make sure its head didn't fall off.

The chipmunk watched the bear hump the fox for a while, seeming to cheer them on, and then it leaned on the hood of the other car, beckoning the shy rabbit to join. The rabbit came, though it still seemed a little timid. They embraced and pressed their bulbous cartoon faces together for a moment, then the chipmunk bent over the hood while the rabbit, finally emboldened enough to take charge, began to hump it from behind, pulling at the chipmunk's tail with one paw and slapping its rounded butt with the other.

"What in the everlovin' fuck is this?" Lane whispered when Teddy had crouched back down behind the bin.

"The fuck am I supposed to know?" Teddy whispered back.

"I don't know. You on the internet all the time. We didn't have this kind of shit before the internet."

Teddy shushed Lane with a finger to his lips. "Hush," he whispered. "They got no idea we're here. We just gotta wait it out, sneak out when they done."

"You think they getting off inside of there? Like rubbing their dicks on the inside of the suit? Or is it just, like, pretend or some shit?"

"Shhhh. Shut the fuck up."

"They can't hear us. We whispering. Plus you probably can't hear shit inside a suit like that." He was quiet for a moment. They were no longer watching, but based on the Disney-voiced moaning and grunting pierced by occasional encouragements to go harder or faster, things were going well.

"Oh shit," Lane said after a while, bringing his hand to his mouth in shock, much like the rabbit had done earlier. "One of them is Anna, probably. I didn't think about that. Lord, don't let it be that fox."

"Don't think about that. Just shut up and be quiet."

Teddy snuck another peek over the top of the bin. They'd swapped partners, the rabbit now humping the shit out of the fox while the bear writhed atop the chipmunk on the floor. "Gonna be a minute," he said, sliding back down beside Lane. "They still going at it pretty hard."

Lane was unable to shut up. "Teddy," he whispered, "I can't

believe I got you in this shit."

"We'll talk about it later."

"I'm sorry, bo. I been a fuckup my whole life. Probably why my wife left for fuckin' Chucky Cheese over there. And here I done got you in this bullshit, and you 'bout to have a baby. I promised your daddy I'd take care of you, but I shoulda promised him I'd leave you the fuck the alone, stay away from you."

"Just please shut up," Teddy whispered back. But it didn't matter, because this time it was him who'd fucked up. At just that moment there was a buzz in Teddy's pocket, and the ringing of his phone echoed all around the cavernous building. It had to be Mandy, he couldn't help thinking as he jammed his hand hurriedly into his pocket to silence it; who else would be calling him in the middle of the night? The cartoon humping noises stopped abruptly, replaced by startled human ones.

"Who is that?" a man barked. Then, more quietly, to his companions, he said, "Quick, y'all get out of here. I got a gun in the dash of the car. Gonna check this out."

Teddy felt concrete harden in his veins. He was unable to move, but Lane sprang into action. "Whatever happens, keep your ass hid behind this dumpster," he whispered to Teddy.

Then he stood up and brandished the pistol toward the menagerie. "None of y'all move or else I'ma shoot every fuckin' one of you. Get your goddamn hands in the air," he said.

Teddy peeked around the edge of the bin, still hidden in the shadows, and watched as four sets of furry arms went in the air. Lane stepped over him and strode over to the edge of the spotlight. The chipmunk had taken its head off, revealing itself to be a man, middle-aged and handsome, face sweaty, hair mussed from being inside the suit. It was Vance.

"Now listen here," Vance said, his anger and fear rendered ridiculous by the mirth of his costumed body.

Suddenly the bear whipped its head off. It was Anna. "Lane, you piece of shit. Put that gun down before you do something stupid."

Lane laughed, sounding crazier than Teddy, who'd heard him pretty crazy, had ever heard. "Holy shit!" he said. "Figured you was the fox getting her pussy eat out on the hood of the car. And I might be a piece of shit, but at least I ain't your husband over here getting nailed in the ass by all the friendly little woodland critters."

"Shut your fucking mouth," she hissed. "You don't know a thing about this. You couldn't ever understand it."

"You right about that. I don't know a goddamn thing about this shit right here. But you the one needs to shut up or else I'ma shoot Alvin the chipmunk over here." He stopped and looked around for a moment. "Reckon y'all need to take off them heads, too," he said, motioning over to the rabbit and the fox.

The fox brought its hands to the sides of its head to comply, but the rabbit took off for the door, flashing its cottony tail as it ran. Lane shot it in the back before it even got out of the circle of spotlight. Its head came off as it twisted to the floor, rolling to the side to reveal a woman somewhat younger than Anna with short, dark hair and a chubby, round face. The fox threw off its own head, and underneath was a man with hair the same Bugs-Bunny gray as the suit. "Julie!" he screamed, rushing to the woman in the fox suit, but Lane shot him and he fell to the concrete floor, whimpering and trying to crawl for a moment before Lane finished him off with one more shot that echoed around the dark garage.

Vance, still in the chipmunk suit, lowered his shoulder and rushed at Lane but pulled up short as Lane swung around and leveled the pistol at him. Anna began to scream, crying real tears and berating Lane with every vile name she had, ranting with the freedom of finally telling him what she'd wanted to say years ago, but he cut her short with another shot straight up at the roof.

"Shut up. Lord, everybody just shut the fuck up and let me think."

"Think? What the fuck is there to think about?" Anna said. "You just murdered two people minding their own goddamn business on somebody else's property. Fuck you, Lane, you stupid son of a bitch."

"You know what?" Lane said evenly. "You're right. Guess there ain't nothing to think about now. Might as well stop dickin' around wastin' time." He squeezed off two shots into the chest of Vance's chipmunk suit and two more into Anna. They crumpled together into a heap, Anna's human head coming to rest on Vance's furry belly.

When Teddy got to him, Lane was in a ball on the floor, crying his eyes out. He sobbed until he was dry and then looked up at Teddy. "I'ma make this right," he said. "Get you out of it."

"Ain't no making it right," Teddy said. "We just got to get the fuck out of here fast as we can. Try to cover it up."

"Nope. There's a way," Lane said. "Take care of that baby, Teddy. Don't fuck around with that copper over there, just get your ass out here fast as you can. Walk home. Ain't that far, just a few miles. Leave the truck here so they think I was by myself, I just came in here and shot up the place 'cause I was broke up about my wife fuckin' a buncha football mascots having some kinda weird orgy or some shit."

"What are you talking about?" Teddy pleaded. "Just come on, let's get outta here."

"No, they'll never stop looking. Ain't no way we'd get away with this."

"Lane."

"I'm serious, Teddy. I done fucked up so much I ain't fuckin' this up, too. Don't make me do it while you watching. Get the fuck outta here. You can take over the lawn business. Ain't much, but it's something, enough to take care of a baby, let that girl stay in school, get y'all started."

"Lane."

"Swear to god, you better get the fuck outta here, Teddy. You 'bout to see something you don't wanna see."

"Fuck that shit," Teddy said. He tried to choke down the sickness spreading in his gut. "Come on, let's go."

"I love you, bo. Always told Big Teddy I'd take care of you. Lemme do it."

Teddy lunged for the gun, but it was too late. Lane raised it to the side of his head and squeezed the trigger with his eyes still open. There was an awful finality to the silence that settled over the garage in the wake of the shot. Teddy stood watching the blood pool underneath Lane's head for too long. Then he turned and went out the way they'd come in and walked all the way home in the rain.

WOMAN ACROSS THE RIVER

Brodie Lowe

The two-toned Blazer cartwheeled four times across a reaped pasture clotted with stacks of hay deposited helter-skelter by balers. The momentum receded as it slowed in its final flip, balancing its weight on the front right tire as if there were a skilled daredevil behind the wheel posing for some half-ready photographer of stuntmen. Then it dropped on its hood and rocked, the suspension whining and the tires spinning in the air and flames already bursting from the hoodless frontend, lapping at new sprigs of green.

Hull grabbed the steering wheel right-handed and kicked open the driver's side window with his boot heels. He crawled pell-mell through the shattered opening on his hands and knees. Rolled over on his back. Ran hands over his torso and neck to make sure a part of him hadn't been pierced in the wreckage. When he judged his blood pumping undiminished, he threw out his arms and lay there on his back, sun-showered and stricken like some shored starfish.

A slack-jawed cow had crossed his path when he was speeding down a long stretch of tar-snaked highway. He had been looking in his rearview mirror and checking the claw marks on his neck. He turned the steering wheel right, the front tire dropping into a ditch. Fishtailing, he yanked again on the wheel to miss an abandoned rotary tiller. That's when his world began to tilt sideways.

He arose. Adjusted the belt around his waist. Checked to see if his toes still pointed straight out in front of him. Then he sprinted for the tree line back-ending the field, patting the thieved photograph in his front pants pocket, and looking to see if the trio were lingering in the pastoral landscape behind him. Out of the corner of his eye, he saw a farmer staking the ground with a pitchfork, watching his harried sprint in disbelief.

The screen door slapped against the front porch's wood-paneled wall as Angie and Brandy ran spraddle-legged down the steps for their older sister. When they reached her, they stood on either side and grabbed her shaking hands, resurrecting her from the muddy drive. After she found her bearings, they caught wind of whatever concussion had taken hold of her and they slid around in the loosened gravel, waving their arms in the air so as not to fall. A passerby might've believed them to be wine-drunk or addled by spirits cast out across the land by spittle-mouthed ministers.

"What did he take off with?" Brandy said. She wiped the back of her hand over the hairless beam of her brow.

Rhonda struggled for footing and wrapped her arms around their shoulders as they crutched her six-and-a-half-foot frame. Her sisters stood eye-level with her elbows, and the trinity looked as if they might've aged beyond what mere flesh could handle.

"Came right through the front door," Rhonda said. "Knew exactly where it was. Like he'd been here before. I was asleep on the couch. Must've stepped on one of those boards right there where the rug needs fixing. That's what woke me up. And I shot up. Took after him."

Angie looked around the property. The seed bell she had hung on a blackjack oak's low branch had fallen and exploded on the ground. "Was that his doing?"

Rhonda marked different areas of the front yard with an index finger, recounting the short-lived pursuit. "Had him grabbed around the collar all the way down the front steps. Scratched him up some. But he tore loose from me. Hurdled over the washtub like a damn gazelle and ran headfirst into that bird food."

Angie undraped her taller sister's arm from around her and let Brandy take on the weight. She walked over to the tree. Stooped at the trunk. Hand-ladled the seeds from the ground. A cardinal watched her from atop the propped elbow of a porcelain gnome that lay sideways in the weed-choked yard. "Spent all day looking around in the attic for a yellow ribbon to tie up with that food so we'd have us some goldfinches come through." She grabbed the three-foot-long ribbon that had been around the waist of the bell and slid its silk body through her fingers. Standing, she shoved it in her pants pocket. "Let's take a drive. See if we can find out where he headed off to."

Angie started off toward the barn. Unlatched the great wooden bar that kept it closed. Stepped through and waved her sisters to follow into the unlit space there beneath the oak tree's far-reaching limbs.

Sunlight parceled the dark as they climbed into their windowless van. Angie slammed it into reverse and backed out. Vinyl lettering on the side of the van was so sunworn that the words were hardly legible. It had traveled many a mile, driving from house to house through storms and snow and floods, delivering casserole dishes to those who needed comfort and assurance. They called themselves Ladies Helping Hands and they liked to show up when nobody expected them.

Hull loped through a long-forgotten, bracken-laced wagon trail. A lulled singing played out ahead of him. A sweet-sounding chorus synced with splashes of water. He slowed when he came to a cleft in a tree line and saw an unmoving river peopled with worshippers in white robes. Some stood waist-deep in the murky depths, running open hands over the tranquil surface, preoccupied with a watchful vigilance meant for water moccasins. The others stood on the bank behind them, shooting heads and arms through more white robes they chose from cardboard boxes labeled by size.

A preacher stepped into the river, moving through the muddy water, grabbing a bobbing limb and throwing it underhanded onto the opposite side of the bank, clearing the way.

Hull looked to the right and left and wondered if he should backtrack. Go further down and cross the river where it was unbothered. But in his deep crouch, he saw the rectangular outline of the photograph in his pants against the curve of his thigh. He took a knee. Reached inside his pocket and withdrew a sandwich bag zippered airtight. When he opened it, he half-believed to be robbed of his breath in the same way storied archaeologists had been when they opened tombs in Egypt's deepening sands. But there was no smell. And his breath did not falter. He grabbed the corner of the daguerreotype by his fingernails, careful not to taint its form, and brought it out of the bag.

The origins of the silver-shadowed photograph had been told and retold until there was no longer any sure path of its heritage. Word was that the picture had passed through the hands of a carny who had an infantile head with squinted eyes and a grin growing from one of his feet where his toes ought to have been. His job was to hold it up, using the deformity as a puppet and talking through the side of its little mouth during stage shows for gawkers who paid for its many jokes and prophecies. This malformed carny had happened upon the picture at a yard sale and slept with it pressed beneath his pillow for a week. After seven days passed, he awoke with a normal foot. The little face had been replaced with five uncalloused toes as if that part of his anatomy had been born again.

A miracle.

There were many stories of how the picture ended up in the hands of those not afflicted but wishing for fortune. The trajectory of their lives had shifted in a way that brought about riches unforeseen. The photograph was said to take away skin burns, bring back fingers lost in textile mills, and dissolve abscesses and goiters until the skin sagged empty and translucent.

Hull had to find out if the tales were true. But he didn't know where to start. And as if by providential aide, he overheard someone speaking of three sisters deep in the wood who had found the photograph in their mother's belongings after losing a battle with death.

He deliberated over the image of a shirtless man who lay sprawled back on a rocking chair in the middle of a dark room, forever frozen and recorded in time. There was no telling if the picture was taken before or after death. The camera's light had caught his eyes in a way that he didn't appear to have pupils, but cataracts. A black liquid rimmed his forehead and ran over his eyes in an oily sheen, coagulating on his jowls. Women held him by his wrists, his open palms facing the cameraman. And in the center of each hand was an amoebae-shaped pool of dark blood snailing down his wrists and forearms. A farmer was on bended knee, his back against the chair's edge, and the man's naked feet were propped up on either shoulder, showing the same injuries as those on the hands.

A prevailing wound of mystery only few endured. And fewer lived to tell.

Stigmata.

Hull wondered how many hands it had passed through. And how many stacks of dollar bills it had brought into the lives of those who had followed its prescription of seven days. How many of the lame could now sprint alongside Olympians? How many of the poor in spirit had been lifted? How many had moved from living on the streets to living in mansions untarnished?

He placed the photo back in the plastic baggie, and as he shoved it in his pocket, he felt bites on his ankles and shins. Standing up, he found that he had been resting a knee on an ant hill the size of a baseball mitt. Red ants spilled out of the mound of dirt, had already found the separation between pantleg cuff and skin, and were sprinting for his groin.

The robed ones heard the cursing before he made his appearance, hopping one-legged down the embankment, through stands of poison ivy, and yelling for somebody to splash water on him and save him from being eaten alive.

"Spirit's done grabbed ahold of him," the preacher said, and he waded back toward the shore. "Spectators are wont to be touched."

Hull tripped over quartz rock jutting from the ground and front-flipped twice, his face landing at the water's edge. He lay still for a long second. Then he raised up, long hair water-combed forward over his face, flailing his arms and sucking air, and they were all much afraid.

The preacher grabbed at this stranger who had invited himself into their clandestine service, but Hull ran ahead, dunking himself under water, unsteered, and snapping his head back. Water roostered in wild arches from his hair and splashed on the people. Little by little, he worked his way across the river in a gargling mess, floundering and side-stroking and bobbing until he reached the opposite side of the river.

He stood and shook his leg out, slapping at his knees and thighs, frog-punching his quad. Wailing for the pain to end. For the ants to die.

The preacher shook his head. "That's not how any of this is done, brother."

Hull looked at them. He believed them to be out of their minds for standing in a place where dead bodies had been found. Where shards of glass bottles were liable to cut through feet. But they didn't move. Only stood there with their hands outstretched, praying for him to come back into the water with them a little while longer.

On his far left, an idling van was parked on a bridge crossing the river. Three shapes stood watching, and he could see the taller sister chewing on her gums and holding fists out in front of her, knuckles up. Spitting over the cement railing. And breaking an imaginary stick as if it were his body.

Turning around, he took off through a deeper part of the woods where lay deadened trees split and struck by lightning, windblown by long-ago hurricanes.

Before long, he came to a gable-roofed house and tested the front door's knob. It was unlocked. He turned it and entered a backwards-built house in which the front room was a kitchen where a living room ought to have been.

"Wasn't expecting a visitor," a woman's hollowed voice spoke from somewhere within the house.

"I'm being chased," Hull said. "Don't want to give you no trouble. Just need a place to hide until things blow over."

"They close behind?"

Hull thought about the three sisters. He had staked out their property for weeks. Watched them move past the windows, restless in the night. Holding the blessed photograph up to their faces in their lamplit den only to replace it in a book on their shelf.

He knew them all by name. On some nights when there was a summer breeze, they cracked their windows open. And he would stand outside in the shadows, listening to them read from a story about four men burning unhurt in a fire.

"Yes."

"Does this house have a neon sign on it saying to bring your troubles here?"

"Just let me go on through then. Out your back door. And I'll be on my way."

"I've got a hungry Doberman back there who hasn't had a meal yet today. What's your name?"

"I'm nobody. Help me hide and I'll be out of your hair."

"Pantry's open."

He rushed over to the pantry and closed the bifold door. He stood there in a pitch-black cell that smelled of cured meat.

The woman shuffled over linoleum and came over to the stove. Long, layered hair cocooned her face in a shifting shroud of black. From the closet, Hull couldn't tell her age or her features. "Wasn't planning on having company." She looked out the window. "Cavalry's arrived."

She moved to the door and opened it to three heavy-breathing sisters.

"Our poor son's done gone and lost his mind. He was being held at the asylum down the road and he broke loose. We have an inkling he might've stopped here for a little refuge. He believes the end times are among us. All he needs is a big enema and a straitjacket and he'll be back on the straight and narrow," Rhonda said.

"I haven't heard anything. But you can have a look."

"Thank you, sister."

She stepped aside. They moved through the kitchen in a hump-backed triad, reverential and awe-inspired by furniture-dragged markings on the floor and darker corners of the room. Amateur detectives studying the place for evidence of his whereabouts.

Brandy stopped in the kitchen's doorless frame. Stretched out her arms. Pressed her hands against either side beam and, closing her eyes, whispered in a different tongue. Her head snapped back and the third steadied her, grabbing the nape of her neck and asking her what she knew. "Where is he? Do you feel him?"

He squinted through the slit in the pantry and inspected their feet for they appeared to be floating, ghost-propelled and tabernacled by some greater spirit who held their shoulders concave, their heads bowed in fervent meditation.

Rhonda pointed to the ceiling. "We're going up. If you don't mind."

"Sure. Be careful up there," the houseowner said.

"You know something we don't?"

"This house has a mind of its own." She worked her hands through the air, outlining a giant globe of no clear boundaries. "I see shadows up there from time to time. That's why I never go up."

"How long have you lived here?" Rhonda walked to the

doorframe and stood between her two sisters.

"Going on three years."

"I'm not afraid."

"Doors open and slam shut at night," the woman said.

Brandy nodded toward the tall one. "This one here gave us a scare on here a while back. Used to traipse around through the woods at night. Ran through the creek and climbed trees with the squirrels. Might nearnt lost her mind."

Rhonda stared at her feet. Wiggled her long toes inside acrylic-chipped pumps. "Suppose I did go a little crazy back in the day."

"Had to chain her to the bed," Angie said. "She threw up everything we gave her to eat. Thought we was helping her keep her appetite. But we was just adding fuel to the fire. All of it shot out green like out of a spigot. You'd've thought she'd taken up painting for a living. Covered the wallpaper."

Rhonda shook her head. "That was then."

"This is now."

"Calmed down a lot since then." Rhonda placed each hand on top of her sisters' heads. Massaged their scalps. They closed their eyes and tilted their faces toward the popcorn-plastered ceiling. "Wouldn't be nowhere if it wasn't for them."

"If you find him, bring him down here and let me have a look at him," the woman said.

And off they went like the rabid and demented. Soon, feet trampled over the second floor above. Doors opened and closed. "I'm waiting," she spoke to the pantry.

Hull opened the door and stepped out. "You didn't have to let them in."

"Going to be confronting each other one way or another. And I'd rather have those ladies up there while we talk. All I've got to do is yell out and they'll be down here ready to take your head off." She parted the hair from her face, and he saw that it was Faye. The woman who he had stood beside at an altar while they were pronounced husband and wife.

He patted the photograph in his pocket. "It works. Sooner

than I thought it would."

"What've you gotten yourself into this time?"

"I'm looking for a miracle. A way to get you back. I think this picture I stole from them just made it happen."

She leaned back on the oven and pushed herself forward, walking across the linoleum toward him. "You've already made a mess of things you can't put back together. And whatever's in that pocket's not going to save you."

"I've quit the drinking. No more gallivanting around. Wouldn't do that to you again. I just want things to be the way they used to be. Taking you into town. Up to one of them fish restaurants. Get you that tartar sauce you like."

She put a hand up. "That's where you found somebody else. And I'm not going back down that road and letting you rip my heart out and stomp on it again. That's why I moved out here. So that I could get as far away from you as possible." She hung her head and closed her eyes. "Your man's down here," she called out.

There was a rustling above him, and the sisters stampeded down the staircase.

He looked back at Faye. "I should've never come."

They rounded the banister, crusading against him and yelling for him to give it up. He ran past Faye. Busted her front door wide open. Ran down the steps. Tripped over a kinked garden hose. Rolling around in the grass, he grabbed at his ankle.

The trio was quicker than they looked. They took off through the front yard in a stiff-legged gallop, their bodies jury-rigged and half held together as if their bones and sinew ran machinations bent on exacerbating the already aberrant into some ultimate totem of deformity. And when they fell upon him, they twisted on his ankles and wrists. Some lesser form of jiu-jitsu.

Angie brought out the yellow ribbon and, coming up behind him, flung it around his neck to hold him in place. She put her mouth to his ear. "Where's our little picture?"

He pointed at his pocket.

Rhonda stooped near his leg and wrenched forth the dampened bag. She took the photo out, shaking it and blowing on it. When she judged it dry and not ruined from his river crossing, she told them to let him go. "I've found our graven image."

Three concussive discharges made Hull's ears ring. Blood-curdled bone meal was already sloughing off the lip of a potted plant.

Hull backpedaled on his elbows, watching the three buckshot-blasted sisters wheeling through the yard, worm-like and gasping for air. They grabbed at their wasted throats and bleeding shoulders.

Faye stood on the top step with a shotgun aimed at him. "I've got more where that came from."

"You know I didn't mean it," he said. "That was the drink."

"I've a mind to just go on ahead and blow a hole clean through your throat so that for the rest of your life, it'd just waterfall out of there before it even hit your stomach. You'd never make a bad decision then, would you?"

"Let me go."

She stepped over Rhonda's quivering body and picked up the dropped photograph. "Tell me what this means."

"Grants your wishes." He stood and ran back through the woods from whence he came. Buckshot chewed away the side of a tree next to his head. He sprinted until he came to the river, high stepping through the muddy water until he was slogging through waist-deep.

"He's done changed his mind," the preacher called out. He squeezed his biceps as if he had been lifting and putting down heavier things than he was used to handling, and he gave a weak wave for Hull to come closer to them. And when Hull got close enough, the preacher stopped him in his tracks, grabbing by the shoulder and turning him around, palming his forehead in a wet clap.

But Hull grabbed his wrist and pushed away. Diving straight down, he disappeared so that he could swim closed-eyed past the assembly's robed legs. Losing his bearings, he found that he was swimming in place, disoriented, not gaining ground, and turned topsy-turvy upside down in the crowded water.

His scalp bumped along the riverbed and then he stopped. Something had grabbed hold of his long hair. A root, washed away and exposed from the mire by years of mighty rushing waters, had now crowned him in a squiggle of knuckled wood.

His voice boomed from the depths as he yelled and grabbed at the root, but it only tightened his bound and ever-knotting hair. The sound that came from his throat jarred his skull and came out in a garbled mess of tongue he did not recognize. Words were blown to the surface in a glug as if the river itself was having a drink.

The preacher ordered Hull to come on up for some air. "You've been down in it long enough."

Hull's peripherals darkened while he held his breath for longer than he imagined his body could handle, and as the seamless beyond reached for him, he felt kin with the carny and the puppet foot, and he hoped that somehow his foot would proclaim his heart's desire in the selfsame honesty through the shoes he wore. Not that of prophecy, but that of sorrow and a way of remaining who he had once been. He wiggled his toes. Believed that part of him to have a voice unfound until that moment. Trusted that the baptized congregating around him would hear of his longing. They pulled on both his blood-drained and needling feet as he fought in the water's embrace. And he felt as if he had been living for years in some stranger's body, a rigored avatar that gloved an earlier part of his personhood where still remained some measure of nobility yet triumphed by maleficence.

In his mind's eye, he could see the woman, his lost love, standing somewhere in the rising timber across the river, throwing down the shotgun and marveling over the spellbound photograph, wondering what power it held and if she would cross paths with a better man in a different part of the world.

A TRAILER ON THE OUTSKIRTS OF TOWN

J.B. Stevens

Glitter fell out of his hair and covered the job application. Doug thought about a sparkling future. Then he felt like an idiot for daydreaming in puns. He brushed the specks away.

Savannah Community College's new term began in a month and he needed to complete the paperwork. He hoped to enroll in the Emergency Medical Technician program. It seemed like a good job. Doug liked the idea of getting paid to help people.

After lunch, he put on a black polo shirt and blue pants, no belt. His belly stretched the polyester. He spritzed himself with cologne and walked into the trailer's living room.

His brother, Andy, was still sleeping on the green corduroy sofa. Andy was a bit taller, a bit fitter, and a bit better looking than Doug. However, Andy was short, fat, and ugly. He was snoring when Doug left.

Doug limped into the janitorial gig before the evening rush. The problem with cleaning Emperor's is the glitter; it sticks to everything. He didn't mind. The sparkle was a nice addition to the daily slog.

Doug said hi to his favorite performers, asked the DJ to put on an Outkast rap song with a pumping bass line, and got to work.

He wiped down the bathrooms and made his way to the VIP area—always lots of cleanup in there. Doug started in booth one. It smelled like warm bodies and fruity lotion.

Doug heard Jim, the owner, and Destiny, the entertainer, in booth two. Destiny was tall and lean and from Russia. Jim was shiny. His skin, suit, hair: it all sparkled. He never missed anything.

Doug watched Jim close. He'd noticed that Jim had a thing for Destiny. Jim put Destiny through nursing school. Jim was good like that. He didn't even expect anything in return. However, eventually Destiny came back to the club. She still went home covered in glitter.

Doug was rubbing down purple velvet chairs and trying to stay awake. He half listened as Destiny suggested she and Jim go target shooting.

Jim talked about avoiding the IRS, using cash and a safe out on his yacht. Jim invited Destiny to come over for some extra-curricular fun and gave the address. Doug typed it in his phone.

Work ended. Doug got in his beat-up Ford Bronco and went back to the trailer on the outskirts of town. Moonlight broke through the oak trees, and the place felt haunted. He heard crickets and smelled the salt marsh. Doug loved nighttime in Savannah.

He went inside the old mobile home. Andy was drunk as hell and relaxing on the couch. Doug kicked an empty Natural Light can.

"Why you laying around? You could at least tidy this place up," Doug said. "I've been out working all night and I come home to this."

"Working, ha."

"I bust my hump."

"Whatever. You know I can't move around too good. Plus, why would I clean?"

"Huh?"

"You're the pro."

Doug threw an empty can at Andy. "Stop milking that slip and fall. We both know it's bull-crap."

"Yea? Then why is disability still paying me?"

"Because the Piggly Wiggly over in Cusawitchee has good insurance, not because you're hurt."

"Says you." Andy frowned. "Enough about me, you good? You look goofy."

"Yea," Doug said. "Pondering on some stuff I heard at work."

"What kind of stuff?"

"I'm not sure."

Andy shifted to face his brother. "Well, spill it."

Doug explained about the safe and the boat. Andy nodded and drank.

"I'm tired of you talking about the place. I want to be around all them girls. How about you get me a job over at the club?"

"Then you'd have to get off disability."

Andy thought about that for a while. "Might be worth it. It'll be less money, but it's not like we pay rent."

Doug went to his bedroom and took off his work clothes. He grabbed a greyish white shirt off the bed. He smelled it—it wasn't too ripe—and put it on along with an old pair of Wranglers.

He went back to the living room. Andy tossed him a beer.

"Sit down," Andy said. "Have a drink. Bigfoot documentary is on."

Doug grabbed the can. "This's warm."

"Yup."

"You drink all the cold stuff?"

"Yup."

"I don't want warm beer."

"Then don't have any."

Doug sighed. He dropped on the sofa and popped his room-temperature brew. The place still smelled like Mom's cigarettes and made Doug feel wistful. Mom was kind. As Doug sipped the drink, Andy handed over a piece of paper.

"What's this?"

"Tax bill," Andy said.

"I work for cash, you're on disability. What taxes?"

"County says we got to pay for the land."

"But we own the trailer and the lot."

"If we want to keep em', we need..." Andy looked at the bill. "$7,323.36."

"Crap."

They watched pro wrestling and tried not to think about money.

Things played out for a while. They got another tax bill. This one had red ink. Doug started to worry. He told Andy his concerns. Andy nodded.

Four days later, when Doug was getting in from the club, he saw Andy pacing.

"I went over to the library," Andy said. "Got online, typed in that boat you told me about a few weeks back."

Doug looked at him and raised his eyebrows. He took a sip of cold beer. "Jim's?"

"It's parked out at Isle of Hope Marina. I think Jim lives there full-time."

"What do you think?"

"You know what I think," Andy said. "You're thinking the same thing."

"Maybe."

"Don't be scared. Just say it."

"We should rip him off."

"Yup."

The conversation drifted to Bigfoot and then the Loch Ness Monster. They drank until both passed out.

They kicked around a plan for a few more nights. Jim was divorced and his kids lived up north with their mama. So that yacht was a one-man show.

"Yachts are small," Andy said.

"Not a lot of places to hide a safe," Doug said.

"We could borrow a boat, hop on his, tow him out a bit, rob him...let him drift. We keep his cell phone. When we get back, we dial 911 from his cell phone and tell the coast guard where he is. Then we ditch the phone."

"Could work."

"Yup."

"Probably be easy."

"Yup."

Two nights later, they decided to take their shot. It was pitch-dark and smelled like rotten shrimp when they got to the marina. Doug could hear boats groaning on gentle waves. Doug had been there before on a hull-scraping job. There was no watchman or security.

They'd snagged hats, gloves, sunglasses, and old T-shirts from the lost and found at the club. Doug wrapped a shirt around his face, gangster style. Andy did the same. Andy grabbed his Remington 870 pump shotgun. Doug had a Hi-Point 9mm pistol.

Doug went to the marina's office building: a sad, clapboard grey thing in the center of the dusty gravel lot. He broke the window and unlatched the door. Doug went inside and found the keys to a fifteen-foot Carolina Skiff.

He waved Andy on. They went down weather-worn planks to the slips. Doug found the skiff. He bounded in, primed the outboards, and fired the thing up.

"All right," Doug said. "You go untie Jim's boat. We hook them up. We tow Jim two miles out. Throw his keys overboard. Take the phone. Take the money. Drive back in and call the Coast Guard 'cause we don't want him to die."

"Don't want to turn this robbery into a murder," Andy said.

"I agree."

"Does this make us pirates?"

"Probably."

"Arrrrr."

"It's a good plan."

"Too easy. We got this."

"We should give some of the money to Mama's church. That way, we're doing a good thing."

"Got to stay right with that. A little donation makes us like Robin Hood."

"What about DNA and stuff like that? We should do something with the skiff."

"Good call. When we get back, we'll point the thing out to sea, pin the throttle, and send her on her way. No evidence."

Andy smiled and nodded. Doug put his hand on his brother's shoulder. Doug felt good.

They untied Jim's big, off-white yacht. They lashed the front to their skiff. The brothers met on the dock.

"All right," Doug said. "You get on his boat and find him and put the gun on him. Once we're out a bit, I'll hop on. We'll get the money, untie, and head back."

Andy nodded and got on the yacht. Doug started the tow.

They got about twenty yards when the skiff's engines started whining. After ten more, they began smoking and cut off.

Doug saw Andy's head poke up.

Andy raised his hands and mouthed, "What the hell?"

"Damn thing's dead," Doug said. "Screw it. Let's get the money and figure it out from there."

Andy gave him the thumbs-up. Doug climbed onto the yacht. His unbelted pants descended. He slipped and fell and dropped his gun. He took his gloves off, threw them overboard, and grabbed the pistol.

It was quiet. The boat's lights were out.

The brothers went inside the humid cabin. There was a whiff of strawberry lotion.

"We're close," Doug said.

An interior door exploded open. Jim stood there naked, shiny, and howling.

Doug yelped and jumped backward. His pants fell. He tripped and hit his chin on a dresser and saw stars. He dropped his gun. He scrambled, found it, and aimed at Jim.

Andy fired a shot into the ceiling.

Doug's ears rang. "Stop shooting."

"Sorry, had to control the situation," Andy said.

"You," Doug said, pointing at Jim and stepping into the bedroom. "Sit down. Where's the safe? What's the combo?"

Jim looked at Doug. Jim's eyebrows furrowed and his face got hard.

"Fat, glitter-covered hands…" Jim said. "What the hell, Doug? You really think this is going to work?"

Doug's heart jumped to his throat. He looked at Andy. Andy shrugged and took off his face mask.

"Damn, it's hot in there," Andy said. "No use coverin' up. We're in deep. What now?"

Doug took off his mask. "How should I know?"

Jim glared at them and sat on the bed.

Andy motioned to Jim. "Whatever. Where's the money?"

Jim spit at Andy. Andy kicked Jim and put the gun to his head.

Doug closed his eyes and looked away. He didn't want to watch.

The shot was loud.

Pain came. It confused Doug. He looked down at his chest. Blood oozed. He got dizzy.

Andy fell to his knees, holding his crotch. Red seeped through his hands. He screamed.

Destiny walked by. She wore a jewel-covered mini-dress and stood over Doug. Glitter fell off her and got in Doug's eyes. Doug watched Jim pull out his cell phone.

"Hello," Jim said. "This the coast guard? Yea…I'm gonna need some help. No…no rush. Two intruders on my yacht just got shot with a small-caliber target pistol. Take your time. Isle of Hope Marina."

Destiny stood on the far side of the room, aiming at the brothers.

"Do you want me to help them? They might bleed out," Destiny said.

"Let 'em leak."

"I've never shot someone before."

"You used a twenty-two. It's basically a BB gun. It doesn't even count."

Doug felt nauseous. Jim took the brothers' weapons and left the room. He came back and nodded at Destiny. She went to her purse and pulled out two sets of furry handcuffs. One was pink and one was zebra-striped. She secured the brothers to the bed. The bed frame was bolted to the floor.

Jim led Destiny out of the room. He turned off the lights and closed the door.

Doug's chest hurt. Andy was screaming. A bit of moonlight snuck through the window. A seagull chattered and it smelled like fireworks.

Doug felt guilty. They were going to lose Mama's trailer and couldn't help the church. It all fell apart. He watched blood mix with glitter on the floor. He brushed the specks away and waited for the cops.

LOW DOWN DIRTY MEAN

Nikki Dolson

When the phone rings after ten p.m. on a weeknight, there was no good news coming down the line. I answered, expecting to hear that one of my husband's buildings was on fire or some developer friend has wrecked their car, was arrested for DUI, has killed someone, and they or their fixer was calling us for help. I didn't expect to hear my sister's voice.

"What's wrong, Anna Mae?" I slipped from my bed to talk to her from the dark depths of my closet.

"I just wanted to say hello, Grace," she said.

This lie from my sister who hadn't returned my phone calls in the three years since I chose to abandon her, my only family, and marry some guy she didn't think was worth my time. We discussed the weather and other nonsense, then she was gone, and I was left with fear growing in the pit of my stomach. Something had to be wrong. So, I did what any good sister would do. I booked a red-eye flight and arrived in Georgia in time for breakfast.

Her street was quiet with mostly tended lawns and big weeping willows and cypress trees casting shade across the homes. The house was tiny but serviceable with tall narrow front windows and a screened-in porch. Through the screens, Anna Mae, in her white night gown, looked like a ghost as she moved to the door to open it for me. She wasn't surprised to see me, only shook her head. "I was about to do my hair. Come have some coffee."

Ceiling fans in the living room and kitchen blurred at their highest settings, saving us from the worst of the morning heat. I was overdressed for the weather and felt sticky. I stripped off my shirt and shoes to sit in my bra and linen slacks at her kitchen table. I watched Anna Mae press her hair straight just like our mother had done for us when we were little, with an ancient hot comb stuck in the flame of the gas burner, a jar of hair grease open on the Formica counter.

"You didn't need to come," she said. "It's nothing I can't figure out on my own."

"Tell me what's going on," I said.

"Nothing. I guess I just wanted to find me a white boy like you did. Someone to sweep me off my feet and pay for everything. Is he cheating on you yet?" She clicked her tongue at me and parted her hair.

"Anna Mae."

She cut me off with a wave of her brush. "I don't expect you to approve of my life here."

"It's your life. I only ever wanted to hear how you were. I've missed you."

She pinned back a finished section of glossy black hair, parted her hair again, and applied grease to the thin line of scalp revealed. She brushed through the section of hair and pulled it taut. Two passes with the hot comb, put it back in the flame, pin back the hair, part the new section. Repeat.

"I met a man. Tyler. He seemed great. Definitely loose with money. Everything was good. I'd work a few nights at the bar; I'd work a few nights on him. I made enough plus some to save. But what I didn't know was that he had a husband."

"How'd you find out?"

"He caught us in his bed."

"Damn."

"Get this. Tyler runs out of the bed and out of the house, stark naked. The husband and me are looking at each other like *who's gonna move first*. He does, though. Just shook his head and left the room. No yelling, just tears. I hear him sobbing in another room."

"Packing that guy's shit?"

"You know it. I tiptoe over and lean around the doorway, intending to apologize then just grab my panties and go. He says 'It's not your fault. I knew he wasn't worth it, but I wanted him to be the right one.' Then we end up talking the rest of the night about the assholes we've dated. He was cool, which only made me feel worse."

"What's the husband's name?"

"Clint. Anyway, a few nights later, I'm working in the bar and Clint shows up. Hangs out. The bar is a dive. They water down the cheap, cheap whiskey there. But he's having a good time. Stays at the end of the bar all night."

"So, you're friends now?"

"Yeah."

"But there's a problem, right?"

She nodded. "That night, my dog Otis was killed. I found her on the driveway near the willow."

I remembered the Lab from a picture on her Facebook page. "Hit and run?"

"Bullet to the head." She sighed. "Did you know they actually have pet cemeteries? I always thought it was something Stephen King made up. I found one. It'd be two grand to bury my good girl, but I didn't have it. Clint gave me the money. I promised to pay him back and gave him three hundred dollars right then. He was there when I put her in the ground. A little headstone with Otissa on it. She was barely five."

My stomach clenched. "You tell the cops?"

"We all talked, but I said I didn't have a clue who'd want to hurt her. They figured it was random."

"But you don't think so. Who do you think did it?"

She shrugged. "It's a short list."

"But why you and not me?"

"Maybe they don't know where you're at. Maybe it's

someone who only knew me."

We had done a lot of things when we were younger. Used our dewy youth and ample assets to get what we wanted from the world. We were always together back then.

"You work tonight?" I asked.

"Yep."

"I'll come with."

Anna Mae's shift didn't start until late and she had errands to do. While she was gone, I tried to narrow down the possible names for the short list. Men and a couple women who felt done wrong by their encounters with us from back when we were professional girlfriends. The ones who were still angry after we moved on because they didn't give us enough to keep our attention. I settled on the ones with the means to come after either of us. I added Tyler and Clint to the list too.

My phone buzzed. It was Mitchum, a man who worked for my husband, letting me know he'd hit town. I asked him to look into Tyler, Clint and, with some regret, Anna Mae. I wanted to know what exactly she'd been doing in this town. I loved her, but I didn't always trust her. She had a talent for finding trouble. Trouble I had always followed her into until I finally got tired of it. Now I had money, a husband, a life worth holding on to, and she didn't even have a dog anymore.

For the other suspects, I called my favorite contact, Gerry. He was seventy years old, smoked a pack a day, and dragged around an oxygen tank for the brief moments when he wasn't smoking.

"Grace! How much do you need?" he said.

"I don't need money."

"Oh, then you're calling because you've finally realized our love cannot be denied."

"Close. I need information on some other men."

He grumbled.

"Please, Gerry. I'll make you the Bolognese again."

"That was good. These guys. Are they local? Or California?"

"I'm not sure where three are at the moment. I need to know

if they have connections down here in Georgia. Someone might be after my sister."

"Sorry to hear that, but I don't do the south."

"Come on, Gerald. Bolognese. With me?"

"With you?"

"Me and my top-shelf cleavage."

"Fine. Give me a couple days." Gerry was a happy man.

That night, Anna Mae installed me at the end of the bar with a beer and a basket of chicken fingers. There was a good-sized crowd. A mix of older regulars and some barely legal drinkers, all of them keeping her too busy to talk to me. Her smile was still plastered on, but it was a calculated smile—not one thrown up to protect her, but to elicit reactions. Buy our alcohol, flirt with the pretty girl, go home.

Clint showed up after ten. My sister gave him the my-goodness-it's-been-forever smile and then efficiently moved him down to the end of the bar and introduced us. Clint was suburban-dad cute, all backyard barbeques and Saturday morning golfing. He was tall enough, had a little belly and an adorable cleft chin; if he was straight and I wasn't married, I might've tried for him.

"I guess she probably told you how we met," Clint said after he downed half the vodka tonic Anna Mae brought him.

"She did. I'm glad it worked out for you two."

He cut a look at me. "Meaning what?"

"Only that I'm glad you're friends now."

"Yeah, she's a sweetheart." He relaxed then and tried to catch Anna Mae's eye. He held up his drink. She nodded at him.

"Have you heard from him lately? Or is he staying low-profile until you're over wanting to set him on fire?"

"Ha! Tyler's not lying low. He came by Sunday, asking to borrow a car. I have this old Subaru I used when we headed out to the lake. He said he had a lead on a job in Atlanta. Haven't seen him in four days, I guess." Clint shrugged. "I was never any good at telling him no. He was beautiful."

He pulled out his phone and located a picture. "Here. Look at that smile! He was a trainer at my gym when we met. I thought we were in love." He let me take the phone.

Tyler was blond with a strong chin, good shoulders, a tiny gold earring in his right ear. He looked like the kind of guy who would see Clint as nothing but a mark. I checked out Clint's other pictures. More pics of him in a kitchen, on a deck, and near a lake where he looked to be unloading a boat. I sent a few to my phone, then handed it back to him.

"He's very handsome," I said.

"Such a good face. He ruined everything. I mean, I knew he would, but I hoped for something more." He put the phone facedown on the bar and finished his vodka tonic. Anna Mae was there with another drink for him.

"What do you do for fun out here?" I asked.

He lifted the remains of the second vodka tonic. "These days, I drink."

Clint was a liability consultant. He reviewed civil engineering practices and advised on all the things they were doing wrong that would get them sued into homelessness. For this work, he traveled six months of the year and made six figures. He was forty years old, without children or an ex-spouse. An only child of elderly parents. They lived in Oregon in a house he bought them. But love, real love, he said wistfully, had eluded him. We drank until the bar closed, then I packed him in a taxi home.

I left Anna Mae to close up and met Mitchum out at his motel. He sat on the edge of the bed, holding a bag of ice against his face.

"What happened?'

"Tyler has interesting friends. None of them were interested in talking to me. Don't make that face. I'm fine, Miss G."

I knew he could handle himself. Mitchum was ex-military, twenty-eight years old, solid, and mildly menacing even when he wasn't trying.

"Best I can tell, Anna Mae hasn't made any friends out here, nor any enemies. They like her at the bar. She has a handful of speeding tickets but that's about it. You were worried," he said.

"I was worried she had moved from what we used to do to outright crime. Drugs or something." Mitchum raised an eyebrow. "Believe it or not, before I became a nice, bland wife, my sister and I were slightly less-than-upstanding citizens."

"Miss G, I have never thought you were nice or bland." There was a sparkle in his eye.

I relayed what Clint told me about Tyler and stood to leave. "Keep looking for Tyler. Find the boat."

"Do you think he really has an interview in Atlanta?" Mitchum asked.

"Anything's possible, though I figure he'll just lay low until Clint forgives him. You take care of that face."

He gave me a lopsided smile. "Yes, ma'am."

"So, what did you think of Clint?" Anna Mae asked the next morning.

It wasn't even eight o'clock yet. I was still mostly asleep on her uncomfortable couch. She sat on her coffee table, legs crossed, foot bouncing.

"Is there coffee?" She handed me her mug. "Clint is nice enough. A little sad. Not that I blame him. He said Tyler was in Atlanta for a job."

"Maybe a job means he's found a Clint replacement. Though that man loved the boat Clint bought for him. I doubt he'd give it up," Anna Mae said.

"Where is the boat kept?"

"Not far from the lake. Some boat storage place."

She patted my leg and scooted out the door. More errands to do. She was working again that night. I sent Mitchum the information about the boat and called Gerry. He didn't let me down. "Here's the lowdown on your dirty boys. Some mean ones on your list."

Frank, fifty-two, our tennis pro with the nice beard and clean fro. He'd liked cigars and Anna Mae in tennis whites. He'd gotten married a few months after we left him, taking four thousand in cash with us. Evidently, he beat his new wife and she divorced him. Now he owned a club in Florida. He was close, but when the men Gerry sent pressed him, he wept and swore he didn't care one bit about us anymore.

Next was Teddy, Teddy, always at the ready. Led cock-first into every room. Gloriously fine half-Italian motherfucker. When last we saw him, he was being sentenced for check kiting. He always blamed us for getting caught. Three years in he got saddled with another ten for killing another prisoner. He didn't have the kind of reach needed to touch us from the inside. Crossed him off the list.

Clint could be the guy, but all Mitchum found was a man drinking his way through a heartache and literally fucking the pool boy. (Bobby, twenty-four, worked a dozen pool accounts and charges them each a hundred bucks each. He fucks some and lives cheaply. I didn't hold it against him.)

And then there was Leland, sixty-three, the one who almost made us settle down. The one who showed me that settling down didn't have to be a bad thing. That there could be joy and comfort in waking up to the same man every day. To fucking the same man every night. We had trouble telling him no more and bailed when he had a heart attack. He might very well hate us, but he didn't feel right for this.

That left Tyler. Age thirty-seven. Local heartbreaker, a cheater, a player. A man after our own hearts. A man who was still missing.

Gerry lobbed one more piece of trivia at me. "I did some digging on your sister. Did you know she has life insurance on you? I hope you're watching your back."

Anna Mae had taken out a $100,000 life insurance policy on

me two years ago. I knew she'd been angry with me, but this was surprising. I didn't even try to process it. Fortunately, Mitchum called and kept me from worrying about it. By noon, I was thirty miles from Anna Mae's place, pulling my rental sedan up next to Mitchum's black SUV out at the boat storage facility. Most of the facility was nothing more than a long metal awning over tarped and wrapped boats on their trailers. The lake itself was a ten-minute drive away. Mitchum was in front of a tall metal building, talking to a short, narrow man sweating profusely in a gray uniform. He had a padlock in his hand. The man in the uniform left as I came closer.

"Who was that?" I asked.

"Mr. Adamson. He hasn't seen anyone drive up here lately." Mitchum twirled the padlock on his finger.

"Then why am I here?"

He rolled the large metal door back on its track. He found a wall switch, and overhead fluorescent lights twitched to life. I followed him in. The room was thirty feet long by twenty feet wide. A tarp-covered boat took up most of the room. In the back was a wooden table.

Mitchum said, "They should pay Adamson more. A hundred bucks and he unlocked the place for me. Tyler never made it to ATL."

I looked at the boat. "He's in there?"

Mitchum turned me to face another tarp-covered thing that was on my left. "In the car."

I yanked off the tarp. There was the Subaru. I could see through the back window the folded body. I could see the tips of fingers. I stepped to the side and looked closer. There was a head right under the side window. The blond hair was dark where the blood had dried. I could make out a tiny gold earring covered with blood. My knees went weak and I dropped my purse.

"Don't touch," Mitchum said. I'd started to put a hand on the car but now I backed away, a scream trapped in my throat. I backed up until I hit the metal wall and slid down to sit on the concrete floor. It felt a little cooler there.

"He's...he's very dead. Goddamn." I hiccupped a sob. I didn't know Tyler, but part of me had been looking forward to meeting him. To see his charm in action.

"Breathe slow now." Mitchum spoke softly to me. "I think I've got water in my car. I'll be right back."

He left and I stood up. I kept my gaze from the car windows as I made my way past the car. I closed my eyes and tried to compose myself. That's why I didn't see Clint walk in.

"You found him."

I opened my eyes, and there he was in front of me, dressed in a Braves baseball cap, a T-shirt, shorts, and docksiders. Suburban stealth. He was pointing a snub-nosed revolver at me.

"What are you doing, Clint?"

"I have to keep my end of the deal."

I glanced behind him. Mitchum had to have seen him walk in.

"Your friend went to talk to Mr. Adamson. He didn't see me. He won't get here in time. Move back there, in the corner by the table."

"What deal, Clint?"

He gestured with the gun for me to keep going. "Your sister had a good idea. I had a problem and she had a solution. She killed Tyler for me because I could never." His voice cracked and his face crumpled for a moment. Then he recovered. "Now I have to get rid of you."

"Me? Why?"

He shrugged. "She said that you chose a stranger over her. She said you were worth more to her if you were dead."

I stopped moving once the table was between us. There was nothing on it or around it to use to defend myself. "You don't have to do this."

"If I don't, she'll call the police and tell them I killed Tyler."

"Did you kill the dog?"

He nodded. "She needed to make it look like she was in trouble. She knew you'd come. I'm sorry."

"So am I," I said.

Mitchum's big hands clapped Clint on both ears. Clint screamed and went down on one knee. The gun fell from his hands. Mitchum looked me in the eyes when he broke Clint's neck. "Sorry he got past me."

"She set me up. Lured me here." Goddamn. She really did want me dead.

"What do you want to do?" Mitchum asked.

I wiped my face and tried to be as calm as he seemed. I picked up the gun.

"Miss G?"

"Let's go home," I said.

I sat in my rental and waited while Mitchum wiped down everything we may have touched. He put Clint in the car with Tyler and covered the car with the tarp again. He locked up. Nothing to see here. He found my purse, and I put the gun in it. I should've left it, but Mitchum said he'd deal with it after he got me to the airport.

It was nearly four o'clock by the time we made it to the house. Mitchum went in ahead of me to make sure we were alone. I repacked my clothes into my carry-on while Mitchum searched the back rooms. I couldn't believe I thought Anna Mae and I were gaining lost ground, but no, she played me like I was any old mark. Used my guilt to get me here.

The front door opened and closed behind me. "You're leaving?"

I didn't turn around. I couldn't face her. I heard her purse hit the coffee table. "Something came up at home," I said.

"Damn. I was hoping we could hang out some more. I took this weekend off." A kitchen drawer opened and closed.

I zipped my luggage closed. "Figured. You need time to move the bodies, right?" I looked at her now. Her hands were hidden below the counter, likely in the drawer where she kept her knives. "I would've given you money if that's what you needed."

"I don't need your money. Why did you come here? To save

me? You thought you were smarter than me. You scored yourself a luxe 'happily ever after' and tossed me aside." She drew a knife out now and placed it and both hands on the counter.

"Look, I'm going to leave now."

"And go back to your very good life? Do you play golf with him? Or do you just get on your knees for him?"

"I love you, Anna Mae." I picked up my purse and extended the handle on my luggage.

"You aren't going anywhere." Before she could grab the knife, Mitchum was there, wrapping a long arm around her neck and pulling her tight against his body. Her hands yanked and beat at his forearm. His other arm went around her torso and he lifted her. Her eyes were wide with terror and anger.

"What do you want to do with her?" Mitchum shook her to keep her still.

She got out a whispered plea, but Mitchum changed his grip so she didn't have enough breath to speak again. I sighed. "Put her down."

Mitchum made a face but set her down and backed a couple of steps away. I walked over and set my purse down. "Is there really only room for one of us in this world?" I asked. I pressed the muzzle of the revolver into her stomach and watched her eyes widen.

Her lips trembled but her voice was clear. "Yes."

I pulled the trigger. The bullet passed through her, just missed Mitchum, and lodged itself in the wall. He stepped over me and took the gun. "There's blood on your shirt. You should change it, Miss G."

I took off my shirt and saw the blood on it. I pressed her blood against my skin. Anna Mae wasn't dead yet, but her breathing was shallow. Tears leaked from her eyes. Mitchum gathered my things while I stood there and watched my sister, my only family, die.

STAND BACK

Curtis Ippolito

Danny Brown shouldn't be surprised his ex-friends hadn't made improvements to the double-wide in the five years he was locked up. They could have installed new siding. At least replaced the trailer's cracked and sun-warped, south-facing front. Used a tiny bit of the five-figure reward his arrest and conviction paid them to spruce up the place. If it were him, he would have used the money to get the fuck out of town. But he's not stupid.

Creeping closer, Danny sees nothing has changed. It's still the same beat-down dump of a home way out in East County they shared as idiot kids. Nostalgia nibbles at the edges of his resolve. But under a white sun, he chomps back, stalks across the gravel driveway to the windowless side of the double-wide.

Danny backs against the front side of the trailer where his old master bedroom had been. Slides ahead to the back half. He, Melo, and Iggy bought the trailer outright three years before Danny's incarceration. All of twenty-three years old, each of them. They spent so many wild, drunken nights here. Shooting off fireworks in the driveway. Lighting up the mountain ranges in the distance. Living so easy. Reveling in their immortality.

There's that fucking nostalgia again.

Danny reaches the rear of the trailer, drops into a crouch. Darts his face around the back to check for any signs of them. They had to know this day was coming. Melo and Iggy. Those dumb shits. Melo, always wearing baggy black jeans and a wife-beater like a tool. And Iggy. That fat fuck was over thirty now and probably still only ate chicken nuggets and Hot Pockets. The balls on them, not making any effort to avoid this eventuality.

Moments after the verdict rang out, Danny pierced his eyes—sharp as the military-grade knife now on his hip—into theirs. They knew what his look meant. The three knew what each was thinking at every moment. Like freaky, unrelated triplets. It made sense. They grew up together. Dropped out of school together. Together they held up convenience stores to get money for booze and drugs. Took up home burglaries in their early twenties, then graduated to grifting. And no matter the job or con, Danny led. He never had to say a word to Melo and Iggy to relay his intentions. Move in, stand back, retreat. Danny's resolute brown eyes were their beacon. Those same eyes spoke truth in the courthouse that day. *When I get out, I'm coming for you with fire.*

Danny performs a metered carioca up the back deck's wooden stairs. He knows every squeaky step to avoid.

The night that kicked off this chain of events, Melo and Iggy were partying a bit too much for Danny's liking. It was a work night, after all. Danny approached what they did like a job, while for his stunted friends, each job merely funded the next party. Still blowing their shares on drugs and cheap women. Prizing the short-term payout instead of calculating a long game as he had. Danny had sights on investing in something bigger. Something legit. A sustainable career he could be proud of. He was close, but the scams needed to continue. That night, Danny tasked Iggy with attaching a skimmer to a drive-thru ATM at a bank after it closed. But Iggy got shitfaced. No way he could have driven the twenty-five miles there and back without wrecking or getting busted. In a rage, Danny ran the skimmer to the bank instead and beat the shit out of Iggy when he returned home.

The scam would have played out as it always had: the skimmer pulling data from every debit card used overnight at the ATM.

The data used to load gift cards to buy high-priced technology to sell on the street at a "discount." Only problem, Danny overslept the next morning. When he raced back to the bank to retrieve the skimming device, he was too late. A bank teller was confiscating the device when he rode up. If that's all it was, Danny would have been fine. They missed out on the data on that skimmer. Fuck it. They had other scams working. But while watching the teller from his motorcycle, Danny realized he didn't wear his helmet the night before. It wouldn't take long for authorities to share the surveillance video with the public.

The same day, his face circulated on TV news and was plastered on the Crime Stoppers blog, in bank branches and post offices. An initial reward of one thousand dollars was set for his identification and arrest. Danny hunkered down at the double-wide more than normal, but he wasn't shaken. One of the main reasons he insisted on hitting banks and gas stations at the other end of the county was to minimize the likelihood of being identified if one of them slipped up. A don't-eat-where-you-shit kinda practice. And it worked for a while. But the reward kept getting raised. Two thousand, then five thousand dollars. Then it soared when authorities linked reports of skimmed data from a half dozen other ATMs and debit card machines to the bank case. They dubbed Danny a "serial skimmer," and the reward was pushed to fifty thousand dollars for his identification, arrest and conviction. Still, he didn't sweat it. He didn't think his own mother, who he hadn't seen since running away from home at sixteen, could recognize his face from the grainy video footage. And only Melo and Iggy could provide enough evidence to make the charges stick if he was somehow identified and apprehended.

Imagine his shock when a Sheriff's Department Special Enforcement Detail stormed into the double-wide's front door early one morning and grabbed him before he could throw on pants. Danny yelled for his friends to run for it as soon as he heard the front porch creak. Maybe they could escape through their bedroom windows. He kept yelling for them as he was led outside, barefoot and handcuffed. Sitting in the back of a patrol car, the muscles between his shoulder blades ached as the cruel truth illuminated: Melo and Iggy weren't even home. Stabbed in the back with a dagger just for some money.

The law laid it on thick: possession of stolen property, possession of controlled substances, making criminal threats, vandalism, burglary, and possession of ammunition by a prohibited person. All tacked on to the fraud charges related to intercepted data using skimming devices. Danny was found guilty on all charges and given a six-year prison sentence.

Danny positions himself on the back deck. Flattens his body against the rear of the trailer, the sliding glass back door to his left. The deck's wood is a duller gray than he remembered. Even in the deck's faded state, it's still the nicest feature of the exterior. They built it together when they first moved into the place. Melo and Iggy called him a homo for planting vines at each post. They weren't complaining the following summer, kicking back with beers under the thick shade canopy that resulted.

Fuck 'em.

Danny had waited for this day patiently. He's been out on parole for two months by now. Checks in religiously with his parole officer, has a cashier job at Tractor Supply, stays within the county, and does all the other things one's supposed to do to assimilate back into society. Never mind the five years taken from him. You're just supposed to move on, right? He would have had a legitimate business humming along by now—had his stash not been seized. Could have had a construction company, maybe running a rock yard. The ones that sold all colors of flagstone, gravel, pavers—that sort of thing. His dream is dead now. He's useless. Destined to live as any other poor-ass East County bum with a felony record. All thanks to the betrayal of the fuckers inside he considered family. So nothing can change his mind. He won't stand back for love nor money.

Danny unsheathes his knife. A Short KA-BAR Serrated he paid a coworker to buy for him. He considered no other weapon.

Guns are for pussies. Guns allow you to stand back, avoid getting physical. A knife carries a different agenda. Danny won't stand back. He wants it to get physical. Wants Melo and Iggy to feel every inch of the fixed high-carbon stainless-steel blade he's about to sink deep into their bellies. He fed off the feeling for five years.

Grabbing the sliding glass door handle, Danny catches his reflection. Shaved head. Face heavily scared; all earned in prison. Sunken cheeks. Crooked nose. The youth in his cheeks, long-since beaten out of him.

He's ready. Fear isn't warping his senses. He isn't drawing deep breaths, not crossing himself or whimpering a useless prayer. That shit's for people who need to psych themselves up. People whose only hope is getting out alive. Neither applies to Danny. It's not that he's resigned to dying. This isn't some sort of suicide mission pact he's made with himself. True, Danny hasn't contemplated the future beyond killing his former friends, but dying hasn't even occurred to him. These dipshits don't pose a risk to him in the slightest. They've sat around and waited for this day to come. They had plenty of time to get out of town. If they didn't think he would come knocking, that's on them.

Danny pulls the door handle and the door gives. Unlocked. Dumb shits. Knowing the door will catch a quarter of the way down the track, Danny moves the knife to his teeth, biting the leather handle. With his free hand, he tilts the end of the door slightly, allowing the door to open as smooth as butter. Knife back in hand, Danny steps into the dining area. They threw so many parties here. Especially when they first moved in. Keggers, his favorite. Fuck. Got to tamp that shit down.

Danny's eyes fall on the carpet. Cream when they moved in, eventually soiled black. But now it's a clean, crisp blue. These two actually made a home improvement, he realizes. He shouldn't feel proud of them, but he does. He chews on what that means for a second or two and turns his head. There are two people standing in the kitchen. But not Melo and Iggy. It's a woman hugging a small child close. Her child. She's a mother. Danny spins his head in every direction, confused. There are packing boxes stacked in all the rooms within view. Others are flattened, leaning against the refrigerator.

Danny straightens up and the mother shrieks.

"Who are? What the—" he spits out. His mind is reeling. Are they moving into the double-wide? And the kitchen has been refurbished. The beige Formica countertops with chunks taken out of the ends from opening beer bottles are gone. They're stone countertops now. Inset specs of quartz reflect the sunlight coming in through the windows. There are doors on all the cabinets, too. Nice, polished cherry wood with brass pulls.

The mother's screaming snaps Danny out of his trance. He reaches out a hand in peaceful gesture but yanks it back, realizing he's still posturing in attack, knife in hand. Danny sheaths the KA-BAR. An apology pressed to his lips, he lifts his face. A figure in orange flashes in his peripheral vision from the backyard. Before he can move away, a .30-06 bullet screams through the open sliding glass door and zips through Danny's head. It strikes his right temple and blasts out the left side of his skull. He crumples to the floor, the inside of his head ringing a deafening tone he's never heard before. A thin line of blood trickles down his face from the bullet's entry point while the three-inch exit wound saturates the new carpet underneath his head. His empty eyes stare at the popcorn ceiling, no longer clouded from years of cigarette smoke, but a brilliant new white.

WHAT'S DONE IS DONE

Jerry Bloomfield

They wait until midnight to dump the body. Less of a chance of meeting anybody coming home off second shift. Around here, middle of the week, late at night, people going to or coming from work was about all the traffic you saw. Wasn't like there were any actual sheriff's deputies to worry about, and the Center City cops never went out past the city limits. State police? Always possible to run across one of them. Was also possible frozen shit could be dumped from an airplane and slam into the car. Sit around thinking about possible, you never get a goddamn thing done.

Bruce Barlow had driven the car to the spot, tall wooded banks above the river, with Steve following behind in his own. It'd also been Bruce who'd muscled the body up and shoved it into the car. Steve was almost checked out, moving on autopilot, just doing what he was told, sitting stiff and staring straight ahead. Understandable. You couldn't blame him after what had happened and all. Bruce, well, Bruce had been fifteen the first time he'd seen a dead body, laid out across the floor of his stepdad's beer joint, blood spilling out between fingers clutching a knife buried deep in his gut. The state police had dealt with that one, had it picked up by the coroner, did their whole thing. The next one wasn't even a year later, and that had went a whole other way. So…

"Bruce."

The kid... He had always thought of Stevie that way, even though Bruce was only a couple years older—two grades in school. They had known each other since middle school, when Steve and his family had moved into the house next to Bruce's stepdad's and Bruce had always looked out for the guy, kept the bullies off his ass. He might not have been worth much, but when the word went around Sutter County that someone was under Bruce Barlow's protection, well, folks tended to leave that someone alone.

Usually.

Steve hadn't been expecting much when he'd opened the app. Center City wasn't exactly a hotbed of gay activity, but he hadn't felt like driving into the city and hitting Lexington's bars, and cruising had never been his thing. So he'd popped on Grindr, figured at most he'd get some pictures, chat a little, someone live to jerk off with instead of staring at porn.

The first shock was seeing somebody on there less than ten miles away instead of the expected thirty or forty or more. The profile didn't show much, barely filled out and another headless torso. A nice torso, at least. Discrete, of course. Which meant either married and hiding it from the wife or deep in the closet. Which wouldn't be a shock, not in Sutter County. The only other out people Steve knew was the lesbian couple that ran the coffee shop slash record store on Main Street. And they'd been there so long that people just looked at them as "our lesbians." Great folks. Men doing...stuff to other men, well now that was just wrong.

The second, bigger shock was when the pictures came in. And it hadn't just been the naked pics. Though those had been quite the pleasant surprise. When he finally got to see the face, it was Daniel motherfucking Stirret. Star athlete in high school in every sport it seemed—except girls softball—starter on the university football team, and from one of the rich, important families in the area. Married to one of his high school sweethearts: a former cheerleader and band drum major. The bane of Steve's high school life. And now an exec in the Stirret family chain of banks. The perfect beautiful all-American family. Photos to prove it right there on Facebook, or on the calendar the bank put out every year, posed up against a big tree or with horses or an old tractor on a farm.

Except the wife didn't put out anymore now that the kids were born and they slept in separate rooms on opposite sides of that big house. And not a goddamned thing he could do about it. He even brought up the word "divorce," his father would kick him in the ass and cut him off from everything. But a man has needs and it wasn't really gay. A bro job they call it. Just one dude helping another dude. All good. Just don't like it too much.

Steve had liked it.

"Stevie! Stevie, you ok, man?"

"I…yeah." Steve's legs gave out and he slumped down to the floor, back against the stove. Bruce put the cast iron skillet in the sink, upside down, and squirted dish detergent over it and turned the water on.

"Good. Then get up here and clean that pan. I'll handle…this."

Stevie did as he was told. There was something comforting in Bruce's calm voice, a steady tone of command. Not for the first time, he thought the big guy could have been so much more than some country thug, but Bruce would just point out that a man can only play the cards he's dealt and that smoking weed and getting into fights wasn't the worst career to have. Then he'd quickly change the conversation.

Steve grabbed the stove and pulled himself upright, then slid his pants back up his legs. If Bruce noticed, he didn't say anything. "You shouldn't have used soap," Steve said. "Mamaw would kill me."

Bruce grunted, pulled the dead man's shorts up his legs and

patted the body down. The guy had dressed like he was going out for a jog: running shorts, fancy tennis shoes, and one of them expensive shirts, make you sweat less or some shit. Nothing on him but keys and a phone, the very latest iPhone model. Could wipe that, take out the SIM card and sell it somewhere.

"What happened here, Stevie?"

Steve glanced over at him. The kid's eyes were still wide. Shook. Couldn't blame him for that, but it would have to wait. Bruce needed him in the here and now.

"We were having some drinks, and um, stuff. You know."

"With Daniel Stirret? After all the shit he done?"

"People can change. And sometimes they act out because they're in the closet and go all hyper-masculine. Also, high school was a long time ago."

"Uh-huh. Or, he's a fucking asshole who just likes getting his dick sucked."

Steve ducked his head, scrubbed harder at the pan. Out, out, damn spot. "Oh, he did like that. But when we were, he was, ah, finished, I don't know. Got all angry and just came at me, yelling shit and swinging. Tripped over his shorts, I made it in here, but he got back up and had me by the throat when you came in."

Bruce squeezed Steve's shoulder and left the kitchen, returned a few minutes later with an old blanket. He draped it over the body and pushed it over, rolled it up.

"Did he drive here? Park in the driveway?"

Steve nodded. "Said there was no need to sneak, nobody to see anyway."

Bruce gave him another squeeze. "I'm sure he was hung or whatever it is you like in your men, but damn you got some shitty taste in dudes. Daniel motherfucking Stirret. I'd rather stick my dick in a hornets' nest than a Stirret." He reached down, pulled Steve's hands out of the water. "Stevie. It's as clean as it's going to get unless you plan on peeling off layers of iron. I'll get the body out, and you mop the floor. Don't use too much bleach. It'll make someone suspicious if they happen to come asking questions."

Bruce stepped back and Steve picked up the pan, forearm straining with the weight of it. Had lived here a number of years, happy to have the house he had more or less grown up in, the place that reminded him of comfort, family, love. Would have thought that old pan would have gotten lighter in that time, but it seemed heavy as ever.

Might have even been heavier.

He set it on the stove, its accustomed place of honor, front right burner. It'd been there for as long as he could remember, often stopping in the kitchen to stare down into it, the surface so black it gleamed and he could see something of a reflection staring back. Mamaw had used it for every meal, and he'd often stood there with her after he had all but moved in. Helped, stolen pieces of bacon, just soaking up the comfort of her, the only family member who hadn't turned on him after he had came out.

Now the pan just sat there, clean but dull, grey. It would have to be seasoned again. Mamaw really would have flipped out over him scrubbing it with soap, said if you used it right, never needed anything more than some hot water and just scrape any mess right out. She'd always been right.

But he didn't think she'd ever had to clean chunks of brain and bone and blood off the thing.

He looked down again. There was no portal, no little version of him looking back from another world. The whole time he was growing up, he'd always wanted to leave. And here he was. Steve unclenched his fists from the oven handle and stepped away.

He wished Mamaw was still here. She'd know what to do.

The car was nice, but not too nice. The Stirretts liked to play the game. It was ok to have money if you didn't show it off too much, nothing overtly flashy. No running around town in a Lamborghini or something. And buy it a year or so old. Nobody had to know it was paid straight-up with cash.

The old man tried to play up the successful farmer bit. Ran around in an almost new Dodge Ram dually, occasionally even hauled dog food in the back. His son couldn't have given a flying fuck about any of that. Had no use for a truck. And wouldn't be caught dead in some family sedan. Wanted speed, performance, something to draw people's eyes. Even hinted that he did the mechanic work himself.

The two men stood in front of the souped-up Honda Civic that looked like somebody took a picture from the *Fast and the Furious* to a car dealer and said, "Give me one like this." Bruce shook his head.

"How in the hell does he not scrape the bottom off on these roads?"

"I don't think he ever drives it very far. Bank, their house, the bar."

"What, you know his whole goddamn life now?"

"We talked some before, you know."

"Before you rubbed your peepees together?"

"Oh, fuck you." Neither had taken their eyes off the car. "Do these things even have a trunk?"

"Not much from the looks of it. But maybe this is better. Give me his keys."

"Make it look like an accident?"

Bruce shook his head. "Are you kidding? Did you see the back of his head?" If anything, Steve thought he would never stop seeing it. "Nah, you gotta keep it simple with these things. Work too much to try and fool them and it just gives them shit to figure it out with. Don't you read any of them books in there?"

Steve flipped him off and went inside to mop the kitchen floor. He wouldn't have been any help anyway, would have just vomited all over the place. Bruce smoked a cigarette and stared up at the sky. It was a clear night and it looked like every star was shining. It'd always been something of a comfort to him, coming home late at night and stopping to stare up at the sky, just how vast and awe-inspiring it was. Compared to all that, you're just small, insignificant. You don't matter. Nothing does. And if nothing matters, well, you get to decide what matters to you.

He flicked the cigarette down the drive, the red end flipping over and over as it bounced down the pavement. He squatted, hoisted the body, and shoved it in the back seat of the car with a grunt. Too bad he wouldn't be able to sell the car. Fetch a pretty good price, but it wasn't worth the risk.

The fight had been what had woke him up. He'd been crashing there a few days, in between jobs and houses. Stevie had said ok without even a thought. Obligation, or maybe he was lonely out here in this big house by himself. Either way, it was a better deal for Bruce than trying to sleep in his shitty old car.

Especially since the house had air conditioning.

He hadn't known what it was at first, thought maybe he'd left the TV on or something. A big crash, yelling. He took the stairs two at a time, loud as hell but it hadn't seemed like it put a stop to anything. When he made it to the kitchen, it was dim, the only light coming from a lamp in the living room. He could see two guys, one of them Stevie. Both were half-dressed, pants around their feet, and the guy had Stevie around the throat with one hand and the other cocked back in a fist. At the sight of Bruce, the guy had dropped Stevie, took a step toward Bruce. "Work fast, don't you? Already got the next one lined up?" he said to Stevie, a sneer across his face. "Maybe I should just beat both your—"

He didn't know if Stevie would remember much of what went on, but Bruce would never forget that sound for as long as he lived. Didn't know the kid had it in him, but he'd scrambled up, grabbed the frying pan off the stove, and swung it with all he had.

Better than he'd ever swung a ball bat. Damn near brought a tear to the eye.

***

The ding-ding-ding fills the air, the overhead light of the car casting a dim light out around the open door. After they had pushed it over the bank, Bruce had climbed down to put it back in gear and unwrap the corpse and toss it down the bank. Bruce couldn't tell if it had sunk, but he had heard the splash of it hitting the water and that would have to do.

"We should have helped him. Called the cops."

"And go to jail for that motherfucker?"

"It was self-defense."

"You think they'd believe that. You think his daddy would let them? 'Specially if they knew what was going on? And that's not even counting me being there."

"Yeah, but, I don't know, man. It doesn't seem right to just dump him like that."

Bruce climbed into Stevie's car and clapped a hand on his friend's shoulder. The kid had already climbed into the passenger seat. "We didn't have any other choice. Not unless you want to rot in jail. Call them now after all this? They wouldn't believe a word you said. All we can do now is get the fuck out of here. What's done is done, man."

The kid's voice was small, quiet, but at least it was steady enough. "Bruce?"

"Yeah, Stevie?"

"I'm sorry I got you involved in this."

"Shit, Stevie. I'd be pissed if you didn't. What friends are for, ain't it?"

Stevie grunted, turned the radio up higher, and turned his head to look out the window. It was too dark to see much, indistinct shapes as the headlights whipped past, the occasional yard lit up by the security light up on the electric pole or a garage light left on. Not like there would have been much to see anyway. Just the odd house, trees, or tobacco fields. Maybe some cows or horses. Everything quiet, asleep, tucked away for the night.

Where he should be.

Where Daniel Stirret should still be. Instead of a corpse bobbing in the river, food for the fish. But maybe Bruce was right. What's done is done. Couldn't change it now, right?

Bruce backs the car up in its usual spot and kills the engine. With the windows down, the sound of crickets merge with the ticking of the motor. The stars are still bright as fuck, diamonds flung out across black velvet.

"His people are going to raise all kinds of bloody hell. You know that, right?"

Stevie nods. He looks a little more present, although still pale. First times could be like that, Bruce reckons. "We done good though, right? There's nothing to bring them here?"

"Should be fine. Especially if you never texted him. Think his wife knew?"

"No. He was clear on that."

Bruce shakes his head. In his experience, wives often knew a fuck of a lot more than their husbands ever thought they did. It just serves their interests to keep it to themselves. At least, until it didn't.

"Then forget all about it. It never happened. If it's not in the newspaper, you don't know about it. Got it?"

The kid nods again, gets out of the car, and disappears inside without even turning a light on. Bruce just lets him go, sits on the hood, and lights a joint. Something to relax, help calm down after all the excitement.

The extra phone in his pocket rings. He tugs it loose, the screen showing HEATHER WIFE. He pops the back, tugs the battery and SIM card loose, and lets it go to voicemail.

TEMPTATION IS A GUN

James D.F. Hannah

Twenty-two years, and the only thing changed since the first and last time Roy stepped into Murphy's Tavern are the posters. Concert flyers, filling every available inch of wall space, a chronology of wannabes and never-weres that have graced Murphy's stamp-sized stage. Cover bands mechanically reciting seven-minute solos note-by-note with the same rote nature as a dog taught to play dead. Faded flyers, ripped edges, and torn corners revealing the previous generation underneath, the present literally plastered over the past. Roy knows none of the new bands that play Murphy's, nor the bands they're ripping off, and it's further proof to him how time marches inexorably the fuck on.

Otherwise, Murphy's is as frozen in the past as those mosquitos caught in amber. The Confederate flag behind the bar looks new and crisp, Murphy's not a place to let a worn stars-and-bars hang long. It's Tuesday, no band tonight, a DJ in the corner knocking out song after song, all of them sounding the same after a while. It doesn't matter so long as it's loud, as long as it drowns out the conversations around you and the voices in your head.

Roy carves out a section of bar all his own. The girl pulling taps busy on her cell, thumbs dancing across the screen. When she finally notices Roy, she sighs, sets the phone aside, cranks up a hundred-watt smile as insincere as a promise made in the dark.

"What can I get you?" she says.

"Bourbon," Roy says.

"Well, or from the shelf?"

"It's been a while, I'll treat myself. Off the shelf."

The bottle's dusty as she takes it off the shelf, wiping the years off with a rag. Murphy's, no one's concerned about the quality of bourbon, only the quantity. What the hell, though, might as well celebrate, right? You don't get out of prison every day, Roy thinks.

The burn from the first sip catches Roy off guard. He breathes through it slowly, letting the tendrils of warmth stretch out through his chest. He sips at it again and sets the glass down, and that's when he notices the bartender watching him, smiling. She's a cute thing, a pile of blonde curls stuffed underneath a large knit cap, with dark green eyes and lots of jangly bracelets on slender wrists and junk jewelry rings on skinny fingers.

She nods toward Roy's drink. "Another?"

He reaches the glass toward her, and she tops it off. Sets the bottle aside and folds her arms across her chest. "Not to sound like that person or nothing, but you're not a regular. I'd know your face, and no one comes in here without a reason."

Another drink. The flush sensation hits him, as comforting as an embrace. Fuck it, Roy figures, and throws back the rest. Deep breath. Almost tears in his eyes. Good reason or bad, there he is.

"Looking for someone," he says, setting the glass down. "You know Lizzie Murphy?"

Roy Hardin, nineteen summers old, sitting in the pickup cab, staring out at Murphy's. The bar's a cinderblock building, a dirt parking lot, just off a country two-lane, but with the noise and the flashing lights, it may as well be a Vegas casino. Roy's willing himself the nerve to go inside, with fifty bucks cash burning a hole in his blue jeans pocket.

The summer help who cut tobacco on his old man's farm tell

Roy about Murphy's, three counties over, where the girls aren't looking for anything but a good time, and a kid like Roy—raw-boned and muscular from years spent working the field—he'll score himself some fun with no problem. Buy a few drinks, they tell him. That's all it takes. It's Jimmy Dale who gets Roy a fake ID. Technically it's a real ID, the driver's license of a cousin who Roy looks like if you squint hard enough.

Roy's spent the last few years messing around with local girls and getting nowhere fast. They've got the sounds of Sunday mornings shoved so deep into their hearts that the only key to unlocking their legs is a diamond ring, and Roy already knows that's not for him. Not yet.

He tells his parents he's taking the truck, driving to Lexington to visit friends at UK, the kids who escaped the tobacco farms and the fields of corn and soybean and are living somewhere with more than two traffic lights. His mom tries to nix it, doesn't want her baby boy out late, driving far. It's the old man who reminds her that Roy's a legal adult—he can go die in war, after all—and she can't expect him to sit on this farm his whole life. He slips Roy an extra ten with the truck keys, winks at him, and tells him to have a good time, but not too good of a time.

Murphy's is jammed elbow-to-asshole when Roy walks in. He cuts his way through the heavy cigarette smoke, past guys shooting pool, past girls in slivers of denim pretending to pay attention, past bikers and farm hands and folks with eyes like predatory birds, watching and waiting and looking for their next meal.

The bar staff's hopping behind the counter, rushing to fill beer glasses and pour shots. There's a round, sawed-off dude, looks like someone's left nut grew legs. Jimmy Dale said that would be Murphy himself, and he's not to be fucked with. Everyone else who works at the bar has a sense of humor, they'll laugh with you, tell you a joke and whatnot. Murphy's as likely to tell you to fuck off as take your money. It's part of the game, Jimmy Dale says. Like those restaurants at the beach where you eat overpriced seafood and the waitresses tell you you're fat and your wife's ugly. All in good fun.

Roy notices the quickest response comes when you have your money out, so he does like the man next to him, a bill folded between two fingers, high up so they can see it.

This catches the eye of a female bartender. "What can I get you, honey?" she says.

Roy realizes he has no clue what to order. He's drunk before, but it's been Mad Dog or corn liquor from a pint jar. He glances over at the bourbon glass being served to someone a few feet away.

"I'll take that," he says.

The bartender smiles. The smile deepens fine lines around her eyes, and Roy sees her age, but there's something sexy about it. Not old enough to be his mother, but old enough to teach him things.

She pours him the bourbon and slides the glass in front of him. Roy reaches the bill toward her and she waves it off.

"First one's on the house."

"The hell it is," a man's voice snaps behind her. Murphy snatches Roy's money. He nudges her with an elbow, and she stumbles sideways like a fawn on its first steps.

"We got customers, Lizzie," he says. Gets Roy his change and lays it on the bar without another word to him. "Move your little ass along." Then he hustles down to the far end and pours a fresh beer.

Lizzie shakes her head, grins a little at Roy before going to another customer, and that's when Roy knows.

Her name's Alma, by the way, which strikes Roy as an old woman's name for a young girl. He tells her as much. She doesn't disagree. This is before she tells him that Lizzie's dead.

"Cancer," she says. "About five years ago."

"What kind?"

"The kind that kills you."

Roy's on his third bourbon. It helps settle in his gut that Lizzie's gone.

"She wasn't here when she died," Alma said. "It wasn't one of those sudden things. She got sick and headed down to Florida, to one of those spa places where they try to fix you with crystals and shit."

"How'd that work?"

"She's dead, ain't she? I'd say it didn't work at all."

The bourbon burns in all the best ways, Roy decides. The first drink, he sputters and his eyes water and it feels like something may explode behind his rib cage. Once he finds a rhythm in the drinking, though, he keeps going, calling the barstool home for the night. People come and go around him. Riffs develop into arguments that turn into fights, and Murphy handles it all with no bullshit. If it doesn't seem they'll listen, Murphy brings a Louisville Slugger out from under the counter and steps his way into the action. That seems to solve whatever the problem is.

The crowd thins out but Roy maintains his post so that by the time the band's packed up and someone's just stuck a CD into the stereo to play out the rest of the night, it's him and Lizzie and a handful of stragglers. Murphy has adjourned into the back to start counting the night's tally.

There's the saying about feeling ten feet tall and bulletproof, and that's Roy right now. Lizzie takes a top-shelf bottle and fills Roy's and one for herself. She raises the drink for a toast.

"To surviving your first night at Murphy's," she says. She swallows it all in one gulp, slams the glass down with intent.

"How you know it's my first night?" Roy says. The words slip out of his mouth like each syllable was greased and kicked across the floor.

Lizzie rests her forearms on the counter. "'Cause I've done this a long while, honey, and if I couldn't tell, I wouldn't be good at my job."

She leans in closer, and Roy smells her perfume push through the stink of stale beer and cigarette smoke. He also sees the faint half-moon discoloration underneath her left eye, purple turning yellow she's tried to cover with makeup. He gestures to her face.

"What happened there?" he says.

Lizzie's body draws tense. "Fell. No big deal." Grabs a rag and starts wiping down the counter. "Shouldn't you be headin' home? Don't you got a farm somewhere to be?"

He does, in fact. He knows he told his parents he'd be in Lexington overnight, but he hadn't thought the lie out full. He hadn't thought he'd be sitting at Murphy's at closing time, drunk as hell.

"What are you and Murphy?" Roy says. "You married?"

"According to the power vested in a Baptist minister by God and the Commonwealth of Kentucky, we are indeed married," she said.

"And he hits you?"

"Who said he hits me?"

Roy twists the glass around. "Being drunk don't make me stupid."

Lizzie clears glasses off the bar. "What if he does? Ain't the only guy. Your dad never popped your mom one? A smack to keep her in line?"

Roy laughs. "My mom'd cut his stuff off with a carving knife, he ever even thought about laying a hand on her."

"Good on her. And thanks for the concern, but tonight's not the night I need saved." A glance at the clock. Two in the morning. "Need to send you on your way."

Murphy comes out from the back office and surveys the area. Hands on his hips. There's not much to Murphy, Roy decides. A stubbed toe of a human being.

"All right, assholes," he says. "Every one of you, haul your asses out of here and find somewhere else to be. Now!" To Roy, he says, "You too, farm boy. Get on along and go back to hangin' off your momma's tit."

Roy pushes himself off the barstool and someone moves the floor before his feet hit it, this sudden shifting underneath, the room dancing faster than he can handle. He slumps and catches himself on the lip of the counter.

"Kid can't hold his liquor," Murphy says, the words stinging with hard laughter behind them.

Roy slings himself upright, staggering toward Murphy. "You think you're a big man 'cause your name's on the sign out front? Smacking your lady make you big?"

Murphy's face burns red. Realizes a group's gathered at the entrance, staring.

"I said to get the hell out of here!" he barks.

The figures linger, curious, then gradually slip out until it's just Murphy and Roy, Lizzie watching, seeming not sure what to do.

Murphy rushes behind the bar and grabs the Slugger, tight grip, raised high, rushes Roy.

Roy can't move fast enough to stop Murphy from the first swing, but Murphy puts no power behind it. Catches Roy on the right shoulder, and the younger man grunts, hits his knees. When Murphy brings the bat back up, there's enough time to drive a fist into Murphy's soft middle. All the air pushes from Murphy, and it gives Roy the chance to wrest the bat from the man's hands.

Roy uses the Slugger to get back onto his feet. Takes it firm in his large hands.

Murphy's all friendly now, steps backward, the smile on his face not masking the fear in his eyes.

"You want money?" he says. "It was a good night. Cash. Go on in back and it's yours."

Roy thinks what a sad little man Murphy is. Wonders when the last time the geezer got stared down by someone bigger than him. Murphy's nothing without someone weaker to pick on. It makes Roy sick to his stomach. It's that or the bourbon.

He throws the bat to the floor, the polished slab of ash rattling against the concrete. He turns and walks out of the bar. In the briefest of glances back, he sees Lizzie watch as he pushes the door open.

The fresh air rushes around Roy, and for a heartbeat he imagines he might be sober, a vague clarity threatening to creep into his skull. Then he hangs his head and retches, and vomit splatters across the ground, onto his shoes, specks flecking across his jeans.

He doesn't remember much after that. Sitting in his truck. A tap on his window and Lizzie's face.

"Move over," she says. "I'm driving."

More blank spaces and Roy wakes up to see the vastness of a thousand tiny stars in the sky, and Lizzie again. This time, her face contorts into shifting expressions of pleasure, of agony, of bliss. They're in the pickup truck bed, his clothes in a ball in the corner, Lizzie straddling him, like nothing he's ever known from the girls before her, before tonight. He barely seems to need to do anything, simply accepting her actions, wordless commands that activate responses in him. She pins his shoulders down with the flats of her hands and in one last thrust onto him lets out a scream into the night that he'll hear in dreams for the rest of his life.

Later, as they lay together, a blanket thrown over them, she points out which stars are which, naming constellations.

"Some of them stars are dead already, burned out hundreds of years ago, and that light's just getting to us now," she says. "All that space and time between them and us, and we'll never know the truth about any of it until it's long since said and done." Buries her head into his neck. "That's the way life is."

More darkness, met with the creeping light of sunrise, and the realization that Lizzie is gone. The drive home is long, but he smells her perfume the whole way back.

Four days later, Roy riding the tractor back from the cornfield when he sees the sheriff talking to his old man, his mother crying, two stone-faced state troopers next to them.

They describe how Lizzie says she found Murphy lying in the middle of the bar floor, skull cracked open. Customers said they saw Roy beef with Murphy. And then there was the matter of his fingerprints on the bat.

"Murphy's in a coma, so that's assault," the sheriff says. Rests a hand on Roy's shoulder. "He dies, that's murder, son. You can help yourself a lot by telling us the truth."

Which Roy does. What he remembers. The problem is, what he says and what Lizzie says, those things don't match up. Lizzie tells them she left the bar as her husband was closing up, that she saw Roy asleep in his truck in the parking lot. She didn't think about it. Sleeping it off in Murphy's parking lot is damn near a rite of passage for a young man.

When the state police come to arrest Roy, the sheriff's with them. "Hate to do this to you, son, but you should have told us the truth."

Murphy dies, and the county attorney turns it into first-degree murder. The trial starts, and Lizzie walks into the courtroom, her hand resting on a small baby bump.

Roy's parents mortgage the farm to pay for an attorney, but witnesses; fingerprints; a pregnant, grieving widow; a drunken farm boy—it's not open and shut, but the jury comes back on the first day with a guilty verdict. Roy hears they waited long enough to get lunch, then told the judge they were ready once the garbage was thrown away.

The bank takes the farm in Roy's third year at Little Sandy, and his father goes to bagging groceries and stocking shelves at the A&P. That's where he has his heart attack, dying while stacking cans of corn and peas.

Roy's mother goes to live with her sister in Whitesburg, and he gets compassionate leave for her funeral a few years later. By then, Roy's earned himself a bad reputation in the prison, fighting and getting shipped to solitary on a regular basis.

When he turns forty, understanding how much of his life he's spent on that side of high walls and razor wire, it stops. He realizes he has no one waiting for him, nothing to hope for past the possibility of getting out one day.

It's Jimmy Dale waiting for him when he walks out of Little Sandy. Jimmy Dale, a hard-looking man all those years earlier, now nothing but yellowing white hair and deep creases cut into granite and a hacking cough with a tell-tale rattle on the end.

"Your people were good to me when I got out all those years back," he says on the drive home in a beat-to-hell pickup with a slipping transmission. "Least I can do, I reckon."

Roy's first meal as a free man is a pancake joint off the interstate. He works his way through waffles and bacon and keeps the waitress busy on refills. Jimmy Dale has nothing but coffee.

"I been where you're at, finally out, time spent thinking what you'd do once you got here," he says. "And it's tough, 'cause you won't know what to do with yourself. I'll tell you, whatever thoughts you got, don't mind 'em. Let 'em go. Because those temptations'll be the death of you. Temptation'll kill you faster than a bullet."

They go back to Jimmy Dale's single-wide, Jimmy Dale setting up the couch for Roy and going on to bed. Once he thinks it's safe, Roy takes the truck keys and drives to Murphy's, thinking he'll kill Lizzie.

But then she's dead already, and sitting there in Murphy's Tavern, Roy wonders what he's got to live for now.

"Get you another?" Alma says.

"Probably not a good idea. Not that good ideas have ever really been my thing." He throws money on the bar. "I think I'll be heading on."

"Got any big plans?"

To his feet. "No, I don't guess I do." He turns and walks out of the bar.

Alma pulls her cell phone from her back jeans pocket, goes

to the messaging app.

That was him.

OMG, really? How you know?

Looked like his picture. Just older.

You tell him?

About Mom dying? Yeah.

He believe you?

Hope so. All I did was tell him the truth.

Good. She said he'd be back. Hope now he'll go away.

Alma slips the phone back into her pocket and pours someone a beer. The phone buzzes back to life.

Hey Alma.

Yeah.

You think we look like him?

THINGS YOU USED TO DO

Joseph S. Walker

You get to a point in life where all you want is a comfortable place to sit and let the world go by. I had thirty years of all the excitement anyone could ask for. One day, like a branch snapping under thickening ice, I'd had enough, and something inside gave way. I was lucky. I saw an opening and I ran.

I bought a bar outside a little Kentucky coal town too stubborn to know that little Kentucky coal towns are supposed to be dying. I named the place Bar, which shows the amount of effort I'm generally willing to put in these days. I sleep in a little room tacked onto the back and spend most of my day sitting at a table in the corner, sipping something and reading.

The drinks and the books are brought to me by my only employee, Billy Muir. Billy taught high school English for forty years. He announced his retirement, at a school assembly, by setting fire to a stack of ungraded essays about *The Red Badge of Courage* and then punching the principal in the nose. It earned him eight weeks in the county joint, which he says was vastly preferable to reading the essays. Now he tends bar and lends me books. Every few weeks, when I've got the itch and his hip is up to it, I take him back to my room for a little horizontal workout. Mostly, though, we sit and read, me at my table, him behind the bar. Except for Friday and Saturday nights, Bar doesn't do a lot of business. It's quiet. Comfortable.

We were doing that one Saturday afternoon, before any customers had shown, when Damien Donovan walked in. He stopped just inside the door to take off his sunglasses, squinting as his eyes adjusted to the dim interior of Bar. His hair was a little thinner and his middle a little thicker, but it was him. There was even the same slight break in the line of the slacks around his right calf, telling me he still favored an ankle holster.

For the first time in three years, I wanted a gun in my hand. I thought about trying to slip out, but he'd already seen me and was sauntering over, grinning a grin that hadn't changed at all. It was charming as hell and showed a lot of bright white teeth, and it didn't come anywhere near his eyes.

"Connie Grace," he said, stopping right in front of my table. "I didn't really believe it until right this second."

I put my book down, using a coaster to mark my place. "The name's Maggie now, DD."

He cocked his head. "Maggie," he said, trying it out. "If you say so." He pulled out the chair opposite me and sat, looking over at Billy, who had put his own book down and was watching us. "Hey, old-timer," he said. "Lemme get a beer, huh? Whatever's on tap."

Billy looked at me. I nodded. He shrugged and picked up a glass.

DD was looking at me, tapping his fingers on the table. "You want to hear a funny story, Maggie?" He put a lot of weight on my new name. "Couple months ago, Mr. Flynn took over a beer distributor. Wasn't really his plan, but somebody owed him money, and that's what they had to offer. You know how it goes. So last week I'm in there to get things in order and one of the drivers starts talking about this bar he delivers to in the middle of nowhere. Says it's owned by an old woman who'd still be a looker except for the patch over her right eye and the stump where her left pinkie should be."

Billy set the beer down on the table. "Thanks, pops," DD said without looking up. Billy looked at me and I tilted my head to let him know he should go back to the bar.

"I said to myself, how many old women like that can there

be, so I drove down to take a look." DD took a long drink from his glass. "What do you think about that?"

"I think I should have gone further away," I said.

"Damn straight," DD said. "Bangkok might have done it." He leaned back. "So, obviously, Mr. Flynn wants to have a word."

"That's flattering. Now that he knows where I am, he can call anytime he wants. I'm generally around during business hours."

"Not how this works, Connie," he said. "My car's outside."

"Gee," I said. "Has it got a nice roomy trunk?"

"I don't get many complaints. Of course, there's another option."

"Enlighten me."

"You give me a hundred thousand dollars, in cash, and I tell Mr. Flynn the driver was wrong."

I barked a laugh. "Look around you, DD. The jukebox is the most expensive thing in here and it's a piece of shit. What makes you think I've got a hundred grand?"

"Come on, Connie." He shook his head in mock disappointment. "It is not possible you're not running some game here. My bet is meth. Just get a couple of the local shitkickers cooking in a camper and have Grampa Time there pass a little something extra to special customers. Am I close?"

I shrugged. "I'll never tell. Even if you were right, though, it would take some time to get that much cash together."

"Limited time offer, babe. I'm not hanging around this hillbilly hellhole for an extended vacation. This ain't fucking Disneyworld."

I sucked my teeth. "Tomorrow. I can have it tomorrow."

DD raised an eyebrow. "How do I know you'll still be here tomorrow?"

"I ran once. I guess I've found out I'm no good at it." I blinked, looked at the bar. "I'm comfortable here. I don't want to start over again."

He stared at me. I was sure he wasn't going to go for it, and my palm itched again for a pistol grip.

"Okay," he said at last. "Tomorrow. When and where?"

"Right here. We're closed Sundays, so it'll be private. Make it noon."

"Noon. You're not here, lady, and I will make you wish I'd just shot you." He stood, picking up my book as he pushed his chair back. "Never pegged you for a reader. *The Iliad*. What's it about?"

"It's about all the bad shit that can happen when you piss off the wrong person," I said.

He chuckled and dropped it on the table. "I always thought you were a cute one, Connie. Be here tomorrow with my money, and you can stay that way."

After DD left, I just sat, staring at nothing, tapping my empty beer glass against the table. Six or seven minutes. That was all the time it had taken for my comfortable life to burn down.

I was broken out of my reverie when Billy set two shot glasses on the table and took the chair DD had been in. He had the bottle of Johnnie Walker Blue we keep underneath the bar for personal use. He tipped out two shots and used the back of his hand to push one across the table to me. I lifted it mechanically and tapped it against his and drank, trying to focus on the taste and the smooth burn down my throat.

Billy set his glass down. "I gotta say, I kind of like the jukebox."

I closed my one good eye and sighed. "How can your hearing possibly be that good, old man?"

"Clean living and the pursuit of modest virtues. Do you have a hundred thousand dollars?"

"Not unless somebody left one hell of a tip last night."

"That's what I figured." He picked up the bottle, thought better of it, and set it back down. "I think we have to get into this, Maggie. I think it's time you finally told me about the things you used to do."

I looked at him squarely. "I used to kill people, Billy. For a crime family up north, the Flynns."

He didn't flinch. "The mob. That's a real thing?"

"Real enough."

"Half of me wants to think you're joking. It's like you're saying you used to work for the Tooth Fairy."

"Well, teeth were sometimes involved."

"And this is how—" He gestured at my eye, my missing finger.

"Yeah," I said. "I got in a knife fight with a guy who knew a whole fucking lot more about knives than I did."

"Yet you're still here."

"Well, he knew knives. I knew there was a gun under my bed."

Billy picked up the bottle again and this time did pour out new shots. "Do I want to know how many?"

I put my hand around the glass but didn't pick it up. "Hell, Billy, I'm not even sure I know how many. I worked for the Flynns for thirty years, and for a lot of it I was blasted out of my mind."

"That seems like a long career for a hitman."

"I started out hooking," I said. I tossed back the shot and set the glass down. "One day Seamus Flynn came to me and said that one of my regular johns was causing problems, and did I know anything about him that might help them out. I said I knew how to make him break his breathing habit, if the price was right. He laughed and told me to go ahead. I don't think he believed I would do it."

"But you did."

I nodded. "Guys are pretty vulnerable when they think they're about to get laid. It was easy. And it was damn sure more lucrative than fucking."

"So it's this Seamus who wants to talk to you."

"Yeah. He runs the family now. DD, the guy who was here, is his right-hand man. Has been for years." I shifted in my seat and reached for the bottle myself. "I didn't just kill people. I did a lot of things over the years. Hijacked liquor trucks, collected protection money. I think Seamus got some kind of a bang out of having a woman enforcer working for him." I filled our glasses for the third time.

"So what do you think he wants you to do now?" Billy had barely moved the whole time I'd been talking.

I laughed. "Die, I imagine. About three years ago I decided I wanted some peace and quiet. So I just took off. The Flynns don't have a retirement plan, Billy. I know things about Seamus that could put him away for the rest of his life."

"Okay," Billy said. "So why didn't this guy today just shoot you?"

I rolled the glass slowly between my palms. "That's a good fucking question," I said. "I've never known him to go behind Seamus's back before." I looked Billy in the eye. "Right now I'm wondering more what you're going to do. You could walk out of here right now. Go to the cops. Might be the smartest thing you could do."

"You'd let me?"

I nodded.

He took in a lot of air through his nose, glanced at the door, and looked back at me. "I got no family. I've got nothing in my life but you and this place."

"It bother you, what I was?"

"Let's focus on what you are. You going to run?"

"Fuck no," I said. I lifted the glass and we toasted and drank the shots. "I was telling DD the truth about that much. I'm too old to start over."

"Jesus, Maggie. You're near on twenty years younger than me. Stop calling yourself old." Billy stood and picked up the bottle and glasses and went back behind the bar. "We're going to need some kind of plan," he said.

"I'm working on it. We expecting any customers soon?"

Billy glanced up at the Coors clock behind the bar. "Probably not. Alex and Jesse are usually the first on Saturdays and they won't get here for another hour."

"Okay then." I stood up and headed for the door to my room in the back. "The first part of my plan is seeing how your hip is holding up today. Thinking about getting killed makes a broad want to live a little."

DD knocked on the front door of Bar promptly at noon the next day. I nodded at Billy and he unlocked it and stepped to the side. DD squinted at him as he came through, dismissed him, and walked toward my table. Billy quietly locked the door behind him.

I was eating from a takeout container of barbecued ribs with sides of fries and corn bread. I had sauce smeared on my hands and around my mouth and there was a pile of soiled, wadded-up napkins next to my mostly empty glass of beer. DD's mouth twisted a little in distaste before he noticed the small athletic bag on the chair next to me.

"Catch you at a bad time?" he said as he sat down.

"Sorry, I should have gotten you an order." I belched, covering my mouth but not enough to keep him from getting the smell. "Little place down the road. Family's been making this stuff since Prohibition. You ought to try it before you leave town."

"I'll stop at the first McDonald's."

"Your loss," I said. I polished off the beer and raised the empty glass to Billy, who nodded and turned to the tap. "You want a beer, at least?" I didn't wait for an answer. "Two, Billy."

"I suppose we might as well drink to our arrangement." DD's eyes drifted to the bag. "Is that my money?"

"Not yet," I said. I picked up another rib and started to gnaw. "First I want to know why I should believe you're not just going to take it and then turn right around and give me to Seamus anyway."

"Connie," he said. "Haven't I always been a man of my

word?"

Billy set two beers down and went back behind the bar.

"The name is Maggie," I said. "And it doesn't seem like you're keeping your word to Seamus."

"What Seamus doesn't know won't hurt you, whatever your name is," DD said. He picked up the beer and drank. "The old man's not what he used to be. He's missing things he didn't used to miss."

"Why, Damien," I said. "You sound like a man with ambitions."

"I prefer to think of it as vision. Maybe inspiration. In fact, I'm having an inspiration now." He took another drink, crossed his arms on the table, and leaned forward. "What if I had a way for you to keep half of that money?"

I put down the rib and licked sauce from my thumb. "I'm listening."

"Seamus always had a little thing for you," DD said. "I'm betting if I did take you back, you could get yourself alone in a room with him. Then you could, you know. Do what you do."

I shook my head. "That's just a slower way of getting me killed, DD. As I recall, Seamus has a son who's gonna take the throne. I don't think much of my life expectancy as the woman who offed his dad."

DD snorted. "Ronan? Kid's soft. Him I'll take out myself. It will be a pleasure."

"Sounds iffy," I said. "Maybe I should get some advice." I raised my voice a shade. "Hey Seamus, what do you think of DD's plan?"

"I think it has some problems," a deep voice growled. DD sat bolt upright, his eyes wide. I pushed aside the pile of used napkins to reveal the smartphone resting on the table with the speaker connection open.

"What the fuck did you do?" DD said.

"Connie," Seamus said. "Kill the cocksucker."

"I already did," I said. "Thirsty boy drank his medicine."

DD looked wildly at the half-empty glass of beer in front of him. He knocked it flying off the table, at the same time leaning forward to reach for his ankle holster. I put my hands against the edge of the table and shoved it hard into his midsection, pushing against the floor with my feet so that my full weight was driving into him. He blew out air and toppled backwards onto his ass, half stunned, and I came scrambling over the table and dropped onto his stomach with both knees, driving out what was left of his wind. Then I straddled him, my knees on his upper arms, and wrapped my hands around his throat.

Missing a finger actually helps with this. Makes it easier to concentrate your force on the vital point.

"Got a little too pudgy for that ankle gun to be a good idea, huh?" I wheezed, putting all my strength into my hands. I don't think he heard me. His eyes were bulging and his hands beat desperately against the floor. I leaned forward more.

When I knew he was gone, I unclenched my hands and fell to the side, breathing hard. I felt completely spent, every muscle aching. "Jesus," I said. "That used to be a lot fucking easier."

Billy was standing between DD's body and the bar, holding the baseball bat we keep behind the bar in case there are disputes over a tab. I don't think he was aware of it. He was staring at DD, and he looked pale.

"Somebody tell me what the hell is happening," said a voice with just the faintest hint of Ireland in it. The floor around us was a confused mess of barbecue and napkins and glasses and pieces of DD's broken chair. I stirred through it and came up with the phone.

"It's over," I said. I scooted myself into a sitting position against the wall.

"You know what I need," Seamus said.

"Yeah." I held out the phone and took a picture of DD's still, blue face. I had to fumble a bit, but I figured out how to send the snapshot to him.

"All right," Seamus said. "You've not lost your touch, girl.

Did you really poison the bastard?"

"What the fuck do I know about poison? I just needed an opening."

That earned me a chuckle. "Always the clever one."

"Seems like I've solved a problem for you," I said. "One you didn't even know you had."

"I had inklings."

"The fact remains."

"So what do you want? You want to come back? All is forgiven?"

I leaned my head back against the wall. "That bridge is burned to the ground, Seamus."

"What, then?"

"I want what I had." Billy had sat down on one of the barstools. He was holding his chin in his hand and he was still pale, but he was looking at me instead of DD. "I want to be left alone to live whatever's left of my life. Can I have that?"

Seamus was quiet for so long I thought the call had dropped. Billy and I stared at each other. I'm not sure either of us was breathing much more than DD.

"For now," Seamus said.

"I'll take that," I said, but there was nobody to say it to. He'd hung up.

I scooted over to DD's body and dug through his pockets until I found his car keys. I tossed them to Billy. He caught them, nodded at me, and headed for the front door. We'd worked out the next steps overnight. He'd pull DD's car around back, and when it was dark we'd move the body to that nice roomy trunk. Then a quick stop at one of the many deep, abandoned holes in this part of the country. I would drive the car to Lexington, Billy following in his truck, and leave it in a parking lot with the keys in the ignition. With a little luck, we'd be home by dawn.

For now, Seamus had said. Okay. I'll take now, at my little corner table, with Billy behind the bar and my shitty jukebox playing Southern rock. What the hell. *The Iliad* was pretty good, and Billy tells me there's a sequel that's even better.

I'll take all the now I can get.

LITTLE MARTHA
Art Taylor

In The Family Room

Bright eyes, dimpled chin, cherub's smile, fairest skin. Tulle tutu, bloomers peeking, smiles all sides, hide-and-seeking. Swerve and shift, sudden lift. Rough hands, rough cheek. Deep voice, soft speak. "What a beautiful girl!" Fraying dolly clutched tight. *Me. Mine.*

In Her Mother's Bathroom

Caked eyeshadow, lipstick thick, Mama's nightgown hanging loose. Hand on shoulder, cooing, laughter. "Goodness, little girl, are you fixing yourself up for Daddy?" Mirror held high, proud smile smeared askew. *Look at you!*

At The Mall

Blonde hair curled and crimped. Pink Lolita lip gloss. Tight black tank, snug jeans, fresh curves. Strutting (not strutting), glancing (not glancing), watching (not watching). And being watched? A faraway chime, text on screen: "Send me a snap?" Shiny iPhone clutched tight, lifted with nonchalance, with badassery, with girlpower, with defenses trembling. *Look at me.*

After The Prom

Mascara streaming, lipstick chewed. Shoulder strap sliding, soul slumped. Dodging side eyes, pointed fingers. Whispers, laughter, words echoing. "Jilted." "Kicked over." "Loser." Lost. Corsage ripped from her arm, hurled hard. *Why me?*

In Too Many Backseats/Dorm Rooms/Studio Apartments/Married Men's Beds

Smeared lipstick, cheeks flushed, eyes shut. Blouse/tee/sweater askew/up/off, skirt/cut-offs/jeans high/low/adrift, hipsters/thong/boyshorts hooked on one ankle/kicked free/forgotten. Rough beard/rough hands, smooth cheeks/smooth fingers, sudden lift, sharp turn, easy pull, quick grab, prod, poke. Deep voice, soft speak. "Martha. Martha Martha. Martha!" Hands clutching at vinyl/leather/silk/skin/air/nothing. *Is this who you are?*

In One Room Too Far

Lips bruised, cheeks scraped, eyes shut wide. Skirt off, thong snatched aside. Kitchen counter beneath, behind, beneath. Coffee maker, Cuisinart, cutlery holder…Not glancing. Not watching. Some song low on the speakers in the next room, familiar, far away. "…goes my baby… my heart…." Glancing. Watching. Cutlery holder. Cleaver. Clutched tight. *Is this…who you'll become?*

At The Courthouse

Seriousness, attention, concentration—as the lawyer reminded. Cosmetics light, conservative—as ordered. Gray business suit—as selected, required, and the ill fit ignored. Armor. Shield. Defenses holding. All eyes targeted, some faraway weeping. A gallery of strangers, one man standing. "Guilty." The pencil she's holding—snapped in two by whose hand? *Mine? Me?*

* * *

Today

Stony expression, sterner concentration. Lines worrying the corners of eyes, corners of lips. No makeup. Blue and white jumpsuit, ill fit unnoticed. Other jumpsuits folded into rectangles, another pile coming from the dryer to the empty table, another wet heap into the empty dryer, another dirty pile into the empty washer, another…emptiness. Cleared throat: "The Man expects you to hustle." A bit of drawstring, knotted, frayed. Clutched tight.

SET TWO: JUST OUTRIGHT BAD THINGS

"Human nature is you work shoulder to shoulder
in a real emotional kind of setting, and there are
jealousies that come up. There's resentment,
and resentment turns to just outright bad things."
—Dickey Betts

NO MERCY, NO MORE
Rob Pierce

She wielded that fiddle like a murder weapon. He loved to watch her play. She stood at the side of the stage, took her occasional solo, more like Paul Warren from Flatt & Scruggs than Charlie Daniels or any other modern motherfucker. It was the guitarist's band and most all the crowd showed up for him, with his tongue extended, eyes to the sky approach. Duane wasn't opposed to all that, just his eyes settled elsewhere. Much as he saw the band and close as he got to the stage, she'd noticed.

This, however, was the first night he'd spoken to her. "Hey," he said, and doffed his Stetson.

She was headed off the stage, just a few steps down the side. "Hey yourself."

"You look real good playin' that fiddle."

"Yeah? You look okay sittin' in that seat. Except it's creepy how much you stare."

"Yeah?" he said.

"Oh yeah."

She stepped past him, and he turned to walk with her.

"You play like Paul Warren."

"I'd like to think I add something to that, but thanks."

She smiled. He hadn't seen that from her much on stage.

"You do," he said when she stood there and waited. "Only I can't say what."

"It's my magic touch."

"You wanna get a beer?"

"Lemme put this away," she said, indicating the fiddle case in her hand. "Meetcha at the bar."

He watched as she went out the back. He strolled to the bar, not knowing whether she'd come back and join him. Usually they didn't. Usually they had to have a couple drinks down already. She drank water onstage. Hard to really drink while playing fiddle, but he'd noticed the rest of the band didn't have that problem. Shit, the drummer smoked.

Didn't really matter though, did it? All that mattered, as he ordered a beer, was whether she'd join him. He knew it was wrong to think of it this way, to put that much hope into any one thing. But he hadn't been laid in a while, like since Mercy left him. That had been how many years? Over how much he drank, of course. And how he acted when he drank "too much." Which according to her was more than two beers. He shook his head at that memory, drank slow from the tall glass before him.

It wasn't too long a lean to his glass, despite that there were no seats at the bar. Place still packed from band night. It would whittle down as the night grew on, but for now, people still thought they had a shot at whoever they'd found attractive during the music. He turned sideways to look at the crowd. Didn't want to settle for one of them, but he would if she didn't show. Be fucking rude of her, and he'd see her next show, but he reckoned women were treated rude all the time.

Then she was crossing the room. He looked at how much beer he had left. She hadn't been that long, he just worried too much. Figured.

"Pick a beer," he said. "I'm sure you know the selection."

"Maybe not so well as you, but yeah. I'm Cheryl."

She held out her hand and he shook it.

"Duane," he said. "Like Allman."

She laughed. That one always went over better with musicians. So yeah, she wouldn't be his first, but the others were back when he was single. Why Mercy married him—funny, smart, good in bed until she ceased to care about that, he never found out why—she'd been a guitarist. He still had a Fender Telecaster she'd left behind. That said something about her unwillingness to compromise and his sentimental nature, he supposed. God knows he'd never play the thing.

Cheryl's beer arrived and she too stood sideways to the bar, close to him. He liked that. It meant she'd at least be loyal to him over the course of this round. Loyalty mattered. He looked at her a minute, tried to take her all in, but she was a healthy Southern gal, too much to take in fast.

"How long," he said, "you figure on sticking with this outfit? 'Stead of going solo."

"A solo fiddle player? Like who, Amanda Shires?"

Pretty gal, Duane thought, both Cheryl and Amanda. But he'd never get Amanda, she was hooked up with Jason Isbell solid. And they were big names. His chance was to get Cheryl before she got too big.

"Yeah, like her."

"I done a couple," she said. "Weekends, bars that make this one look like Mercedes-Benz stadium."

That was where the Falcons played, in Atlanta. Actually *in* Atlanta, not like a lot of these stadiums in the outskirts or wherever the hell the land was cheapest.

"Yeah?" he said. "In town or out?"

"A little ways outa town."

"Tell me next time. You'll get an audience of at least one."

"Shit, do me more good if you brought friends."

"ZZ Top," he said, "had an audience of one once. They played their whole set for the guy. Worked out for them."

"Only they had a label by then, right? I ain't."

"Still. You get an audience of one, you play your whole set, right?"

"Ain't had that yet, but I reckon I would."

He'd be her audience of one, he knew that. She could play

her set, she could play solitaire for all he cared.

He kissed her.

"No." She pushed him away, both hands on his chest. "Not yet."

He liked that phrase. Not yet meant later if he didn't fuck things up. He nodded, as though in agreement. "Sorry. Guess I've been looking at you too long."

"Maybe look away a while," she said. "Admire the room."

"Admire?" His eyes stayed on her. "Kinda hard to do. Met my wife here."

"You're married?"

"Was. She left me. Seems I drank."

She nodded. Not enough information to determine whether he was worth a long-term relationship. Or to even decide whether to believe him.

"So," she said, "your wife."

"Yeah. I'd divorce her but ain't no one found her. Couple more years I think before it's official abandonment." Not that he had any desire to be legally single again.

"She ran off," she said.

"Just fuckin' disappeared. One night we're arguin', felt like the millionth straight night, next night she's gone."

"Hm."

"Zackly." He downed the end of his beer, waved to the barkeep. "You ready?"

She looked at her drink. Half of it left. "Yeah," she said, and proceeded to drink like a musician.

He smiled at her. "Long night?"

"Long life, sometimes. Don't want it to end, but it could use a few more highlights."

"Always." He raised his empty glass to hers. With nothing in them, they toasted and he took her glass. Good. He hated few things more than talking with a pissed-off woman, least when she was pissed at him. "Name a lowlight."

Her turn to look uncomfortable. She didn't know him well

enough. 'Course, if tonight didn't pan out, what would he have? Information he could never use was all.

"You notice the bass player?"

"Sure," he said. "Different guy than last time. Why?"

"Todd. He was with me. Took up with some bimbo he met at a Lucero show. Mobile, it was. Soul Kitchen, I think. Whatever. He never made it back."

"Shit," Duane said. Golden opportunity to feign sympathy. "He left *you*? What an ass."

"Good guy up 'til that, I thought. I thought…" Her voice trailed off.

"Yeah," he said. Their beers arrived. Thank God. Even feigned sympathy has its limits. He passed her glass, raised his. They toasted for real this time and drank.

It was light beer, something to fight the heat with. That's all you could do around here some nights. Like you could ever win a fight with the heat. And anyone says it ain't the heat it's the humidity can go fuck themselves. It's both, asshole. Always both.

"That why you played so ferocious tonight?"

"Did I?" she said. "Felt like I played same as always."

"Crowd mighta reacted that way. Ya know, your guitarist ain't that good."

"What?" she said. "Tommy's fantastic."

He shook his head. Some of the crowd had noticed who she was by now, tried to cut in on the conversation. It was all "Hey" and "Hey, baby" so far. He didn't know how much she should put up with. Knew he wouldn't put up with much.

"Look, asshole," he finally said to one, "you don't know the lady, back off."

"And you know her?"

He guided her away by the elbow but the guy he'd called asshole followed. "You know her? Tell me."

Duane stopped near the front door, turned to look at the guy. "Go on, get your beer. We'll talk."

The guy walked back to the bar. Duane and Cheryl drained

their glasses and walked outside.

"We go to my place," Duane said.

"Can't leave my fiddle behind. Get in your car, I'll follow."

Duane pointed out his Chevy, walked to it, got in, and waited for her. She'd just gotten behind the wheel when the tall asshole came out, ran to her. Duane got out of his car, cut in front of him. "She don't wanna see you."

"Let her say it."

Duane shook his head, grinned, turned his back on the guy, and mule-kicked him to the knee. The guy went down and Duane followed.

The asshole grabbed him by the throat and Duane smacked him upside his head, threw a left then another right, checked him down to his ankle, pulled two knives, rolled him over, and grabbed the .38 shoved in the back of his pants.

"You must have a way with the ladies, needin' all this shit."

He stood, kicked the asshole in the head, glanced at Cheryl.

She saw the whole thing, smiled. "Your place." She started her engine.

He got in his car and pulled out the lot. She followed, right behind him. Nothing wrong with a little bloodlust.

His place. Small but it had a basement, it was fine. Mercy's Fender hung on a living room wall. He didn't play at all, hadn't touched it since she left him except to afford it that space. He'd thrown away the case. No sentiment attached to that.

He walked in, left the front door open, grabbed a couple beers from the fridge and the Wild Turkey and two glasses from a cabinet. He set it all on the table in front of the living room couch, walked to the stereo, started to put on Lucero, remembered her story with a smile and put on The Complete Jimmy Rodgers. It was a long disc, wouldn't need interruption.

The beers were open, the bourbon was not. He'd wait on her approval for that. He figured she drank it but he knew she drank beer. Hell, who don't?

After a couple minutes, she was inside. Opposite the couch was nothing until you got to the TV. She sat next to him, grabbed the bottle of Wild Turkey, and poured herself a glass. "You want some too, right?"

He nodded and she poured. "You were right not to assume," she said. "If I didn't want bourbon, I'd have been so offended." Her eyebrows lifted. "Ooh, that's pretty."

She stepped to the Fender on the wall, reached out for it.

"No!" he shouted.

"What?" She turned her head to him.

"It was Mercy's."

"So? It's a guitar. It ain't sacred."

"No." He pulled her away from it. "Sit on the couch. Drink."

She sat. "Subject changed." She drank Wild Turkey, then beer. Looked at the guitar, though. What was special about it. He that sentimental about his wife?

"She's gone, right? She left you?"

"Yes." He couldn't look at her.

Cheryl looked at him, though. Looked at him acting so stupid over a goddamned guitar. Didn't make no difference to her, only any thoughts of a long-term romance were out. Guy was still crazy about his ex. Well, maybe tonight he'd call her Mercy, or something stupid like that. She could always accuse him later, accurately, and walk. Wouldn't be no fun to play that club no more, but maybe she'd be sparked to embark solo in another town. He knew where she played only when she was here.

He looked up. "Sorry. I promised her no one else would play it."

"You did that and she left it with you."

"I know. It's weird. I think she hoped I'd pick it up. Never could figure her out."

"So, no one would play it but you."

"Or her if she came back for it."

"You held the guitar hostage."

"No. It was hers. She could have it if she wanted. She never said. And she never came back."

Made no sense. Didn't affect her agenda, only the timing of it. She drank, watched as he did too.

"Anyway," he moved closer to her on the couch.

"Yeah." She leaned in.

They kissed and he pushed himself against her, his chest on hers. She felt his power, leaned back and looked up as he crawled on top of her. She saw the guitar, saw dark stains on its underside.

"Mm," she said, scooted back farther and sat up. "So, your wife. When you say she left you…"

"Yeah?" He pulled his head back, surprised.

"She moved away?"

"Not exactly. But basically, yeah."

"Basically. Means what?"

He didn't answer.

"Where's the toilet?"

He pointed down the hall.

She walked past the kitchen. Bedroom door was to her right. It was open. She opened a door on the left, stepped inside.

"Not that door!" he hollered.

She pretended not to hear, stepped in, and flipped a switch. The room lit up. Steps led down. And it reeked. She turned back, flipped off the switch, wondered why the room was unlocked. She went farther down the hall, opened the next door. The last door. She walked in, turned to lock it. No lock.

She kept her skirt on, stared down the door for a couple minutes. She turned on the sink, ran cold water for a couple minutes, gave herself another minute to dry them, and walked back.

He stood outside the kitchen.

"What *was* that?"

"The basement. I forgot."

"Huh. Smelled funny."

"Somethin' died down there," he said. "Ain't been able to get it out."

She nodded, walked to him. They kissed. She looked over his shoulder, let him go, and walked past, into the living room.

"The guitar on the wall." She looked at it.

He turned his head. "What about it?"

"Got a loose string. Okay if I tighten it?"

"Loose string? How?"

"Don't know," she said. "But that A string..."

He looked again, didn't know which string was the A.

She stepped to the guitar. "This one," she said, licking her finger and running it along the second string from the bottom. She picked up the guitar from the wall.

"No!" he shouted. Second time tonight, but this time his shout was cut short as she swung the guitar like a baseball bat and smacked him across the head.

It was one hell of a swing, and he collapsed. Blood spurted from one temple. She got his pants off, stroked his dick until it was hard enough for a condom, slipped herself on top of him with both hands at his throat. She rode him. He started to wake and her fingers tightened. She fucked him until she came, over and over, her fingers getting ever tighter as she did.

She checked his pulse and got off him, put her clothes back on. She dragged his body to the basement door, then down the steps. To where his wife lay, stinking to high heaven. She dropped him short of her, took a step past and up the stairs.

His wife had left him the way Todd had left her. Left for dead.

NOT MY CROSS TO BEAR
S.A. Cosby

The evening sun was beginning to dip behind the copse of oaks and maples that ran behind his house when Rev. Emory Prosser heard a car make its way down his lane. The way to his house was an orange clay road that slit its way through a clutch of pine trees that hid his house from the main road. The trees served as a sound break for the house. It kept away the sound of rickety transmissions and worn-out engines and the chest-rattling thump of boys with more bass in their cars than gas.

The car pulling into his yard had no bass. It had four doors, and each one was a different color. It had started life as a Crown Vic, but it had so many pieces and parts that didn't really fit but were just forced into place that now it was a creature of its own singular design. It parked in the shade of the magnolia tree Rev. Emory had planted fifty years ago when he and Alice had built their house. They'd had so much help that every window, every door was a different size. Rev. Emory shifted his weight on the stump of the cherry tree that had served as his outside seat for fifteen years. He leaned forward and rested his arms on the weathered table where they used to pick crabs years ago. Old Man Arthur Ritis had put an end to that a long time ago. His partner Father Time was busy putting an end to everything else.

Rev. Emory heard the car door creak open, then slam with a ferocious commotion. When he turned his head, he expected to see pieces of the door flying through the air like iron butterflies.

Instead he saw his nephew stomping over to the table. Sonny was leaner than he remembered. Or maybe he was always rangy and weathered like a piece of beef jerky. Rev. Emory wasn't rightly sure. He was wearing jeans and brown boots. A red plaid shirt hung on his narrow shoulders. His brown face was as taut as a new catcher's mitt. His eyes were black flinty chips set way back in his head.

He pulled up a cinder block, sat it on its end, and used it as a seat. It seemed to Rev. Emory that once upon a time he had planned to do something with that old cinder block, but its purpose was gone from him now. Sonny crossed his arms.

"What you want with me?" he asked. His voice was a whisper trying to become a scream. It strained against his vocal cords and came out like a bobcat in a trap. Fearful, angry, and desperate.

"How long you been out?" Rev. Emory asked.

Sonny studied his face. His uncle was clean-shaven and bald-headed. The folds around his eyes and under his neck were the only bellwethers that hinted at his advanced age. Rheumy brown eyes seemed perpetually on the verge of tears.

"About a month. What you want? Eddie Boo said you told her you needed to see me. Said it was important. Gave her fifty dollars down at the store to deliver your message. I'm here. What you want?" Sonny asked.

"You been home a month and you ain't seen fit to come by and see me or your aunt?" Rev. Emory asked.

"I saw Aunt Alice. She was coming out the Western Auto and I hollered to her."

"Where you staying? You over with that white girl? What was her name? Cindy Leigh?" Rev. Emory asked. Sonny scratched his chin.

"Cindy Leigh died not long after I went in. OD'd. I'm staying with Anne Wilson. Buggy Wilson's girl. She trying to get me a job at the shipyard," Sonny said. His uncle's eyes flicked to the right, then the left, and Sonny knew he was deciding whether to press him about working at the shipyard. Sonny knew his uncle knew the yard didn't usually employ ex-cons with a manslaughter charge. But Anne said she had pull. Sonny doubted a black woman had any pull at the shipyard, but he didn't have anything else to hang his hat on, so he was riding it out until the wheels fell off.

"Oh. I didn't know. I'm sorry," Rev. Emory said.

"I'm not. She testified against me. Even though I was taking for her pill-popping ass," Sonny said.

"People let us down. The world lets us down. God lifts us up," Rev. Emory said. Sonny let out a long sigh.

"What you want? I got things I gotta do," Sonny said.

"Like what?" Rev. Emory asked.

"What you mean 'Like what?' Things," Sonny said. He stood.

"I'll see you later," he said.

"Sonny. I'm not doing too good," Rev. Emory said. Sonny put his hands in his pockets. He bit at his bottom lip, pulling off a piece of dry skin and spitting it into the autumn wind. He hesitated, then sat down again.

"That's why you asked me over here?" he asked. Rev. Emory saw a flock of black birds fly overhead. Their triangular-shaped formation blotted out the light from the setting sun for a moment. Soon the light would be gone and the birds would be flying blind. Rev. Emory swallowed hard.

"Doctors say I got Alzheimer's. It's just starting, but they say I got the fast kind. I reckon I got about a year before I forget my own name. Some days it's not so bad. I feel almost regular. Other days I stare at the phone on the wall and can't think of what you call it to save my life. I mean, I know what it is. I know what it do, but I can't think of the word," Rev. Emory said. Sonny rubbed his thumb against his forefinger.

"What that got to do with me?" Sonny asked. Emory looked at him. He blinked his eyes several times. Batting away the tears.

"Your aunt and me done got behind on the taxes here at the home place. Well, that ain't really right. I got behind on the taxes. It just...slipped my mind. More than once. They planning on putting it up for auction in a month," Emory said. Sonny shook his head.

"I'm just out the joint. I ain't got two red pennies to rub together. That's Anne's car I'm driving. Ain't nothing I can do for you," Sonny said. Emory reached out and grabbed Sonny's hand. The younger man snatched it back. He flexed his fingers.

"I think there is," Emory said. A few dogs started howling in the distance. The wind changed directions and the sickly sweet scent of the last magnolia blossoms inundated Sonny. They smelled like a dead body just before it went all the way bad.

"Oh yeah? Tell me what that is?" Sonny asked. He felt like all he'd done since he'd got here was ask questions. Emory reached under the table and down into the waistband of his khakis. He pulled out a six-shot pistol and placed it on the table between him and Sonny. Sonny stared at the gun with ever-widening eyes. It sat there as mute as the Sphinx, exuding menace like a coiled rattler.

"Ten years ago, I took out a life insurance policy on me and your aunt. The boy who sold it to me said if I died in an accident or, as he put it, had a death by misadventure, your aunt would get double. That's more than enough to pay off the taxes and leave her something to live off. She might even be able to get your mama out the nursing home. Bring her back here and let her live her last days around people she knows," Emory said.

"What the fuck you want me to do with that piece?" Sonny said. Emory didn't speak for a few minutes. When he did, his voice had dropped an octave and he cast his eyes downward.

"You know," he said finally. Sonny leaned back, balancing his weight on the cinder block. He rubbed his face, then ran his hand through his close-cropped hair.

"You done lost your fucking mind," he said.

"No, but I'm working on it," Emory said. Sonny felt his chest tighten. His breath came in deep, chugging exhalations.

"I just did twelve fucking years in the joint behind some bullshit. I'm not putting a bullet in your head because you afraid of drooling on yourself," Sonny said.

"Watch your mouth, boy," Emory said.

"Watch my mouth? You sitting here talking some fool-ass shit and you worrying about my mouth? I tell you what, you can watch me leave, that's what you can watch," Sonny said. He stood again. Emory grabbed his hand with a strength and quickness that seemed long since lost to him.

"I can't do it myself. The Good Book tells us it's a mortal sin," Emory said. Tears slipped out of the corners of his eyes like little rivers.

"Tell me where it says that," Sonny said.

"What you say now?" Emory asked.

"Tell me where it says that. What chapter? What verse? I ain't never seen that in no Bible I read. You scared to do it, say you scared, but don't put it on the Bible. Now let go of my goddamn arm," Sonny said. Emory released his grip.

"All we done for you. I ain't never ask for no repayment. I ain't never asked you for nothing. We took you and your mama in."

"And you ain't never let us forget it. Made us feel like it was our fault my daddy died. And we both know that won't the case," Sonny said. Emory saw the way the tight knots and hard angles that made up his form seemed to be in a war with themselves. His anger came off him like heat from a trash fire.

"I know what my part in that was. And if we made you feel like you owed us, I'm sorry. It was our Christian duty. Your mama was my brother's wife. I couldn't see her and his only child out on the street. Times got hard and we was living right on top of each other, but I never meant you no harm. I never meant to throw it in your face. But now I'm here coming to you and asking for one thing. Only one thing," Emory said.

"It won't your Christian duty. It was your guilt. And nothing you did for us adds up to me picking up that piece and putting a bullet in your head," Sonny said. Emory reached under the table again. He pulled out a brown paper bag and sat it on the table.

"There's twenty-three hundred dollars in that bag. All the

money I got in the bank. Your aunt is over in Kilmarnock 'til Sunday. Ain't got no neighbors. Ain't nobody see you come down here. The only person that knows is Eddie Boo, and who gonna believe her? She been high since '83."

Sonny opened the bag. He saw a few stacks of hundreds tied up with rubber bands. He closed the bag and took a step back.

"You think so little of me that you figure I'll risk my freedom for twenty-three hundred dollars? You want this, you gonna need to find you another boy. I got enough blood on my hands. I don't need yours," Sonny said.

"All your life, you done used them hands to hurt and maim. Drink your rotgut and smoke your left-hand cigarettes. Take the virtue of good women just as easy as you take off they panties. Sling your dope and beat people right down to the ground. All I'm asking is once in your life full of inequity you use that Devil inside you for something good," Emory said. Sonny placed his hands flat on the table and leaned forward until they were eye to eye.

"You about as two-faced as a dollar bill. You ran women with my daddy. Played your numbers down at the store. Knocked Aunt Alice around if the gravy had too many goddamned lumps. Then one night after YOU drank your share of rotgut, you flipped that shitty-ass Chevy and sent my daddy flying through the windshield. Then…then that was when you found the Lord. What makes you think I'd do anything good for you? What makes you think I'd give you what you want when I can never get back what I want? What makes you think that I'd ever let you out of your misery when you was the one that gave me mine?" Sonny said. Emory straightened up. His shoulders shook and trembled like he was catching the Holy Ghost.

"I know what I've done. You ain't gotta tell me what I've done. That don't excuse the choices you done made," Emory said.

"Who said I had a choice?" Sonny asked.

"We all got a choice. God gives us free will. That's our choice."

"God took my daddy when I was thirteen and gave my mama

a stroke when I was fifteen. Now ask me again about choices," Sonny said.

"We can't question God's plans, boy," Emory said. Sonny laughed. The sound made the flesh on Emory's arms pucker up in gooseflesh.

"You remember when you and Aunt Alice would make me help you drag Mama to that church over in Surry? They'd be all laying hands on her and gibbering in tongues and then at the end of the service when she didn't get up and tap dance down the fucking aisle, they'd tell her that her faith needed to be stronger. Now I ain't no almighty man of God like you, but I seem to remember a verse about mustard seeds or some shit. My Mama had more than mustard seeds. But you gonna tell me it was in his plan for her to not get her legs back. It was in his plan for her mouth to be tangled up like chewed licorice. Alright. Maybe it's in his plan for you to lay up in that room up there and forget how to breathe. Maybe that's his fucking plan," Sonny said. He was nearly gasping for air. His hands were balled into fists so tight his forearms ached.

"I don't know, Sonny. You're right. I'm scared. Is that what you want to hear? I'm not scared to die. I'm scared to wither away to nothing, like corn husk drying in the field," Emory said, and now the tears were flowing freely.

"Look at you. Crying like a new fish on the block. Inside, them tears would get you a boyfriend. When I used to cry for my daddy, you gave me the business end of your belt and told me to man up. Did me crying for him remind you of what you'd done? I tell you what. Right before your mind goes blank and you can't spell cat if somebody spots you the C and the T and you filling your grown-up diapers with shit and piss, I want you to think about God's plan," Sonny said. He headed for the car.

"Sonny, please! I can't go on like this! I don't know what day it is. I can't remember my brother's name. I don't know if Alice been gone two days or two weeks. Please, Sonny," Emory pleaded.

"That's not my burden, Reverend," Sonny said. He opened the car door.

"He hated you and your mama," Emory hollered. Sonny locked up like a Chevelle with a bad oil pump.

"Don't," Sonny said. Emory stood. He grabbed the gun and tossed it on the ground between them. He squared his formerly quivering shoulders.

"He hated being married. He used to say your mama tricked him into it. Trapped him with them butter-pecan bowlegged thighs. That's why we stayed out late Fridays and Saturdays. He couldn't stand being around a big-legged woman who was just getting big and a whiny crybaby boy who still wanted bedtime stories at twelve damn years old," Emory said. Spittle flew from his lips like sparks. Sonny faced him. He felt a black cloud roll across the secret garden of his heart. Words that he knew had to be false stung all the same. Pierced the rugged hide inside him that protected his softest places.

"Shut up. Shut your goddamn lying mouth," Sonny said.

"I'm a lot of things, but a liar ain't one of them. He was gonna leave y'all. We was drunk and we was arguing about it."

"Stop it."

"We was fussing and fighting about it when he said he was leaving your mama for someone else."

"Shut the fuck up!" Sonny said.

"He told me he'd been sleeping with Alice," Emory said. The tremulous tone of his voice sounded like tin cans crashing against each other in the back of a pickup.

"SHUT UP!" Sonny screamed.

"So that was when I hit the gas and turned the wheel hard to the right."

Sonny knew he had to be lying. He knew every word was an ugly fantasy bred from fear and desperation and helplessness. He knew this as well as he knew he was born to die.

He knew it.

He knew it.

But then he found the gun in his hand. He found his finger around the trigger.

All six shots rang out like Gabriel's horn. Sonny wiped the gun clean and dropped it down the outhouse in the backyard near the woods. He grabbed the bag from the table and got in Anne's ramshackle jalopy. He drove out of Mathews County and into the city. He found a bar across the street from a motel. He dropped a hundred dollars on the bartender and told him to keep them coming.

Some wayward angel dropped a few coins in the jukebox and played "Not My Cross to Bear" by the Allman Brothers as Sonny threw back his first shot of rotgut. He wondered if he would see his uncle in his nightmares later that night.

He wondered if his nightmares were a little glimpse of the Hell that awaited him.

MIDNIGHT RIDER
Christopher Swann

Cassandra checked the hot dogs rotating on their metal grill, blood-red and sweating under the heat lamp. She squatted and gripped the ten-gallon tub of nacho cheese and, with a grunt, lifted it onto the counter. With a plastic ladle, she scooped out a few globs of processed orange cheese, plopping them into the stockpot, and then lowered the tub back to the floor. She took a plastic bag of hot dog buns from a drawer and lay it next to the stockpot, then checked her station. The stainless-steel counter was already wiped down, the napkin box stuffed. The hot dog chili was full, and nobody ate it anyway. The mustard, ketchup, and relish were all good. She smiled, satisfied.

Behind the cash register, slouched against the magazine rack, Kenny snorted. "That's A-plus work there, Miss Cassandra. Must be proud."

Cassandra flushed, equal parts embarrassment and anger. "Got to be proud of something."

"Oh, God, yes," Kenny said, standing up off the magazine rack. The plastic sleeves that held the magazines clung to his back for a moment before peeling away. "Forgot how much pride means to you, your daddy bein' a deputy and all. Must be proud of *him,* sure. Must feel like a step down, workin' in a dump like this."

Cassandra turned from him and opened her backpack, her hair hanging down over her face, hiding her reddening cheeks.

She had no time for these opening salvos of Kenny's. Her term paper was due in two weeks.

"Yeah, it's a dump all right," Kenny said behind her, speaking now to the empty convenience store, its silent shelves of Funyuns and beef jerky and cell phone chargers. "What my uncle saw in this place, I don't have the next goddamn idea."

Kenny's uncle, Max, who owned the store, had heavy jowls and a bad combover but treated Cassandra with courtly politeness, asking about her family when interviewing her for the part-time job. "Family is so important," Uncle Max had wheezed, dropping a hand on Kenny's shoulder. Kenny managed a crooked smile that made Cassandra blush. She covered that up by talking about her daddy, which was how Kenny knew he'd been a deputy. Uncle Max had shown Cassandra the store, apologizing for its shabbiness while clearly proud of what he had managed for thirty years. "But my doctor says I have heart problems, so it's time for me to step back," he'd said. "The world is for the young," he added, gesturing at Kenny and Cassandra. Max had hired Cassandra on the spot. At the time, Cassandra mistook that as a stroke of good luck.

Kenny continued his rant from behind the cash register. "Thought he'd make a fortune pumpin' gas and sellin' Snickers bars, and now he's worthless as a flat tire, coughin' all damn night, leavin' me here to work alone."

If I didn't need the money, I'd walk right now, Cassandra thought. But she did need the money. She was down to searching the couch for coins. Her roommate Libby thought she was exaggerating. She'd even asked Cassandra if she couldn't just call her parents for help. That was easy enough for Libby to say, whose daddy was a corporate banker in Atlanta. Cassandra's father, who had retired from the sheriff's department after blowing out his knee, was still paying off the surgery and couldn't send any more money. And now her mother was talking about going back to work at Kroger so her brother John could go to Valdosta State. God, Cassandra hated money, hated needing it even though she'd earned a scholarship. Hated needing to work with Kenny. She'd actually thought he was sort of cute at first, like a moody Tom Holland. But now that she'd worked here every Friday and Saturday night for a month, she wanted to kill something.

"Getting low on candy bars," Kenny said. "Should put a few more out, Cass."

Cass. Goddamn him. Cassandra dropped her pen and went back to the supply room, ignoring Kenny's smirk.

Around nine-thirty, Libby swept in through the single glass door, wearing something clingy and black, red hair pinned in a messy updo. "Hey, girl," Libby said, high heels clicking on the tiles. "How's life in Nacho Land?"

Cassandra held up her copy of *Jane Eyre*. "Working on this. Stocked some shelves." She shrugged, then glanced over at the cash register. Kenny was ignoring them by reading a *Penthouse*, although he was scowling. "How about you?"

Libby shrugged. "Party at Wade's, some kind of costume thing. I'm not wearing a costume, obviously."

"You look gorgeous," Cassandra said. She marveled at how Libby always looked effortlessly sexy in a way she never could.

Libby looked down at herself and opened her hands—*what, this? I just threw it on.* "You should come later when your shift's over." She glanced at Kenny, then back to Cassandra. "He giving you any shit?"

"The usual." Again, Cassandra shrugged, trouble sliding off her like rain—you get wet and it's annoying, but that's all. "I get off at midnight. Maybe I'll meet up with you?"

"Definitely, girl."

Kenny rattled the magazine in his hands. Loudly, he asked, "You check the expiration dates on the milk today?"

Libby smiled. "Tell me, Kenny, I'm doing a survey on chronic masturbation. Do you jerk off alone, or with a partner?"

Cassandra stifled a giggle. Kenny just stood there, eyes blinking rapidly as he processed what she'd said.

"Alone? Thought so." Libby nodded as if in confirmation. "Well. Have a great evening." She winked at Cassandra and flounced out the door. Cassandra bent over her notebook to hide her smile.

"Nice girl," Kenny said finally, after Libby had driven off in her BMW. "Oughta tame lions or somethin'. Hey, you checked that milk yet?"

Business was slow, mostly people getting gas. Around ten-thirty, the door opened and two fraternity boys walked in, one in a green polo, the other wearing a T-shirt from a Christmas party last year with a reindeer on it collapsed drunk around a keg. Their voices rang off the walls. "So Sam, he takes the keg, and I tell him to take it upstairs," the one in the Christmas T-shirt said. "And when he gets to the top, the fucking *top* of the stairs, he says, 'Oh, shit,' and drops it, and the keg bounces *down* the stairs—"

"No," the boy in the green polo said.

"Swear to God, and it goes right through the fucking *window*, just shatters it, glass everywhere, and he says, 'Oops.'" Both boys burst into laughter. "'Oops,'" the boy in the polo said, and they laughed harder.

"Hey," Kenny called out from the register. "This ain't a nightclub."

The two boys stopped laughing and looked at Kenny. "Sure, whatever," Christmas T-shirt said. They walked to the beer coolers and got two cases of beer, walked up to the cash register, and then Christmas T-shirt pulled out his wallet to pay. The boy in the green polo saw Cassandra further down the counter, behind the hot dogs. "Hey," he said in recognition, moving his hand in a wave. "How's it goin'?"

Cassandra smiled tightly and glanced at Kenny. "Hey," she said.

"You go to school here, right?" the boy asked.

She relaxed her smile a fraction. “Sure do,” she said. The boy was cute, blue eyes and red cheeks, nice full shoulders. She fingered a strand of her hair, wishing it were a darker blonde rather than a shade of Swiss cheese.

Kenny glowered at the fraternity boys. “I need to see your IDs,” he said, and then paused dramatically. “Both of ’em.”

Christmas T-shirt rolled his eyes but handed Kenny his driver’s license. The other boy winked at Cassandra and gave Kenny his ID as well. Kenny made a show of checking their faces against the ID photos, then held the licenses up to the light as if he could see straight through them.

“Hey,” Christmas T-shirt said. “It’s cool. We’re both twenty-one.”

Kenny fixed him with a stare. “Can’t be too careful,” he said coldly. “I sell you beer and you turn out to be underage, I lose my license. Might go to jail. You ever been to jail, hotshot?” When neither of them answered, Kenny shoved their IDs back at them. “Twenty-six even,” he said.

They paid and left without another word. The boy in the green polo with the nice shoulders did not look back at Cassandra. When the door swung shut behind them, Cassandra said, “What did you give them a hard time for? You’d sell beer to a baby if it had the money.”

“Frat boys,” Kenny said, his nose scrunching. “Look at you like dirt if you ain’t in their little club. I know frat boys, believe me. Cocksuckers. Threw me out of a party once, just tryin’ to get a beer and meet some girls. You know? They saw me comin’ and threw me out. Cocksuckers, all of ’em. Think they could handle a night in jail?”

Cassandra shook her head and bent over her copy of *Jane Eyre*. She could understand why they would have told Kenny to leave their party.

“They’d piss themselves they got in jail,” Kenny said. “I got arrested, cops beat me black and blue. They took me off the street, no reason, and threw me in a cell. Three of them held me down and a fourth put a phone book over my head and then got out a nightstick and *pow!*" He slammed his hand down on the counter. "Hit me over the head with it. The phone book kept the bruises away, see? No evidence, my word against theirs. Sons of bitches. When I sell this place, I'm *out* of here."

Cassandra looked up from her book. "I thought your uncle Max owned this place."

Kenny shrugged. "He does, until he dies. Willed it all to me." He assumed a faraway look, his eyes round and glassy. "I'll sell it and go to Vegas, make a shit ton of money at the tables, then just keep on drivin' down that road, free as a motherfuckin' bird. Won't catch me again, no sir."

Cassandra pushed her book away and plucked a local newspaper from the stack on the counter in front of her and opened it to the want-ads.

"That's seventy-five cents," Kenny said absently.

Cassandra dug into her pocket, retrieved three quarters, and slapped them down on the counter, then went back to the want-ads. Agricultural engineer, baseball coach, car mechanic. She circled *baseball coach* with a blue pen, then saw it was a volunteer job and crossed it out.

The door opened and a Korean girl came in, her eyes wide and shy. She stepped tentatively to the cash register. "I would like some change," she said in a barely audible voice to Kenny. "Some quarters, yes?" She held up a limp five-dollar bill.

"You have to buy somethin'," Kenny said.

The Korean girl shook her head and smiled. "No, thank you. I am not wanting anything other than change, please." Again, she held up the bill.

Kenny's voice rose as if he were speaking to a deaf person. "You have to buy something first." He leaned forward, towering over the girl from behind the counter. "No change unless you buy something. Understand?"

The girl shrank back, looking around nervously.

Cassandra picked up a lollipop from a jar on the counter.

"Here," she said, and both the Korean girl and Kenny turned to look at her. "You can buy this and get change. It doesn't cost very much."

The girl's eyes grew wider, and she smiled. "Thank you," she said, and she took the lollipop from Cassandra. Turning to Kenny, she announced, "I will buy this." She held up the five-dollar bill. "And change?"

"Yeah, yeah," Kenny said, ringing her up and handing her change to her. She smiled again at Cassandra, then hurried from the store.

"Gooks," Kenny muttered under his breath. "Oughta learn the goddamn language 'fore they come over here."

There was nothing in the want-ads. Cassandra threw down the paper, then sighed and reached into her backpack and took out her dad's old handheld voice recorder.

"What's that?" Kenny asked suspiciously.

"Voice recorder. I tape my class lectures."

"Why?"

"So I make sure I don't miss anything."

Kenny said nothing, and Cassandra turned to a fresh page in her notebook.

"Why don't you just record on your phone?" Kenny asked.

Cassandra grit her teeth. "Because I don't have a smartphone."

"You don't have a smartphone?" Kenny said, frowning.

"No."

"Huh. Don't know nobody doesn't have a phone."

"I have a phone," Cassandra said. "Just not a smartphone."

"Okay, but—"

"I'm on scholarship, Kenny. I don't have the money for a smartphone. It's why I've got a shitty flip phone and drive a shitty car and work at this shitty job with you."

As if on cue, her flip phone buzzed on the counter. She opened it and saw a text from Libby: *When U coming.*

"Haven't seen one of those in a while," Kenny said.

Soon as I can, Cassandra texted back. *Done at midnight.*

Then she closed the phone and dropped it in her backpack. She felt flushed and angry at Kenny and with herself. She didn't care about being poor; she just didn't want it shoved in her face all the damn time. She took a deep breath, blew it out, then put her earbuds in and pressed the *Play* button.

"I ain't payin' you to do homework," Kenny said.

Cassandra pushed *Pause* and turned to face him. "No, your Uncle Max is paying me, to clean up, restock, and basically do whatever it is you don't want to do. I've done it tonight already. If you have something else you need me to do, tell me and I'll do it, but get off my back."

Kenny leaned back against the register and let out a low whistle. "Damn, somebody's touchy."

If he asks if I'm on my period, Cassandra thought, *I'll shove every last one of these hot dogs down his throat so he chokes to death.* The thought shocked her, but it also broke through her anger and almost made her laugh. She took another breath and picked up her voice recorder and pressed *Play.*

"Actually," Kenny said, "there's beer needs to be restocked. Two cases, I believe."

Cassandra pressed *Pause,* took out her earbuds, and stomped back to the cold storage, where she grabbed two cases of beer and then shoved them into the cooler. She went back behind the counter, sat down, and put her earbuds in again, trying to shut the rest of the world out.

For an hour, the store was quiet. Kenny shifted restlessly and muttered to himself behind the cash register. Cassandra kept copying notes and listening to the voice recorder, then rewinding and listening again. Dr. Allison's voice was old and kindly and often drew a laugh from his students. She worshipped this man and often spoke to him after class about graduate school and teaching literature. It was a dream her parents shared with her and supported, but she wouldn't get anywhere near it without getting straight A's.

"Damn it," she whispered—she'd missed something Dr. Allison said while she was dreaming about being a professor. She stopped the recorder and rewound a few seconds.

"Getting lots done?" Kenny asked, cleaning out an ear with his pinkie.

"Yeah," Cassandra said, hoping he would go to the restroom and finish cleaning out his ear in there.

"You think I'm a real prick, don't you?" he asked.

She sighed and put her pen down. "What, is this feel-sorry-for-me night?"

Kenny put his hands in his back pockets, jaw set, eyes narrowed. "You're so high and mighty, sittin' there judgin' me," he said. He thrust his face toward her. "Goin' to college, got your mamma and daddy at home all proud of you. Bet you never had your daddy hit you with a wrench when he was drunk. Never had a mamma who just sat and watched soap operas when it happened and then told you not to be a baby." He laughed, but Cassandra could hear the bitterness, the dark thread that ran through his words. "So I got the hell out when I was fifteen, come up here and worked for my uncle. And now he's dyin'. You don't know nothin' about me, girl." He took his hands out of his pocket and clenched them into fists. "You don't know nothin'." He suddenly quit talking as if he had run out of words and turned back to the cash register. He grabbed a magazine from the rack, chewing on a thumbnail as he savagely flipped the pages.

Cassandra stared at him, then reached for her voice recorder and pressed *Play*. She tried to concentrate on Dr. Allison's voice but instead caught herself thinking about Kenny's words, about her own dad and his broad face and tired smile, how he would unclip his revolver from his belt and lock it in his closet before turning to her and giving her a hug. What if he had yelled at her? Hit her with a wrench, or worse? She shook her head angrily as if trying to shake the thought out. She glanced over her notebook at Kenny, still slouched in the corner, looking at a centerfold without interest. Behind Kenny she could see through the plate-glass windows the road that went off into the night. It was a state highway that ran for miles before merging into other roads, roads she had yet to see that went on forever. She was struck by an image of driving in the dark, down a road with no signs, no map, nothing. The thought frightened her. And she realized that may be how Kenny felt, too—for all his talk about driving away and being free, he was afraid of being in the dark, alone, lost. She brought her eyes back to Kenny, who was folding his magazine back up. He shoved it back in the rack and then turned to see her looking at him.

"I'm sorry," Cassandra said. The words hung overhead like the fluorescent lights, half of them burnt out, the other half glaring down.

Kenny stared at her, then said, "I don't want your damn pity."

Something snapped like a cheap rubber band and anger surged in her. "Oh, shut up," she said, the words out before she consciously thought of them. "I don't pity you. I'm showing empathy. I'm trying to be a human being and you act like an asshole. Just forget it." Angrily, she went back to copying her notes.

"Hey," Kenny said.

Cassandra ignored him, copying Dr. Allison's words: "*...in the instance of the split chestnut tree Jane and Rochester sit under when he finally reveals his passion—*"

"Cassandra," Kenny said. "Hey."

She stabbed the *Pause* button. "What?" she demanded.

He looked blankly at her. "Sorry."

They looked at one another across the tile floor, the fluorescent lights glaring down.

"Okay," she said finally. She nodded, as if something had just been concluded, although Kenny kept looking at her. She bent back over her notebook and pressed *Play,* copying her professor's words.

"—what to do with this scene? Is Miss Brontë trying—"

There was a dull metallic *snick* at the edge of Cassandra's conscious hearing, and she half-raised her head, but she wanted to finish copying Dr. Allison's point down.

"—obviously a woman of passion herself—"

A hand brushed her hair. She jerked and turned. Kenny stood right there. He took her by the shoulders and kissed her on the mouth. She froze, shocked, Kenny's lips pressed against hers. She broke away and slapped him. The smack of her hand meeting his cheek was as startling as the slap itself, but Kenny just leaned in and kissed her again, his tongue pushing into her mouth. She tried to pull back but Kenny pressed against her, his mouth still on hers, and he picked her up by the waist and sat her on the counter. She registered her notebook being swept away, her voice recorder falling to the floor, but she was overwhelmed by Kenny, his smell of hot oil, his probing tongue. She turned her head away, breaking off the kiss. "Get off me!"

"Come on, Cass," he said, his voice pitched to a whine. "I've seen you look at me." He still held her on the counter. Her short legs were off the floor and he stood between them, too close for her to kick him. His breath was hot in her ear. "You haven't wanted this? You haven't thought about being fucked right here? Come on." She hit his ribs with her fists, then tried to hit the side of his head. He caught her arm and pinned it down. "Stop it, Cass," he growled. "I'm not joking. You want this, too." His hand slid from her waist to her breast.

"No!" She turned her head to look at the door, willing someone to walk in, to stop this, and with horror she saw that the OPEN sign on the door had been flipped to CLOSED and the bolt was thrown, locking the door. That realization crashed over her like a wave, and she struggled wildly.

"Goddamn it, you bitch, settle down." He gripped her upper arms and shook her. She was appalled by his strength, his hands clamped on her arms like an iron press. Then his right hand was pawing at her blouse, his mouth on her neck, forcing her back onto the counter. She stared up at the glare of the lights. With her free left hand, she groped around on the counter. Her fingers touched the plastic handle of the nacho cheese ladle and closed around it. She forced her body to relax.

"Yes," Kenny breathed, taking this as a sign of submission, but when he raised his head from her neck to look down at her, she brought the ladle around in a clumsy swing and smacked him in the side of the face. The cheese, now runny and hot, spattered across his cheek and nose.

"Shit!" He fell back, letting go of Cassandra and raising his hands to wipe at his face. She braced her hands on the countertop and kicked. Her foot connected, and Kenny buckled. He staggered back against the magazine rack, *Penthouses* and *Clubs* falling at his feet. He sank to the tiled floor, hands covering his crotch. "Oh, God," he groaned. "My nuts."

She slid off the counter, her face burning. "You asshole!" she screamed. "What the fuck is wrong with you?" Rage shot through her. If she'd been holding a gun right then, she knew she would empty it into him.

Kenny got to his knees, one hand on his crotch, the other swiping at the nacho cheese that ran down his face like bright orange snot. He stood awkwardly. Cassandra took three steps back, balling her fists, but Kenny raised a hand in surrender and retreated to the cash register. She was panting as if she'd just finished a run. "Why did you do that?" she cried.

"I thought…that you liked me," Kenny said, still clutching himself.

"And *that's* how you show someone you like them?" A dark fury gripped her. Her entire body shook.

"I'm sorry," Kenny said, wiping a final glob of cheese off his cheek and smearing it onto his jeans.

Cassandra began to cry. She flung up the hinged countertop and rushed out and down the chip aisle to the bathroom at the back of the store. From the bathroom door, she looked back, afraid Kenny was following her. He was still half-crouched behind the cash register, looking dazed.

There was a rapping on the entrance and Cassandra saw someone standing outside, a man wearing a sweatshirt with the hood pulled up, hands cupped around his eyes as he leaned against the glass door, peering in. Kenny straightened and moved toward the door to unlock it. Cassandra went into the bathroom. She closed and locked the door.

Her face was a blotchy mess, her eyes swollen and leaking like red sponges. She turned on the sink faucet and cupped her hands to lift water up to her face to wash it off. There were no paper towels in the dispenser to dry her face, so she used toilet paper. Bits of it tore and clung to her cheeks and she wiped them off. She could still taste Kenny on her lips. She gagged and leaned over the sink for a moment, but she didn't throw up, and gradually the nausea faded. She concentrated on breathing in through her nose and out her mouth, trying to calm herself. She couldn't stay there. But she had to get her bag—she couldn't afford another backpack, another copy of *Jane Eyre,* another voice recorder. A customer was in the store now, so Kenny couldn't do anything. She would simply walk out, grab her things, and leave.

When she opened the bathroom door, the customer was at the counter, his back to Cassandra. He was speaking softly so she couldn't hear him, but she heard Kenny as he stood behind the register. "No, we don't have any," he said as if repeating himself and tired of it. "We're out of cartons. You can buy a pack and—"

The customer shifted, his right shoulder and arm moving inside the sweatshirt, and Cassandra saw Kenny's face pucker with fear, his mouth shrinking to a disbelieving O. The customer said something.

"Y-yeah, I'm alone," Kenny said, his eyes focused on something in the customer's hand. "Don't shoot, mister, please."

Jesus, Cassandra thought, her pulse quick and hot in her ears. She crouched behind a shelf, peering around the edge down the aisle.

"Gimme the money," the man in the sweatshirt said, his voice strained.

"We got a time safe," Kenny said, his voice ratcheted high. "I can't open it 'til—"

The man raised his hand and placed the barrel of his revolver against Kenny's forehead.

Oh, no, Cassandra thought.

"I said gimme the money now, motherfucker." The man with the revolver shifted to his left so he could see both Kenny and the front door. Cassandra now saw he had a bandanna over his face. He was sweating, nervous. "Right now."

"Okay, shit!" Kenny stabbed at the cash register, the drawer popping open with a cheery ring.

Cassandra remembered her father describing convenience store holdups. Most thieves left the cashiers unharmed. But this man with the revolver definitely looked like he belonged in the other group. The revolver wavered, his gun arm unsteady. She looked around her—Doritos, Sweet Tarts, packets of peanuts, hardly an arsenal worth considering.

"Put it in the bag, man!" the thief screamed. She heard Kenny sobbing as he opened up a paper bag.

Her eyes fell on a fire extinguisher on the wall behind her. Without thinking, she crept across the floor, reached up, and took the extinguisher off the wall. When she turned back around, she brushed against a tall can of Pringles on the end cap and knocked it off its shelf. She grabbed it with her right hand before it hit the floor. Then she sank to the tiles, her breath released in a ragged gasp from her throat.

"Come on!" the thief shouted.

Cassandra put the can of Pringles down and stepped one aisle to her left, putting a row of shelves between her and the thief. Then she crouch-walked to the end of the aisle. She pulled the pin on the extinguisher and gripped the lever at the top.

When she peeked around the shelf, Kenny was crying and

stuffing cash into a bag. The thief's back was still to her. But Kenny saw her, his eyes widening with shock. The thief noticed and whirled around, his revolver coming to bear. Cassandra squeezed the lever. Yellow powder sprayed out from the extinguisher into the man's face. He cried out, and then Kenny latched onto the thief's gun arm, yelling. The thief cursed and struggled to free himself until Cassandra brought the extinguisher down on his head with a solid *thonk* and he collapsed, the revolver hopping out of his hand and skittering across the tiles.

Cassandra held the extinguisher up in case she needed to bash the thief again, but when she was sure he was unconscious, she lowered it to the floor. Her arms were shaking and her mouth tasted like dirty pennies. The store smelled like ammonia, sharp and acrid. Kenny fell back against the counter. "Holy shit," he said, his voice thick with rage and fear. "Did you see that?" He looked revolting, face screwed up in a grimace, eyes wet and wild, nacho cheese on his shirt. "God, I grabbed his gun. And you beat the shit out of him with a fire extinguisher!" He laughed, a ragged, uneven burst of sound. He drew an arm across his face, wiping away tears and snot. "Jesus, you clocked him good."

The thief moaned and Kenny leaped back as if stung. Cassandra reached for the extinguisher, then saw the revolver, a .38, on the floor. She picked it up and pointed it at the thief, who tried to sit up, one hand rising to his head. The front of his sweatshirt and bandanna were covered in yellow dust from the fire extinguisher, and the thief pulled the bandanna off his face and started coughing and wiping his eyes. When he finally opened his eyes, they immediately crossed as he saw the barrel of the .38 pointed at his head. "Don't shoot," he said weakly, holding his hands up.

"Don't shoot?" Kenny shouted. "You cocksucker! You deserve to have your balls cut off! I oughta kill you right now!"

Cassandra saw her notebook and voice recorder on the floor behind the hot dog station, where they had fallen when Kenny had knocked them off the counter. Still covering the thief with the .38, Cassandra crouched down and picked up her things one at a time, placing them on the counter.

"I'll get some duct tape or something," Kenny said. "Tie up his hands and feet. You got him?" Cassandra nodded and Kenny hurried down the aisle that held household goods and hardware.

Cassandra picked up her voice recorder, then paused. She glanced at the thief, but he was still on the floor, trying to wipe the yellow powder off his face and out of his eyes. She turned her attention back to the voice recorder. A tiny red light indicated it was recording. It must have started when it fell to the floor. She stopped it, then rewound and listened to a couple of seconds. Her face hardened.

"Here," Kenny said, stepping out from the aisle and holding up a roll of silver duct tape. "Let's hogtie this sumbitch."

Cassandra pressed *Stop* and stepped away from the counter, looking down at the thief. "Stand up," she said. The man rose shakily to his feet, and Cassandra took two steps back to stay out of his reach.

"Turn around, motherfucker, so I can tape up your hands," Kenny said.

"Get out of here," Cassandra said to the thief.

Kenny's mouth dropped open. "What?"

"Go," she said.

"You gonna shoot me if I run?" the thief asked.

"I'll shoot you if you don't move in the next three seconds," Cassandra said, and the thief bolted, plunging out the door and into the night.

"What the *fuck*?" Kenny said. He shook the roll of duct tape at her. "Why'd you let him get away?"

Cassandra turned the .38 on Kenny, who immediately paled.

"Give me the money," she said. "The bag he made you get."

Kenny stared at her a moment, then snorted, half in contempt and half in disbelief. "Or what?" he said.

She raised the pistol and fired into the ceiling, the flat *crack* causing Kenny to jump and drop the roll of tape. Cassandra brought the .38 back down and leveled it at his chest.

"What the fuck is this, a *game*?" Kenny screamed.

"Get the bag," she said.

Eyes on the .38, Kenny sidestepped to the counter, grabbed the paper bag, and threw it at her feet. "Go ahead," he said, licking his lips. "Take it. Deputy's daughter stealing from her employer? That'll make front-page news. Your ass'll be in jail for a long time, you bet."

Cassandra bent down and retrieved the bag of money, then reached across the counter and grabbed her backpack. She put her novel, her notebook, and the bag of money into the backpack and slung it on her shoulder, all the while keeping the .38 trained on Kenny.

"Fucking go to *jail*," Kenny said, louder this time. "Locked up where you belong, you bitch."

Cassandra held up her voice recorder, rewound a few seconds, then pressed *Play* and held it up to Kenny as if she wanted him to speak into it. From the recorder came the voice of her professor, interrupted by a loud, violent sound like cloth being ripped in half, then voices. Cassandra thumbed the volume up. *"—off me!"* her voice said from the recorder, followed by Kenny: *"Come on, Cass. I've seen you look at me—"*

Kenny flushed, then went pale. "That—that don't mean nothin'," he said.

"—haven't thought about being fucked right here? Come on."

"It's *nothing*!" Kenny shouted.

"No!" the recorder played, followed by, *"Goddamn it, bitch, settle down!"*

She pushed *Stop*. Kenny stood before her, snot and tears running down his face.

"You got robbed," Cassandra said. "Then you jumped the guy and fought him and sprayed him with a fire extinguisher. You ran him off. You'll look like a hero. Or you can make up whatever story you want. The main thing is, I wasn't here. I'd already left. Or this tape will go to every news station in this state, and you'll go to jail for attempted rape. And everyone will know what a piece of shit you are." She paused, but Kenny just stood there, crying, so she left him, walking out the door for the last time. She got into her ten-year-old Ford Focus, tossed the backpack onto the passenger seat, and drove away.

She drove three miles before pulling off to the side of the road, where she wiped the .38 clean with a rag and tossed it out the window into the woods before driving on. There was two hundred dollars and change in the paper bag, enough to last until she found another job. Her heart beat strong and fast, but instead of fear, she felt exaltation. She knew this moment was the most singular of her life so far, and she also knew she would never do anything like this again. It was enough to know that she could. She would keep the memory of this stored away, only taking it out when she needed to remind herself what she was capable of. She looked at the clock on her dash—five minutes to midnight. She gave a little grin. If she hurried, she could still catch Libby at Wade's party.

MULTI-COLORED LADY

Raquel V. Reyes

NW Georgia Bugler
October 23rd, 1990

Another headless body has been found on the banks of the Coosa. Officials say wet weather and erosion have contributed to these recent discoveries.

"Melvin. MELVIN." Thom knocked harder. A slate blue paint chip embedded itself into his knuckle. "Lazy son o'bitch. I'm fixin' to break this door down and raise your scrawny ass from that bed like one of my mama's cat head biscuits on a Sunday morning."

"Hold your damn horses. I'm coming." Melvin opened the door and stepped onto the bowed porch.

"Who are you, the Gorton's Fisherman?"

"They're waders. Last time, my overalls got ruint. Washed 'em five times and they still had dark stains."

"Be more careful next time."

"I'm wearing 'em."

"They're yellow."

"So?"

"Private property. Trespassers will be shot."

"I thought you said it was public land."

"It is, it is, it is. But we have to cross through the old Ledbutler farm to get to it."

"Nobody's gonna be out in this God-awful weather except us fools. Come on, let's go. I ain't worried."

"You got the shovel?"

"Yeah. You got the pickaxe?"

"Yeah."

"A'right, let's go."

Thom turned his 1978 Ford off Black's Bluff Road and into a hidden driveway. The brown truck bucked and whinnied like a mare shucking a saddle as it went from asphalt to rocky clay. Thom took the shovel from the flatbed and Melvin got the rest. The overgrowth and grey sky made the driveway cave-like. They walked up the track to a gate sealed shut by kudzu. The vines, like dark braided hair, dripped with rain. The tears of an abandoned woman. They threw their stuff over and climbed the five-foot gate.

"How far we gotta go? This bag ain't made of feathers." Melvin shifted the strap of the stained duffel bag.

"Quit your griping. It ain't far. A little ways past the slave quarters that's the property line. The public trust land starts there. That's where you'll see the mound."

"Lead on, Pocahontas."

Thom laughed and it sounded like a tree splitting. A sound that made the hairs on the back of a person's neck prickle to attention, anticipating a two-ton crash. But it wasn't a Georgia pine about to fall. It was only harmless good ole boy humor.

The men didn't talk as they slogged up the wooded path. It was hushed. No birds chirped. No squirrels scurried. It was a place fit for only ghosts and thieves. Thom stopped and pointed. Three cabins, the size of playhouses, were ahead of them and a peek of clearing beyond them. They stepped up their speed. Melvin set the bag on the cabin's tiny porch and rested his rubber-clad butt on its edge. The cabin's timber was rotted and its roof caved in.

"Watch yourself; there's bound to be a nest of cottonmouths holed up under there."

"That's another reason I wore these waders. Snakes."

"Sssssshh, you hear that rattling?"

"Stop fooling. I'm not falling for your snake shit."

"I'm not fooling. I heard something." Thom put his finger to his lips to shush his friend. He crept over to the furthest cabin, the only one with an intact roof and a door, and entered it.

Melvin waited. He studied the quarters that would have slept a dozen or more each. Supposedly, the Ledbutler plantation had had a hundred slaves during its heyday. The story goes that Nathan Ledbutler had been meaner than a yellow jacket. Five minutes passed and not a peep from his friend. He went to investigate for himself. As he neared the threshold, Thom charged through the doorway with a pair of antlers held to his head.

"Took you long enough." Thom chuckled.

"What the hell?"

"Looks like somebody's set up camp. I found these"—He waved the two-point buck antlers at Melvin—"and a bunch of other shit that wasn't here last time I was here."

Melvin poked his head into the cabin for a look around. There was a snakeskin nailed to the wall. An old Coca-Cola crate filled with mason jars was in a corner. He lifted a jar from its corral. It was filled with roots. Another had dirt. A third held a possum skull. "A little witch-doctor creepy if you ask me." He ran his hand over a mobile of rusty skeleton keys like it was a harp. "Was that what you heard?"

Thom shrugged and toed a dented Charles Chips tin. It rattled. "That's more like it." He tipped it over and a dozen pecans rolled out. "We're wasting time. Let's get on about our business."

The men gathered their tools and walked into the clearing. The land rose and then leveled. Thom put his boot heel on the shovel and pried the earth open. Melvin dropped the duffel on the wet ground and knelt to unzip it. From the plastic bag within it, he removed the egg-shaped sensor and assembled the metal detector.

"What makes you think we're gonna find anything here?" Melvin asked.

"You remember about ten years ago, when those guys found that Spanish sword?"

"Yeah, the de Soto sword."

"Ok, so, it was just down the road from here that the Spanish attacked that Indian village. And I'm thinking this here mound is part of that village."

Melvin looked at him with doubt. "Are you sure it's even a mound? I thought we were hunting for cannonballs."

Thom wiped the wet from his brow. "That'll work, too. Treasure is treasure. Come on, get that thing beeping. Finders keepers."

NW Georgia Bugler
October 26th, 1990

One of the decapitated bodies found on the banks of the Coosa has been identified. Marshall Cooper, a partner in the Harben & Cooper Auction Company, missing since January, was IDed thanks to a surgical screw in the deceased's wrist.

"Please welcome to our Chiaha stage, the only all-female Allman Brother's tribute band, direct from Macon: Duane's Peaches!"

The audience, seated on hay bales, applauded and whistled. Thom stood in back with Melvin.

"Another crappy cover band," he said to Melvin, who was running the mixing board for the arts and crafts festival.

"Actually, from what I heard in the soundcheck, they're pretty good. That girl there plays a mean slide guitar." Melvin pointed to the woman on stage with a blue bandana.

The band started their set with Statesboro Blues. Several members of the audience got to their feet and swayed along. A few braver souls moved into the small dance area in front of the stage.

"Damn, she's mighty fine."

"The lead singer? Yeah, she's hot." Melvin's attention was on the musicians.

"Nah, that hippie chick dancing up there."

Melvin followed Thom's gaze. "Really? I thought you like 'em bleached blonde and wearing Daisy Dukes." The woman who had captured Thom's fancy had black plaited hair and wore a green tie-dyed skirt.

"I like them any way I can get 'em." Thom watched the woman shake her hips to the gritty guitar. "Damn, I wanna get me some of that brown sugar. Where has she been hiding?" He followed her skirt like it was a burlesque dancer's as she gathered a handful of fabric and sashayed. Her movements revealed a tease of thigh, a tattoo. Three letters. Large.

Melvin handed his friend a paper napkin. "You're drooling."

The band went through their repertoire of Allman Brothers hits including Whipping Post, Melissa, Midnight Rider, and Ramblin' Man.

"Alright folks, this song is not usually on our setlist, but because we're here at the lovely Riverside Park in beautiful Rome, Georgia, we had to. If you know the words, and we're pretty sure you do, sing along." The lead singer stepped away from the mic while the guitarist gentled plucked the introductory chords. When the keyboard came in, she stepped back to the mic and sang.

Got on a bus in Memphis, destination Rome.

The audience cheered at the mention of their town. Most everyone knew the words, and arms were in the air, swaying to the ballad about a broken-hearted bride.

Multi-colored lady, you ain't like no rainbow I've ever seen.

Thom leaned close to Melvin. "I never got this song. Angry red, I get. But, passion blue and shades of green? What the hell is that supposed to mean?" The men exchanged looks of agreement. "Hey, look at my girl. Who's she with?" She'd linked arms with another woman and the two sang to each other.

"You know her. Becca. She went to Model. Worked at Schroder's Deli. She went off to Athens for a spell and came back with some fancy degree."

"Yeah. I remember her." Thom smirked. "Bikini Becca with the Grateful Dead tramp stamp. I hooked up with her a couple of times tubing at Little River."

At the last line of the song, the crowd raised their voices to belt it out in unison.

Come go with me, I'll take you to my home. Oh, by the way, I'm bound for Rome.

The audience jumped to their feet to clap and blocked Thom's view of the dance area. When they settled, the woman was nowhere in sight.

"Where'd she go? I don't see her." Thom searched left and right. "I'm going to go talk to Becca and see if I can get Brown Sugar's name." Thom slapped Melvin's back to say goodbye and sauntered toward Becca. "Hey, girl. Where you been hiding?"

"Thomas Bedford? Is that you?" Becca asked, not rushing to close the distance between them.

"In the flesh." Thom grinned. He looked as cheesy as Bandit smiling out the window of his Firebird. "I haven't run into you in a while. What you been up to, girl?"

"Bettering myself. I graduated from UGA. Now I'm back and working for the auction company."

"We're gonna have to change your name from Bikini Becca to Brainy Becca." The expression of annoyance on her face flew over Thom's head. "And speaking of names. Who was that you were dancing with?"

"Iris Ledbutler? Tsk. You should probably leave her alone." Becca removed the bulldog hoodie from around her waist and began putting it on.

"Ledbutler?" Thom's surprise caused him to draw his head back like a turtle retreating into its shell.

"You heard me. Ledbutler. Iris Garcia Ledbetter. But she pronounces it weird. Ear-Reece. Spanish or something. She's the heir to the Ledbutler estate." Becca stuck her hands into the pouch and started walking to the apple cider booth. Thom followed at her heels like a hungry puppy. "Remember that notice that was in the paper after old man Ledbutler died?"

"No, not really. I heard he'd died and didn't leave a will."

"He didn't have any kids. And he didn't leave a will because the house and property are in a trust from back when it was a plantation. It's crazy. I'd never heard of anything like it. The place passes to a direct descendent of Nathan Ledbutler. And that's how come they had to post that public notice asking for relatives." She took a sip of the hot spiced juice.

"Wait, so this girl just shows up and says she's a relative and gets a million-dollar property for free? Damn."

"Um huh."

"That can't be right. She's a Ledbutler? I'm more likely to be Nathan's long-lost love child than that girl. Sssshiit."

"Why? 'Cause you're white and she isn't?"

"Nah, 'cause she ain't even from around here. Who's her mama? Where'd she come from?"

"She had the proof. She's his great-great-great-great-great-granddaughter."

"Proof?" Thom stopped her so that they were facing each other. "What proof? Nathan Ledbutler's been in the ground at least a hundred years."

"I work at the auction company. I fact-checked the provenance."

"Pro-what? You speak French, now?"

Becca rolled her eyes. "It's like this: if an heir can't prove they're legit, then the estate goes to public auction. I met her because I had to check her papers—family Bibles, birth certificates, newspaper clippings, bank records, all that kind of stuff. Believe it or not, she is a direct line. Mr. Cooper was right pissed he didn't get the contract to auction the estate. He had me triple-check every document. He didn't believe her. I think it gave him a mental breakdown. No one's seen him in months."

"Damn. She gets the land and the house and everything."

"Yup."

"Have you seen that house? Shit, I bet there's silver hidden in the attic and coins under the floorboards. Gawd, I'd like to get in there and have a look. Is she planning on staying or selling?" The pair resumed their stroll through the arts and craft booths.

"She's staying. Told me she wants to connect with her roots. Restore the place and set the history straight."

"Restore it? There's an idea. Get her to hire me." Thom nudged Becca with his elbow. "Don't give me that look. I'm good with tools."

"That look had nothing to do with your handyman skills and everything to do with your sticky fingers."

"I don't steal. I find. There's a big difference."

"Tomayto. Tomahto." Becca motioned to a display of carved gourds and antler-handled knives across the lane from where they stood. "That's her booth. I'll introduce you, but like I said. I think you should stay away from her."

"Why?"

"She's coming off a bad breakup. Some asshole named Derek dumped her pretty hard."

"Rebound booty is my specialty." Thom squeezed Becca's ass. "Remember?"

"Keep your willy in your pants." Becca hip-checked him and slapped his paw off her. "And your hands out of the sugar bowl."

Thom smoothed and tucked in his plaid shirt. "You know I've got a sweet tooth." He ran his fingers through his hair. "Introduce me to that sweet brown sugar."

"Incorrigible." Becca wagged her head.

***

NW Georgia Bugler
October 28th, 1990

Identification is proving difficult without the heads. The second body does not match any local missing persons. Officials are asking the public to come forward with information.

Thom drove his truck through the ornate brick and iron gates and up the grand driveway lined with oak trees. The two-story Ledbutler house had six white columns, dark green shutters, a wide porch with several rocking chairs, and brick steps. The house and the driveway were exact opposite in both scale and care to the slave quarters and servant's entrance Melvin and he had used the other day. Half a mile from one another but worlds apart.

At Chiaha, they'd chatted between browsers and buyers. Thom had complimented Iris on her knives and craved crafts. The blades were etched with symbols. "They're Tsalagi. Those three letters mean *Cherokee*." He figured she must be one, being from that area in North Carolina. He'd never had an Indian chick, and that made her hotter. Thom had offered her his handyman skills, anything to get into her house and her pants. They'd made a date.

"Oh, hey. I'm almost done laying the drop cloths." Iris met him at the door. She wore overalls and a headscarf with an off-center knot that looked almost like a flower. Iris's two braids were tucked out of sight. She had a roll of masking tape in one hand and some tool in her bib pocket.

"Follow me." Iris's voice was soft and sweet like the scent of garden roses. She led him through the foyer. They weaved around a set of sawhorses and stepped over a circular saw.

In the parlor, Thom looked up at the sixteen-foot ceilings. A dusty chandelier hung on a long chain from a cracked plaster medallion. "We're gonna need a bigger ladder." He chuckled. He lowered his gaze and took in the bottom half of the room. The hardwood floor and antique furniture were covered in plastic. A large fireplace with a marble slab mantle commanded the east wall. He drew a quick intake of air when his eyes landed on the mantle's centerpiece, a sixteenth-century conquistador's sword. "Wow. That's a mighty fine replica." He tried to play it cool, but his voice cracked.

"Oh, it's not a replica. It's real. It was found on the property in 1817." Iris moved a five-gallon paint bucket away from the two others in the corner.

Thom inched closer to the polished blade. It was in impossibly pristine condition. His hands began to sweat. "Somebody's pulled the wool over your eyes. No way that's real." He stopped himself from touching the bulbous end and the cage-like guard that looked like tendrils of smoke.

"Nathan Ledbutler kept a meticulous diary. Actually, his obsessive notes proved my birthright. It's fascinating reading. Do you read history?"

Thom looked at her. She was cute. "I'm not much into book-learning. I just kinda pick stuff up from here and there."

"There are thirty-four volumes. He filled a diary per year. He lists the amount of cotton harvested, the weather, the births and deaths of livestock, the health of his slaves, and even his copulations." Iris looked Thom in the eyes and laughed harshly. "Can you imagine that fat old man fucking his wife? And that's not all he fucked." She pronounced the hard K with such force that her upper teeth bit into her lower lip.

The way her voice had changed from dulcet to vulgar had excited him. He could ignore her anger. He saw the passion in her. He salivated watching her lick the bite mark from her lip. Thom was caught between desires. He remembered why he'd wanted to meet her at the festival before he'd known she was an heiress. Maybe he could have both things he wanted, the sword and the girl.

"Let me show you the rest of the house before we get started." Iris's tone was honey again. The tour of the house was short and only the first floor. There was a library filled with leather-bound books and civil war artifacts. Thom's head spun, dizzy with the relics and treasures around him. On a sideboard, there was a brass bowl filled with arrowheads and flint tips.

"Were those found on the property, too?" Thom had been right about the land. He just hadn't had enough time to excavate it.

"Yes. It's in one of his early diaries. They were plowing a new field and found a burial. Nathan ordered one of his slaves to throw the bones into the river. The man didn't want to. He was afraid of stirring up ghosts. Nathan had him whipped."

"Damn. I guess the legend is true. Meaner than a yellow jacket." Thom fidgeted. He didn't like hearing the old man had thrown away the Indian bones.

The room off the study was a bedroom with a four-poster bed. Framed black and white photographs hung on the wall. A picture of the house in earlier days caught his eye. The people in the portrait were in 1800s clothing. A large, bearded man sat in a chair and a well-dressed woman with curled hair stood beside him. Two children in frilly bows and buckled shoes sat at his feet. Behind the landowners, there was a Black man in a suit and a Black woman in an apron.

Iris stood next to Thom and looked at the photograph with him. "1868. That's Nathan." She put her finger on the girth of the man in the chair. "And that"—she stroked the glass over the aproned woman—"that's my fifth great-grandmother."

Thom shifted from one foot to the other. "We should probably get cracking on the painting."

"Yeah. It's a big room." Iris smiled. "I'm going to get us some tea. I'll meet you in the parlor."

"Sure thing, ma—" Thom ate the word he'd naturally had said. Master. He went through the study on his way to the great room and pocketed a few arrowheads and musket balls. Waiting for the iced tea, he stared at the sword and schemed a way to get it. If she trusted him, if he painted all the rooms, he could walk out with it one day. She didn't need it. It wasn't really hers. She'd lucked into it. He cared about what it was, how much it was worth. He deserved to have it.

"Here's your tea." Iris startled him from his daydream.

He took his glass and drank from it, never taking his eyes off the sword. The sweet liquid coated his throat. He finished with a loud ahh. "Delicious." He used the back of his hand to dry his mouth.

"You like it?"

"The sword? Hell yeah, I like it. Wished I found it. Think there's any more buried treasure in the field?" Thom handed her his empty glass.

"I don't know. I doubt it. Nathan probably took all there was to take. But that doesn't stop folks from trying. I think I saw someone digging around in the lower field near the river the other day." Iris turned her back to him. She put her full glass and his empty on top of the two buckets in the corner. She pointed to the one she'd moved to the center of the room. "That's the paint for this room. The top's a little tricky to get off."

"No sweat." Thom bent and tried to remove the lid. It was crimped shut. He knelt and began prying the edge with a screw-driver.

Iris stood behind him and watched him work. He was struggling. "I told you it was a pain in the neck." She took the antler-handled knife from her bib pocket.

"Got it!"

Thom lifted the large lid off as Iris leaned over him. With the knife in her right hand, she drew the blade across Thom's neck and pushed his face into the gelatinous paint. She wiped the blood from the blade and put it back in her pocket.

"Graverobber."

Iris got the electric saw and finished the job. She watched as Thom's head sunk into the once white, now pink paint. She sealed the can with a hammer. Dipping her index finger into a puddle of spilled paint, she wrote a T on the lid before moving it to the corner with the others. Each bucket had an initial. D. M. T. Before rolling his body in the plastic drop cloth, Iris dug into Thom's pockets and retrieved the items he'd taken. She'd bury this body further away from the river.

NW Georgia Bugler
October 30th, 1990

The Etowah Mounds Museum received an anonymous donation yesterday. A genuine conquistador sword believed to be from Hernando de Soto's 1560 expedition was delivered with a request that the item be buried on sacred ground.

"Damn. Thom is gonna lose his head when he hears this."

Melvin snapped the newspaper in the air and tossed it on his kitchen table. He went to the wall phone and dialed Thom's number.

"Pick up the phone." He let it ring several more times. "Where the hell have you disappeared to?" Melvin hung up the phone. He hadn't seen or heard from Thom in two days, which was unlike him. He should have been knocking on Melvin's door with some grandiose plan to find a treasure trove of antebellum silver saved from Sherman's March to the Sea.

Melvin flipped open the phone book and dialed Becca's number.

"Hey, Becca. Do you have that girl's phone number?"

"What girl?"

"That hippie chick you introduced Thom to?"

"Who?"

"You were dancing to the Allman Brothers with her."

"Multi-colored Lady. Love that song. That's my friend Iris."

"Yeah, that's the one. What's her number? Thom was headed out there to do some painting for her and I haven't heard from him since."

"Melvin, don't worry about Thom. He's a tomcat and that's probably exactly what he's doing. Even though I warned him to respect Iris and give her some space."

"What do you mean?"

"Nothing. Don't worry. He'll turn up."

"Yeah, you're right. I'll probably find him by the river with a six-pack."

BLUE SKY

Michael Farris Smith

James walks into the hallway where I'm leaning next to the women's bathroom door, waiting on my daughter. I saw him come into the sandwich shop as we got up to move toward the bathroom. He's with his two boys in their high school baseball uniforms. I thought I'd hang out here until they sat down, and then slide by them and out before he noticed. But here he is, taking off a blue baseball hat and wiping his forehead and shaking his head.

"Win or lose?" I ask.

"Won today, but that's only the third one all damn season. Feels like I care more about it than they do, and it eats me up."

We shake hands and I say, "How's Marilyn?"

"Good. Cleans out the pool usually while we're at the ballpark. Baseball bores her. Can't sip on a margarita in the bleachers."

He knows I know this. Knows I've sat around their pool a hundred times while Marilyn sipped a margarita. Sat around their pool a hundred times while the kids were younger, Katy older and bigger and letting the boys take turns standing on her shoulders, and while they splashed we talked about what we liked and didn't like and James always took up for baseball while Marilyn said it made her ache it was so slow but she liked the tight pants they wore. And we'd laugh and drink some more and watch the kids and swear it was hotter this summer than last.

"Let's play golf some time," he says. "It's dry out, but course is in decent shape."

"Sounds good," I say.

James puts his hat back on his head.

"I'm serious," he says.

"Okay," I answer, then tap on the bathroom door. "Katy? You okay?"

James reaches out and puts his hand on my shoulder. "It's been a while, you know. I'll buy the beer and cigarettes."

"It ain't that," I say.

"I'm just saying. It's been a while."

"I heard you the first time."

I know how long it's been. I wake up and when I'm riding to work, I hear the man on the radio give the weather and the date. I have anniversaries and birthdays marked on the calendar, and they pass and that means years and I know how damn long it's been. I know how old my grandchildren might be if I had any and how many years before I can retire, and every January I watch the Super Bowl.

James backs off but then says, "Let me and Marilyn have you and Katy over for dinner. Katy can splash around in the pool."

"She's not a dog," I say, then apologize, know he didn't mean it like that. "Call us."

"I will. Tomorrow. Marilyn can come over and be with Katy. I'll spot you five strokes."

"And buy the cigarettes and beer."

"I said it. I'll do it. Call you in the morning."

"But don't call early," I say. "Sometimes mornings are difficult."

The bathroom door opens and Katy comes out and her shirt is soaked in the front. I smile and say, "At least you tried."

"Hi, Katy," James says. He touches her arm, winks at me, and goes into the men's room.

"C'mon," I tell her, and I take her hand. We walk back to our table and I take some napkins and wipe her hands and face and neck. Someone has cleared away the drinks we weren't finished with, so we leave and stop on the sidewalk in front of the sandwich shop.

"What now, Katy? Go to the park? How about a ride? We can roll down the windows and listen to the radio?"

She nods and says, "Ride." Her hair is in a ponytail but strands have come loose and fall across her face. I tuck them behind her ears and then we hold hands and walk across the parking lot to the car, the sun behind and our shadows leading us.

They tell you to take some time for yourself, don't try to do too much. Take breaks. You have your own life and you can't ignore that. That's what they tell you. Then they tell you to snap out of it and live life again. But they don't give you the card with the schedule that tells you when one stops and the other starts. I don't like twenty-four-hour nurses, and if she's going to be closer to what she was, then I have to be there. And now they tell me I'm holding the reins too tight. But they don't see the same life in her that I do. There *is* a slight twitch in her eyes when I walk in the house after work, I don't care what they say. They said you couldn't fly out of a car and bounce and live either, but she did. They never thought she'd walk and talk, but we did it. Started from scratch, right foot before left, fork to mouth, c-a-t spells cat.

I open her car door and buckle her in the passenger seat. I get in and we listen to a country station that plays Loretta Lynn and Conway Twitty. It's late Saturday afternoon and we drive out to the state park and ride around the lake. Damn near every camping spot is filled with pop-up campers or massive driveables that look made for rock stars. We pass a steady stream of kids on bicycles and moms pushing strollers. Dads stand next to grills, holding beers and spatulas. Playgrounds are scattered through the park, and kids are up and down slides and hanging from monkey bars and building sandcastles in the weed-infested sand.

We wind through and stop at the park store, and I buy two Cokes and two oatmeal pies. I unwrap and pop tops and give

Katy her share. She looks out the window and says, "Birds."

"Where, honey?"

She points across the parking lot, but I only see a truck and a fat sunburned man on a kid's bike. She stares past him, and I wish I could see what she sees, accept the innocence of her imagination without feeling helpless. Even now, as before, her mother's squint is there, the corners of her eyes wrinkling together as if they were being pinched. Katy was a mature teenager, handled her mother's passing easier than I did, when it would have been easy for her to ride around with boys and smoke in the backyard when I was at work. Maybe she did all that too. At the funeral I watched her move with grace, shaking hands and letting herself be hugged by friends who believed she needed it, and I remembered myself at sixteen, wild with hormones and lusting for parking lot fistfights, and I wondered how she came from me.

I never believed that she would be anything but special.

We ride again and we pass by the basketball courts. No one is playing, but a kid in a go-cart rides circles around the court.

"What?" she asks and points.

"That's a go-cart. Like a little car." She waves to the kid and he waves back.

We make one more loop around the park, then go home.

When we walk in the door, the phone is ringing. I walk Katy to the couch and grab the cordless and it's James's sister-in-law Sharon. Though we haven't met, I've heard all about Sharon as she's juicy gossip, at her peak and proud of it. James gets bits and pieces of her escapades from his wife, then adds details that make her adventures more flamboyant and unleashes them to the boys on the golf course like he's on a locker room soapbox. He's been telling me that she's what I need, that she could show me what it's like to play again. That I wouldn't do nothing but smile.

"Thought maybe you'd like to have a drink tonight?" she says.

"It's kinda short notice and I don't know if I could get a

nurse for Katy this late."

"What would you say if I said I had one for you already?"

I know she's not desperate, but she certainly sounds that way, and I bet James is standing there poking her with a stick.

"Who's the nurse?" I ask though I know this is opening the door to this happening, and I don't really want it to.

"I have a girlfriend who works at the nursing home who said she'd do it."

I look at Katy. She's staring at the only wall in the living room that doesn't have any pictures on it. "Okay," I say softly.

"What?"

"Okay. I said okay."

She tells me to get shined up, don't eat nothing between now and then, and she'll pick me up at seven and the nurse will be with her.

I sit down with Katy and tell her she will have a visitor tonight, but that I won't be gone long.

"Okay the TV," she says. I tell her yes but that we've got to eat and bathe before our friends arrive.

Katy, once a slim girl though her favorite dinner was Pringles and chocolate ice cream, has gained close to fifty pounds in the two years since the wreck. She can be clumsy, so I help her in and out of the tub, but she's hard to convince that the bath serves a purpose. I close the toilet lid and sit down, try to make sure she washes but instead she smacks her flat palms on the water, then wets the bathroom floor with a stream that shoots out of the mouth of a rubber fish that I should have never given her.

"Make everyday events entertaining, something to look forward to," the therapist had told me, so she's got a tub full of rubber fish and mini-basketballs that she shoots at a hoop suctioned just below the showerhead. She's one out of four when I ask her to stop and wash her hair.

She does all her washing and I help her up. I help her dry off and then help her to get dressed in jogging pants and a T-shirt. She comes into the kitchen where I'm making spaghetti and she sits on a stool in the corner.

"I want a go-cart," she says.

"I don't know," I answer and am surprised that she remembers. "Do you know how to drive?"

She nods and puts her hands at the ten and two position. I laugh it off, seems like we had this conversation during her sophomore year in college when she said she was tired of biking and walking and catching rides. When I bought her the car that twisted and flipped and ejected her like a torpedo.

I pour a jar of sauce over the browned meat, and she comes over and takes the wooden spoon out of my hand. I ease behind her and sit on the stool. She stirs with both hands, and concentrates on her motion, careful to keep a steady rhythm. She'll stir until I ask her to stop, but for now, I like watching.

"They say the way to a man's heart is through his stomach," Sharon says after the first round when I mention I'm hungry.

"I didn't mean it like that," I say.

"Let's get a steak." She waves to the waiter for menus we already turned down. She orders us another round when he brings them. I've already told her I'm not much of a drinker but she doesn't pay attention.

"What time is it?" I ask.

"Your daughter's fine. Leslie is a good nurse and a good woman. I like mine bleeding. You?"

"Done. Well."

The waiter comes back with two more bourbon and Cokes and we tell him about the steaks. Sharon folds her arms across her big bosom and squeezes like she's missed herself. She could pass for thirty-five, maybe even thirty in the right light. Even if all you could see of her was her neck, shiny and snake-like, you'd still know she was a looker.

"Are we having fun yet?" she says. "Do you like to dance?"

"Probably not the way you do. I've got a feeling you can

shake it."

"Few more of those and you'll be ready."

"Not tonight. Katy goes to bed early. I'd hate to keep your friend."

She leans over and runs her fingers across the top of my hand. "That's what she's for," she says and I wonder how much it cost James to put her up to this. "Let's just see how it goes, okay?"

I nod.

The steaks are delivered, and before the waiter can get away, she gets us another round.

"I was thinking we'd go to the bookstore for coffee after dinner," I say. This will lose her for sure.

"Sounds good," she says. "How's the cow? Mine cooked a little long."

"Mine not long enough."

"You should try it redder anyway. James says you have a daughter. Kathy? How old is she?"

"Katy. And she's twenty-three."

"I've got a son. Did I say that already? Sometimes I repeat myself."

"You didn't say it," I answer, and I don't want to be a son of a bitch but can't seem to help it. I know there's an etiquette to these situations that would be very easy to follow. From what I remember, I'm supposed to smile and give a little descent humor, but it's like a foreign language I knew once but let slip away over time in bits and pieces.

I eat several bites, then say I'll be right back. There's a payphone next to the restrooms and I call home. The nurse answers on the first ring.

"She's fine," she says. "Cinderella is on cable. She likes the colors."

"Did she finally eat some spaghetti?" I ask.

"Every bite," she says. "Have a good time," she says and hangs up before I can ask anything else. When I turn around, Sharon is there. She holds out her hand and I take it and she walks me back to the table and she smells like peaches. When we get to the table, a man in a black suit is in my seat.

"Well, damn," he says and stands up. "I saw you over here, Sharon, and thought you were alone. Thought I'd join you."

"Didn't you notice the other plate?" she says as she leans over to kiss his cheek. He's a knockout. Taller than me. Younger than me. More hair than me. And dressed like a hitman.

"This is my friend Gary," she says.

I reach out and shake the tall man's hand. "Pull up a chair?"

"Nah, won't mess you two up," he says.

"Maybe some other time," Sharon says and rolls her eyes at me, but I don't know why as they make a striking, sharp couple.

"Really," I say. "Grab a seat."

"Let me grab my drink from the bar," he says. Sharon watches him walk away, then licks her teeth.

"I'll be going now," I say.

"This isn't the way the evening is supposed to go," she says. "You were here first."

"But *look* at the man. Look at you. I should be going anyway. I'm sure your friend has something better to do with her Saturday night."

"If you don't like me, drop the diplomacy and say so," she says, and people from other tables are watching. The only thing to do is cut clean and run.

"I like you. I had a ball. Tell James I said hello."

"You tell him," she snaps.

"I'll take a taxi home." I hold out my hand but she doesn't give me hers. I force a smile and step through the tables and have the hostess call a cab, then wait on a bench outside the front doors.

I count to two hundred and seventy-seven before it arrives. I walk over to it and the restaurant door opens behind me and Sharon comes out alone.

"You know," she says, "I'm not like they say I am."

"I don't know what that means, Sharon," I say. "It's nothing against you."

I climb in the cab and she hasn't moved, her hands crossed in front of her. Her crimson dress clings to her figure like Saran wrap. I open the cab door and say, "C'mon," and she gets in with me, forgetting about her car.

She sighs only a little when I give the driver my home address. The driver has the radio tuned to an oldies station and they're playing a live performance from the Temptations. We let down the windows and she sways and rolls her arms and claps like she's seen them perform on television. I want to move along with her, but the rhythm has never visited me so I avoid the embarrassment and enjoy the show. Her hair spray won't hold in the wind but she doesn't complain. By the time we make it home, she has resorted to a rubber band she found on the floor of the cab to pull it all back in a ponytail.

We go inside and Katy is asleep on the couch, the nurse asleep in my recliner, though it's only a few minutes after nine. I walk over to Katy and brush her hair away from her face, kiss her forehead, think that maybe her way is better. Closer to bliss. Sharon walks around the living room and over to her friend, but when she reaches out to wake her, I say, "No. Wait." I motion her over.

We go out and at the end of the driveway, take a right on the sidewalk.

"Where are we going?" she asks and slides her hand in mine. I look at her and ignore the twist in my stomach.

"Just walking," I say. "It's good for you."

"I've heard that," she says and she stops us, reaches down and pulls off her heels, and heaves them back toward my front yard. "Okay."

"Pretty good arm," I say. "For a girl."

"I had three brothers," she answers. After a block of quiet strolling, she asks how old Katy is. I tell her she already asked but then say twenty-three again.

"That's how old I was the first time I got married."

"The first time?" I say, and we laugh together.

"I didn't mean anything back at the restaurant," I say. "I just haven't been out much and I think I forgot how—"

"It's okay. Nobody really knows anyway."

Soon we're blocks away from the house. We dodge cars pulling in and out of driveways, swat away mosquitoes, make fun of the pink flamingos in a flower bed. There's no moon as the sky is cloudy, and I hope it will rain so I won't have to make up something to put off James and the golf course tomorrow. But he won't give up even if I avoid it.

"Let's turn back," I say. She had dropped my hand but she grabs it again, walks faster, says, "I'll race you." She starts to hop, then breaks into a run, dragging me along, and I haven't run in umpteen years and my legs won't go as fast as my brain wants them to and she lets go, dashes out in front of me, and though she's getting away, I hear her shouting, "They're not gonna catch her! They're not gonna catch her!"

She wins by half a block. When I finally make it to the yard, she's sitting on the front steps, her shoes dangling from her hands as she crosses them over her knees. I sit down beside her and look at her slick legs.

"Do you see your son much?" I ask.

"Not really. He's off at school."

"Which one?" I ask. She thinks, doesn't know. Mumbles something.

"You're wearing me out with all this running," I tell her and ask if she wants something to drink.

"What you got?"

"I think I got some bourbon in there somewhere. Might be old."

"Shelf life," she says. "It never runs out on a good drink."

She nods and I get up, but before I go in the front door, I turn and look at her, the ponytail, the bare feet, and she could be a little girl.

HIGH COST OF LOW LIVING
N.B. Turner

License plates scare me. Have the past three days. Before turning off my ignition, I search the parking lot for any trace of Indiana. If there's even one plate showing evidence of a Hoosier, I leave. Find another place to eat, or drink, or use the toilet. This diner is no different. I scan every car before I feel comfortable going in. Maybe it's safe. Another day of driving and maybe I can relax. Maybe Mississippi is too far for someone to follow me. And maybe I can live long enough for my clients to stop wanting me dead.

When I walk in, the place is almost empty. One guy at the counter but no other customers. The waitress at the front asks me if I'm alone. I nod, so she grabs a menu and shows me to a table. It's too open, too exposed. Someone could sneak up on me there. "You mind if I take a booth against the wall?"

"Sure, why not? Place is pretty open right now," she says.

I slide into the booth, edging my duffel bag toward the wall, and start looking over the menu. Everything's fried or smothered in gravy, ready to turn my arteries to concrete. But what does my blood pressure matter now? Might be dead in a couple days anyway. I saw an Indiana plate in Tennessee yesterday, out past Nashville. Too far from home to be there by accident. Despite my diversions and side trips off the highway to try and dodge him, Travis was still following me.

Ring ring goes the bell above the door. My eyes shoot up

from the menu. An older couple walks in. A man in flannel with camouflage suspenders hobbles to a table, his arm looped in the crook of a woman who looks like she's about to topple over with him. Nothing to worry about.

Air rushes into my lungs as I try to calm down. My heart keeps knocking at my ribs like a kid begging to be let out of his room. I dread the chance that I'm going to look up and see someone I know.

The waitress comes back. "What are you thinking for tonight?"

"Chicken fried steak," I say. "And you guys still serving this evening?"

"Yep."

"A cup of coffee, then," I say, passing back the menu.

"What's with the duffel?" she asks.

"Books," I tell her. "Like to keep them close. I go through them quick."

"Fair enough." She goes to the cook with my order.

I pull a small black notebook from the side pocket of the duffel. My old clients' names cover the pages, side by side with a dollar amount, a goal they wanted to reach. I was their financial advisor and investor, their link to the stock market and Wall Street's money. I was their friend once. For five years, they trusted me with their money and retirement plans. For most of those years, I was there for them, putting their money into the market with care and concern, happy to take the meager commissions when their investments paid off.

The names in the book change after a few pages. My neighbors vanish and the names of my "creditors" take their place.

Gambling can be an expensive habit. You start small and catch a hot streak. You think you can't lose, so you bet more and more. Then the faithless Lady Luck turns on you. You lose and lose again. You try to plug the hole in your wallet, but you can't. So bad money follows bad money until you're so deep in the hole you can't see a ray of fucking sunlight.

My penchant for Chicago strip clubs didn't help my little habit either. Anytime I went to the city, inevitably I'd end up there. When things got real bad, business meetings were just excuses to drink and see the dancers. Expensive ways to ease expensive losses. Sometimes the people I was meeting would pay, and then eventually I always did.

Add in a wife who became an ex-wife after finding out you slept with one of those dancers, and you've got the past two years of my life. After selling a cheap time-share and liquidating a few other assets, I was still in the red. Particularly with my divorce lawyer, who was more interested in billing hours than making sure my ex-wife didn't take everything I owned.

That was when the commissions were no longer enough to pay the bills, and the money my clients gave me to put into the market started going into my pocket. Small chunks of cash at first (one or two hundred bucks at a time), then more and more when it was clear my clients weren't catching on to me. After the cash proved insufficient, I sold their stocks and collected the payoff "on their behalf." Whoever said numbers don't lie never saw what I could do with an excel sheet and the newspaper stock prices.

At first, I told myself I'd put their money back in the market when I was out of debt. Now, I see how badly I was lying: to my clients, to myself, to anyone I spoke with. I've been out of debt for three months, and my neighbors hadn't gotten a dime back. I was too focused on rebuilding the life I had before all my debts took hold.

The number on the last page of the notebook reminds me how much I've got to live on: one hundred thousand dollars. Chump change in some places, but it's enough to help me get on my feet in some backwater part of the south.

Ring ring. Another look at the door. A man. But no one I know. He takes a seat at the counter without waiting for the hostess.

Must be local. Nothing to worry about then.

I take some more deep breaths, trying to remember those meditation courses my ex-wife had forced me to take years ago. "Deep breathing can help calm anxiety and bring you back from anger and stress." My ass, it can. Each breath just reminds me that I have reasons to be anxious.

A blue oblong plate of chicken fried steak clatters onto the table in front of me. A black waterfall of coffee streams into a ceramic mug next to my hand. "Miss," I say.

"Call me Sarah," she says.

"Sarah, would you happen to know if there's a motel nearby? I'm looking for a place to stay the night."

"Yeah, cheap place just about a half mile up the way."

"Perfect."

"Let me know if you need anything else."

Yeah, sure. A time machine would be nice. I'd go back and fix all my shit. "Will do," I say instead.

The steak's tough chewing, but the gravy makes it a bit easier to swallow. A good gravy can make anything tolerable. But it was nothing like what I could get back home: my old diner made a steak tender enough to melt in your mouth. The owner had been an old client, willing to give me a discount for my services. I doubt she'd serve me now. I doubt anyone back there would help me. Hell, if I was drowning, they'd probably fling a boulder on top of me.

I shove the black notebook back inside the bag. Cash bricks poke against the inside wall. It was everything I could draw from the bank before I ran. Getting far enough away that I could buy a different car or a shack and lay low for a while was the best plan I had.

The cops don't scare me. They're easy to avoid. Laws sometimes protect the guilty as well as the innocent. My clients are different. They don't care about whether or not the prosecutor could prove I was guilty. They only care I stole their retirements, their savings, their lives.

The fear of one has had me driving for the past two days: Travis. A mechanic with scarred knuckles, cold eyes, and a voice that stayed rock-steady no matter his mood, he made me nervous even before I'd done him any wrong. I can't explain why I felt cocky enough to take his money; money he needed to pay for his mother's cancer treatments. But I can understand why Travis blames me for her death.

Travis was the hardest client I ever earned. When I first approached him, he said, "I don't need some kid who got all his know-how from some Chicago college to tell me how to handle my hard-earned cash." Took me two years to wear him down and make him trust me. Had to go bow-hunting with him to do it (and prove my lack of hunting prowess in the process). I constantly reminded him that I was from the same town, and that I was one of his folks, and the fact I'd left town to go to school didn't matter, on and on and on.

Eventually, another client had let slip that he was saving his money to help take care of his mother. With that piece of information, it was easy to convince him that I could get him enough cash to give his mother anything she needed.

What a shame she was diagnosed with cancer right when everything started going downhill. For weeks, Travis told me that he needed to get his money out of the market. I told him I'd sell everything, but it would take time for things to go through. "Might be a bit before it reaches your bank account," I told him.

"Just get it done. Her treatment's expensive. And she can't pay the bills on her own."

He believed the half-lie: I had sold everything, but the money wasn't going to his account. Rumors were filtering through some of my clients: I was a thief, a scam artist, a miserable bastard, and that I'd taken every dollar they'd given me for my own gain. People eventually started asking for their money back. That was my cue to take the money and run like hell. Then a week ago, after days of phone calls from people asking after their money, he came to my house. I'd been drawing out cash for a while, getting ready to make a move out of town. The safe behind my bed was stacked with thousand-dollar bricks. Maps of towns in Mississippi and Florida were strewn on a table near the door. Real estate options for the next step.

Past midnight, his fist railed against the door like he was trying to knock it from its hinges. "Where's my money, Brent?" he said. He didn't raise his voice. It was the most frightening thing about him.

"In the market," I told him. "Why are you at my house?"

"Someone told me you've been swindling us all. That your investments are garbage. Tell me it's not true. And then tell me where my money is."

"It's in the process of transferring to your account."

Fingers wrapped my throat like a noose. Travis was big, but I'd never realized his strength. His grip felt strong enough to crush my throat. "Say that again." His tone was begging me to lie once more. He wanted a reason to kill me.

My hand grasped for his and tried to peel it off my throat. There was no space beneath his palm, no give in his wrist. Solid as a rock on my trachea. "You're right. It's not," I said, voice scratching past his hand. He loosened his grip. Air never tasted so good, even though it reeked of his body odor and dip-scented breath. "But I don't have it here. Give me some time and you'll get the money."

"Do it fast. You've wasted my time and my mom's. If I'd had that money, I could have taken her somewhere else. Somewhere better. But you decided to jack me around..."

"I'll get you the money! You can take your mom anywhere with it."

"If she dies, it's on your head."

As he drove off, I locked my door and ran to my liquor cabinet for a bottle of vodka. My hand shook so bad, I poured three ounces into a glass and spilled three ounces on the carpet. *That redneck's gonna kill me,* I thought. I packed my bags, wrote a note for my ex-wife, telling her the house was hers. Cash in the duffel, I sped out of my driveway. Travis was the first to threaten me, but it wouldn't be long before the rest of the town was ready to kill me as well.

I was thirty miles out of town when Travis called. *"My mother just died,"* he said.

"My condolences."

"Fuck your condolences, you son of a bitch." The click at the other end of the line was the starter's pistol: I was in a race for my life.

The chicken fried steak is cold on my plate now. I'd lost my appetite for it. Dredges of coffee and cream line the bottom of the mug, almost every drop drunk. My eyelids are heavier than lead weights, sinking over my eyes like theater curtains announcing the end of the show. Two days with almost no sleep does that.

Sarah comes back and I don't even ask for the bill. "How much do I owe?"

"About twelve bucks."

I open my wallet, peel off a twenty, and slap it on the table. "Any change is your tip."

"Thanks. You all right?"

Sliding out of the booth feels like trudging through wet concrete. My body wants to stay put, to sleep. Cash inside the duffel shifts as I sling the straps over my shoulder. "Fine. Why?"

"You drank about three cups of coffee and you look tired enough to fall over on your face."

"I'll be fine." My feet drag like weights as I shuffle to the door. "Half mile up the road?" I ask Sarah.

She nods and points out which way "up" translates to on a flat road.

I reach my car and start driving that way. I see a liquor store on the way to the motel. God, I need a drink. I pull in, forgetting to check the plates. In and out fast is the goal. I go in and that beautiful black label is right at eye level. The bottle of Jack Daniel's is in my fist and on the checkout before the next customer comes in the door. I pass the next guy as I leave. Pulling out, I see an Indiana plate. The thought of driving on into the night crosses my mind, but the weight of my eyelids reminds me that sleep is non-negotiable. I couldn't leave Indiana and run for two days only to crash on the highway. I drive down to the motel and park somewhere my plate is hidden from the highway.

The woman in the office lets me pay cash for the night. The office opens to the back parking lot: a level plain of gravel stretching to the edge of a forest. I take only my duffel of cash and the bottle of Jack Daniel's inside the room. I'll keep my friends and my enemies on the opposite sides of a locked door, thank you very much.

Drawing the curtains blocks the afternoon sunlight. It'd be dusk soon anyway. Bad diamond-patterned wallpaper grates against my back as I slink down behind the bed. Out of sight from the door and the windows. The carpet's stiff as steel wool. When my hand rubs against it, I feel like it's going to peel away skin. Three nights ago, I'd slept on silk sheets. Now I'm just trying to figure out how to avoid getting shot in the middle of the night. How quickly things go from high to low.

The bottle of Jack twists open, cracking like a boxer's knuckles. It's a beautiful sound to me: speaks of possibility, newness, things yet untouched. Breaking the seal sounds like hope, and it feels like the only hope I have left. One sip and I start to pretend I'm home again, or at one of those clubs. It's all just pretending now anyway. I know I can't run forever. But maybe I can run for just long enough to feel free.

I wonder how my clients figured out what was going on. What did I screw up on those fake returns I'd given them? Maybe I didn't give them enough credit. Maybe they'd suspected something all along and just needed a bit more proof before calling me a thieving bastard. Maybe it doesn't matter now and thinking about it is just a waste of time. One more sip of whiskey and all the questions shift into sleeping dreams. Questions and dreams do me no good though. Sleep is the only thing I need. Sleep and then I can run some more.

Sunlight pierces through the crack in the curtains. It doesn't strike me, but I see it on the wall just above the bed. The Jack bottle is tipped on its side, half of it spilled into the carpet. The cap is lost somewhere under the bed, and I don't bother searching for it. I check my watch as I take a long morning piss. I'd stolen twelve hours of sleep. *I could make Mississippi on that,* I think. Hopeful, I grab the duffel bag and head out to my car.

Hope vanishes when I notice my car almost flat on the ground. Every tire had been deflated. Nails in the sidewalls. *Maybe I could reach a shop,* I think. *Get it fixed and then keep driving to the coast.* An arrow punctures my leg before my hand can open the door.

Searing pain shoots through my leg and into my hip. Nothing else compares to this: it's sharp and intense and every time I twitch, it hurts worse. My knee buckles, more pain barrels through my hip, igniting nerves all the way into my back. Weak fingers grip the door handle, then the next arrow pierces my shoulder.

I don't want to scream, but I can't help it. A deep, guttural sound shoots from my throat. "Goddamn it!" I fall to my side. The barbs cut deeper into my muscles and I scream more. My head turns toward the forest at the reach of the parking lot. Just past the tree line is nothing but shadows and leaves. My eyes scan it like I'm searching *The Wall Street Journal*, and when I find the glint of an arrowhead, I scream. "He—" It breaks into my chest before I complete the word.

Gravel grinds into my leg and my side as I try to drag myself toward the office and away from the forest. Travis struts out from the trees. Camouflaged legs appear first against the grey stone of the parking lot. The closer he comes, the more I see of him: legs, then hips, then torso, and finally his head standing over me. "I warned you," he says. He steps on my stomach, pinning me flat.

I try to speak but nothing comes. Nothing that makes sense anyway. Any gasp of air hurts like hell. Each hesitant gulp of oxygen is smaller than the last.

The duffel bag of cash is beside me on the ground. Travis glances at it. When he opens it, his face twists like a bad theater mask: deformed and wrong and evil. "A thief to the end, huh?" He zips it back up and slides it behind him, out of my reach. Then he drops his knee on my stomach and brings out the knife.

My left hand rises and swings for his face. The arrow in my shoulder burns as I twist. Travis catches my hand. "Just don't fight, Brent," he says. He levels the blade, pointing it at my throat. The knife breaks through my windpipe, and I feel the blood trickle down the side of my neck. He pulls out the blade and the trickle grows.

The last thing I see is Travis gripping the duffel bag of cash, his money finally back in his hands. I hope it satisfies him. It's too late for it to give either of us what we wanted. It couldn't bring back his mother, and it couldn't give me back my old life. Cost of bad business: everyone loses something.

MELISSA

Jessica Laine

He used to call me sweet. That was back in high school when I was an honors student and Troy Clayton was a jock who'd been kicked out of two schools before landing at Our Lady of Sorrows in Saint Petersburg, Florida.

My parents, Ernesto and Yanice García, were strict. I worked almost every night and wasn't allowed to date, but I played the piano and could participate in Sorrows' annual talent show. My senior year, both of my parents had to work at Con Tí Ki, our family-owned bar, so I drove myself.

I knew who Troy was, but he didn't know me. He was everything that I, the daughter of Peruvian immigrants, would never be—blonde, popular, and sure of his place in the world. We stood next to each other behind the stage curtain, and I felt his eyes on me as I crossed the stage to the piano. Normally, I performed classical numbers but as my parents weren't there, I played a slow version of "Crazy in Love" by Beyoncé in a minor key instead. As I left the stage, Troy thrust a piece of paper into my hands. "Call me," it said. As he and his band, Crossroads, filed onto the stage with their instruments, I found a seat at the back of the auditorium. It smelled the way all school auditoriums do, like bubblegum mixed with sneakers and hormones at their peak.

There was something about the way Troy carried himself, like he was something special and you were lucky to watch him perform. He walked up to the center mic and adjusted it, his pecs straining against his tight T-shirt. Then he adjusted his guitar and nodded at his band. I recognized the opening chords of an old song:

"Crossroads, seem to come and go, yeah,

The gypsy flies from coast to coast..."

Was it my imagination, or was he singing to me? His voice was crystal clear and rang throughout the small, packed auditorium. The band was good, but Troy was something special. His hair shone like gold under the spotlight as he hit all the right notes. Watching him perform, I realized I'd never wanted anyone or anything as much as I wanted Troy Clayton. Until then, everything in my life had been about things my parents wanted: good grades, long hours of working at the bar without complaint, no boyfriend. Their careful planning went out the window the night I met Troy.

"You're a gifted musician," he told me as I drove him home from the talent show.

"Thanks. You are, too." I didn't dare look at his handsome face as I drove; I was afraid I might veer off the road.

"I liked your version of 'Crazy in Love.' It was romantic."

I felt my face flush red.

"Are you seeing anyone?"

I was sure he knew the answer but shook my head.

His sapphire-colored eyes stared at me. "Can you stay out a while longer?"

It was March in Saint Pete, already hot and muggy. I drove past faded bungalows on small city lots filled with lemon and orange trees until he told me to pull into the parking lot of a greenhouse that had gone out of business. I lost my virginity surrounded by the steamy scent of jasmine, which blew in through the car window. We were inseparable for the rest of the school year.

Almost inseparable.

Troy had band practice and football practice. Sometimes, I'd hear whispers that he'd slept with some girl at an out-of-town gig or at an away game. One night when I was feeling insecure, I brought up the rumors.

"They're just jealous of our love," he said, tucking a strand of my black, curly hair behind my ear. "Now, let's work on the arrangement for my new song."

Crossroads uploaded videos of themselves playing the songs Troy had written (well, that Troy and I had written) to Myspace. Within a few months, they were signed to a record label and had a handful of hits. People say their songs remind them of The Black Crowes. Nowadays, their songs remind me of how stupid I was not to insist upon a signed contract before handing over my sheet music and lyrics to Troy.

During the past twenty years, our lives had diverged from the paths we'd set out on. For Troy and Crossroads, the hits stopped coming. Each year, they'd play in smaller and smaller venues. I was studying to be a marine biologist. When my father died, I had to drop out of college to manage my parents' bar.

Con Tí Ki is tucked along a curve off Beach Boulevard. Tonight, about thirty people are seated at the Formica bar that sits in the center of the tented building. I'm wiping down the bar when I feel someone watching me and turn to find Troy standing near the cash register.

Although a small beer belly has replaced the flat abs he had in high school and the lines etched across his brow are deepening, he is still a handsome man. He's wearing a Hawaiian shirt and his hair is slicked back. It's dark outside but he's wearing the Ray-Bans I bought him for his birthday, which makes me wonder if he's still getting high. He promised me he was going cold turkey before he left town six months ago.

"Hey," he says.

"Hey, yourself."

He hugs me. When he feels me tense up, he pulls away and gives me the once-over. "You're gaining weight," he says. "You might want to lay off the jalapeno poppers."

"Ha, ha." I cross my arms over my stomach. "How was

Belgium?"

Crossroads has an almost cult-like status in Belgium. Even their newer albums hit the top ten on the Belgian music charts. Troy's been on a European tour for the past six months. Sometimes when he comes home from touring, I need to go to the doctor to get a two-week prescription of penicillin.

"Belgium was great, babe. You should come with me next time."

"Hmmm." I used to get excited when Troy would ask me to go on tour with him. Sometimes, I would even get someone to cover for me at Con Tí Ki, but inevitably he'd find a reason why I couldn't go: too many people, not enough hotel rooms, etc. When he asks me to go on tour with him now, he doesn't get much of a reaction. I can tell it irks him.

Mom, who is working behind the bar, hands me a fizzy water and pours him a Bud Light from the tap. When Troy leans across the bar top to hug her, she dodges him, scowling.

"It's good to see you, too, Yanice," he says as she walks away. "What's up her ass?"

My mother has disliked Troy since day one and says he's *malcriado*, or rude and uncivilized. She also says he's a *pendejo* and a loser who won't ever settle down.

I shrug. "Who knows?"

"Not drinking?" He points at my fizzy water.

"Trying to cut back," I say. "Tell me about Belgium."

"Not much to tell. Can you get me a burger, babe?" He doesn't even look at me as he makes his request, his eyes undressing a group of young women instead. When I return from the kitchen with a burger cooked the way he likes it, I find a giant bear of a man wearing Troy's sunglasses. The man's inebriated girlfriend gathers me in a tight embrace. "These glasses are fucking great," she says.

"Yeah, I know. I picked them out."

"You. Have. Fucking. Great. Taste." She gives Troy a look. "Do I know you from somewhere?"

Troy turns on the smile he reserves for women with big breasts. "Maybe. Ever heard of the band Crossroads?"

"Oh my god, that was my favorite band when I was a little girl!" The woman screams in my ear.

Of course it was.

Later, the Crossroads fan glances admiringly at Troy and tells me, "I can't believe I've just met Troy Clayton."

I drink the rest of my fizzy water and say in a flat voice, "Believe it."

Troy shoots me a dirty look.

The woman looks at me. "I told your boyfriend I'd give him a blow job if he gave me his sunglasses."

This is what I hate about Troy. No matter how old or fat he gets, women still try to get into his pants. He must give off a pheromone like a skunk in heat. I touch Troy's shoulder. "We need to talk." Just then, his phone rings. "I better take this outside," he says as he rises from his barstool.

Next to me sit an older, well-dressed couple and a regular named Emmett whose fleshy jowls and mutton chops remind me of the cartoon character Droopy Dog. He tells them he does construction work in Tampa Bay. "Here's to the economy," he says. As they toast, Emmett splashes some of his beer on the wife. "Whoops." The husband looks annoyed and quickly settles their tab. After they leave, Emmett turns to me. "I'm sorry, Melissa."

It's a slow night and the bar can't afford to lose two paying customers. "It's all right, honey," I say. "Just—don't talk so much to the tourists, OK?"

"When I'm drinking, these things come out of my mouth, and I drive people away. I'm sorry." He looks at me with his hang-dog eyes.

"I know you are, sweetheart." I look at the clock on my phone. Troy's been gone for a while now. "How are you doing, anyway?"

"Not great. One of my very good friends just died."

"I'm sorry to hear that."

"Yeah, well. Colby and I hadn't seen each other in a while, but once upon a time, we were real tight." Emmett crosses his finger for emphasis. "And I can't attend his funeral."

"Why not?"

There's a pause and then he says, "Transportation problems."

DWI? Revoked driver's license? No car?

"I wanna be there so bad. I've known his kids since they were this high." He points to his knee.

"Why don't you mail his kids a card instead?"

"That would be nice. I could do that, but I probably won't." We sit in silence for a while until he says, "I see your ex is back in town."

"Technically, he's still my boyfriend, I guess."

"If you were my girlfriend, I wouldn't leave you here by yourself." He blushes as he says this.

I give him a small smile. "Thank you."

"Life is short." Emmett glances at my stomach as he stands up. "Well, I better get home."

Once he's gone, I step behind the bar and help my mom serve drinks. I have no idea where Troy is, but I watch as the giant scans the bar, looking for his girlfriend.

Typical.

A band called Larry and John is playing tonight. Larry plays the synthesizer and John plays the guitar and they both sing. Their musical selections are eclectic: "Save a Horse, Ride a Cowboy" by Big and Rich; "Disco Inferno" by The Trammps; and "Key Largo" by Bertie Higgins. I hear them play a classic R&B tune and sing along:

"She's a brick…haowsssse.

She's mighty, mighty, just lettin' it all hang out."

Within minutes, the small dance floor is packed. A blonde woman in her mid-twenties waves me onto the dance floor. She looks a little like Cameron Diaz if Cameron Diaz smoked a pack of cigarettes every day. Cameron and I twist, salsa, and tango our butts off until Larry and John take a break. As the music comes to a grinding halt, Cameron grabs my face.

"What's your name, sweetheart?"

"Melissa."

"Melissa, you are a wonderful person. You really are." She smells like a brewery. I really need to talk to Mom about not serving people once they're hammered.

"No, I'm not."

Cameron gives me a big hug and stares deeply into my eyes. "You are really wonderful," she says.

"Well, thanks." When Cameron and her crew take their seats at the bar, I see her pointing at me and saying, "She is so sweet." One of her friends looks at me, rolls her eyes, and deadpans, "Thanks for being *so sweet.*"

I wink at her. It doesn't feel like that long ago that I was in my twenties like Cameron and her friends, but I'm thirty-eight. Has it really been a decade since I last went out with my girlfriends and raised hell? Probably. Most of them are married with kids now. I watched from the sidelines as they graduated from college, met nice men, and got pregnant—while I waited for Troy to propose. Our calls to one other grew shorter and more infrequent until they just stopped. I miss them, but I get it. We've been in different worlds for a while now. I think back to a call last year with my friend Ella. "I wish I could see you, but the kids keep me busy. You know what it's like." Following an awkward silence, she said, "Hey, I'm sorry I said that." No, I didn't know what it was like, and if I stayed with Troy, I probably never would.

Some tourists settle their tab. As they leave the bar, a man yells, "Yeah, that's right, go back to Michigan or wherever. This place is for *real* drinkers." Embarrassed, the man's companion shushes him, but I agree: Con Tí Ki *is* for real drinkers. I'm tired of the hours, the noise complaints from nearby residents, and the occasional bar fights. Serving people alcohol at nine o'clock in the morning was never my jam either.

Kyle walks in. His dark brown hair hangs down past his shirt collar and I watch as he pushes a stray lock off his face.

His job as a contractor keeps him fit and tanned. I admire his backside as he gives Mom a hug.

When we met, he'd just broken up with a girlfriend following a tempestuous, fifteen-year relationship. "I have one lady now who is the true love of my life, and that's the Gulf of Mexico," he said. He told me about his cheap, two-bedroom apartment on the beach. "Life is amazing. On weekends, I peel out of my work clothes and wear nothing but shorts and flip-flops. Friends come over. We barbecue, suntan on rubber rafts in the Gulf, and drink."

"But I just drink on the weekends," Kyle clarified while we were on our first date. "For a while there, things weren't looking so good for me. I stuck seventy-thousand dollars' worth of cocaine up my nose and had to file for bankruptcy. I got divorced and lost contact with my daughter. It was hard, but I pulled it together. A few years ago, my daughter and I got back in touch. She's a sophomore at Emory." He pulled out a worn photo of a young woman with doe eyes, dimples, and a toothy smile. "Isn't she gorgeous?"

His smile as he held that photo of his daughter broke my heart. And when he told me that he liked me and wanted to see me again, I believed him. Don't let this one get away, I thought as he walked me home that night.

"Have you told him?" Kyle asks me after I give him a quick kiss.

"Not yet."

Troy stumbles back into the bar with the Crossroads fan. She makes a beeline for her giant boyfriend, who looks mad as hell. Troy frowns when he sees me sitting so close to Kyle. "Who's this?" he says.

"I'm Kyle." Kyle looks like he's about to say something else. I put my hand on his chest. "I've got this."

"¿Estás segura?" Mom calls out from behind the bar.

I nod.

Troy looks at the three of us and doesn't seem to like what

he sees. "Wait," he says. "I want to sing a song for you."

"Don't," I say, but he's already walking toward the stage, which is empty while the band is on break.

"¿Está loco o chiflado?" *Is he crazy or what?* Mom asks.

Troy picks up John's guitar. John looks at me and I shrug. John goes back to drinking his beer. "This song is for my sweetheart," Troy says into the mic. He tunes the guitar and sings:

"But back home he'll always run, To sweet Melissa."

Troy's Hawaiian shirt strains across his belly as he hunches over the guitar, sweat pouring down his face. This is the person I've wasted most of my life pursuing: a man who doesn't call or write while he's on a six-month tour of Europe; a man who accepts a blow job from some strange chick in the parking lot of *my* bar when he finally lands back in town. Still, he never struggles to hit the high notes. If I close my eyes, I can picture him standing on stage at the high school talent show, the spotlight shining down upon his golden hair. A small sigh of regret escapes my lips. Kyle places a steadying hand on the small of my back. I flash him a quick grin to let him know I'm fine.

When Troy is done singing, I grab his arm and say, "We need to talk." I lead him away from the bar, down a long corridor, and into my office. "Long story short: I want you to give me back the part of the business I turned over to you when you were struggling so I can sell the bar." I set a contract in front of him and hand him a pen. "Sign here."

"Whoa, wait a minute," he says, holding up his hands. "Why would I sign this without running it by a lawyer?"

I try to hold my temper in check. "Because it's not your bar and we're never getting married."

"Who said we aren't getting married?" he says.

"The past twenty years, you *hijo de puta*!" Mom stands in the doorway with a shotgun that's almost bigger than her. I told her to sell the damned thing, that we were more likely to accidentally kill each other than an intruder, but she obviously didn't listen to me. She tips the shotgun toward the contract. "You better sign that piece of paper, *pendejo*, or I'm going to shoot you in the *huevos*. Not that you have any," she adds.

I can tell Troy is wondering if she's serious.

Mom takes aim at a clock advertising coconut rum, which is right behind his head. The face of the clock smashes into a million pieces and tiny slivers of glass fly across the room like miniature projectiles, piercing the exposed skin on the back of Troy's neck and arms.

"What the fuck, Yanice!" Troy looks at me, hoping I'm going to save him from her wrath as I have so many times in the past.

"You heard the lady," I say. "Sign it."

With trembling hands, Troy signs the contract and tips over a chair trying to get away from us. "You're both fucking crazy!" he yells from the doorway.

"Fuck you, Troy!" I yell back. When my heart rate is back to normal, I turn to Yanice. "I told you I don't want that shotgun around here. It's too dangerous."

"I know."

"Mom, you could have killed him."

She sets down the shotgun. "Everything is fine, *hija*. I prayed to la Virgencita and asked for her help. It felt good to wipe away Troy's *cara de culo* or stink eye."

Part of me wants to argue with my mom, but secretly I enjoyed the look of terror that crossed Troy's face as she shot up that ugly clock. I hope he crapped himself. I start to giggle. Before I know it, we're both laughing until tears run down our faces.

"Promise me you won't ever pick up a shotgun again," I say.

"I can't. I'd do anything for you." Mom hugs me and strokes my hair like when I was a little girl. "Just like you'll do anything for your baby when it's born."

I pull away. "You know I'm pregnant?"

She nods. "And I know Kyle is the father. *Las madres siempre saben*. Mothers always know. That's why we're mothers. *Te quiero, hija*."

"*Te quiero, mamá*."

"Why don't you go home?" she says. "I'll close up."

"You sure?"

"I'm sure."

I give Kyle an abbreviated version of events. He says that Larry and John's second set muffled the sound of the shotgun blast. "Let's go." Kyle wraps an arm around my waist. "You and the baby need some shut-eye." Beach Boulevard becomes a little unruly at closing time as people spill out of the bars. It's late and we don't want to walk, so we call Ben's Free Beach Ride transportation service. A few minutes later, a white golf cart pulls up in the parking lot. "Buckle up," the driver says. Con Tí Ki fades into the distance as we zoom down the street and head for home.

IN MEMORY OF ELIZABETH REED

C.W. Blackwell

Roy was drunk on his ass and it was causing us a lot of trouble.

Beth and I apologized for him three times since the first round of drinks, and I nearly fought some college kids on his behalf. The bar was crowded, and Roy wasn't being careful with his elbows. He just couldn't keep himself steady. I wanted to leave, but we'd all come to see Beth's new boyfriend play bass with the house band and I was everyone's ride home.

Lucky me.

When the final song ended and the bartenders shouted last call, I couldn't have been more relieved. Drunks spilled into the parking lot, smoking and hollering, bumming rides into town. It was early spring in central Georgia. The night was cool and clear, fruit trees flowering in the orchards. Blossoms crowded our feet like confetti.

Roy sat in the dirt with his arms crossed.

"Get your ass in the car, Roy," I said. I just didn't have patience for him anymore. I'd been up since 5:00 a.m., worked a full shift at the auto shop. I was too damn sober and too damn tired.

"This place can kiss my sweet ass, Hal," he said.

"Not their fault," I said. "I would have cut you off, too. Sweet ass or not."

"Man, let's get drunk somewhere else."

"Buddy, if you were any drunker, you might catch fire."

Beth shuffled across the parking lot, cool and pretty with her bass-player boyfriend following behind. She looked happy. Dimples showing, Pall Mall glowing at her lips. She introduced me to her new boyfriend, and I shook his hand even though I didn't want to.

Nobody bothered with Roy.

"Can you give us both a ride into town?" said Beth. "Tommy's got a few bucks for gas."

"Is he a good babysitter?" I said. "Roy's about due for a diaper change."

I could tell Beth was good and buzzed by the way her face lit up. When we were together, I'd make her laugh any chance I could. You couldn't fake a laugh like that in a million years.

Tommy set his bass in the trunk of my '72 Plymouth and climbed into the back seat with Beth. I looked around for Roy but he'd disappeared. I checked the front seat, circled the car. Couldn't find him. I opened the driver door, stepped onto the chrome threshold, and scanned the lot. I was this close to leaving his ass behind. All I wanted was to go home, crack a beer, and listen to music while I fell asleep. Maybe I'd pretend it was last summer when Beth would lay catlike beside me, long red hair spilled over the pillows like the bed had caught fire—like the whole damn world had caught fire.

Then I heard it.

A scuffle a few cars down.

An exchange of threats and oaths.

When I came around the back of the car, Roy hit the ground with a brutal groan, nose fouled with blood. The man who stood over him was shirtless and lean, fists balled at his sides. Tattoos of an eagle, a crucifix, and a disembodied pair of titties spilled over his hairless torso. He hauled back and kicked Roy in the ribs.

"All right, he's had enough," I said.

"I'll say when he's had enough," said the man.

Roy wasn't getting up. He touched his face and looked at the blood on his fingertips. I guarded him, my own hands curled into fists. I didn't want to fight, but I wasn't afraid to. A small crowd gathered and someone shouted: "Kick his ass too, Freddy!"

I guessed Freddy had more friends than I did.

He faked with a pulled-punch, then another. Putting on a show. Then he squared off and gave me a hard stare. The eyes of a speed freak. The eyes of a prison-yard brawler. His jaw clenched, and I thought it was as good of a tell as there ever would be.

When he swung, I was ready. I dodged and clipped him in the eye with my elbow, then came up hard under his ribs with my left.

It was enough to send him to the ground.

But Freddy wanted more.

He lunged for my legs and his face met my rising kneecap.

A loud crack. Broken nose.

Everyone winced.

"Get in the car, Roy," I growled.

Roy scrambled into the Plymouth, and Beth and Tommy pulled him through the door. Freddy teetered on his hands and knees, spitting blood. Two of his buddies pushed through the crowd. These guys were much bigger. They looked feral, *bloodthirsty.*

"You're a dead man," said one.

I hurried to the car and shut the driver door before they could reach me. They slapped at the windows, pawing at the locked handles. They pounded and kicked at the door. I fired the ignition and gave the Plymouth some gas. I don't think they were ready for the 440 big-block, because when the RPM needle hit red, they jumped back like they'd just tripped on a rattlesnake. I dropped into reverse and cut into the lot, pitched the wheel, and shot onto the road with the mufflers screaming.

Beth leaned forward from the back seat and touched my shoulder. "You okay, Hal?"

I gunned the straightaway over Lake Tobesofkee, gave Beth a

wink in the rearview. "Not a scratch."

Roy moaned from the front seat. "I got a few."

"You asked for it, dipshit," I said. "At least you picked a fight with the skinny one."

"I always pick the skinny one," Roy said.

I tilted the rearview to get a look at Beth's boyfriend. He sat with his hands in his lap, watching the pines race by. Like he was somewhere else. Beth was such a free spirit, and it surprised me when she dated guys with no personality at all—and Tommy had less personality than a dead bug on a windowsill.

But there was something else in the rearview.

Headlights coming up fast.

I half-expected police lights to commence, but the headlights only drew closer.

Too close.

"I think those guys want a rematch," I said.

Beth looked out the back window. "How far are we from town, Hal?" She sounded worried.

"Not far," I said. "Maybe ten minutes now."

The car swerved into the oncoming lane and attempted to pace us. A red Chevy Nova with stripes down the hood. Fast off the line but nothing much at highway speed. I let them pull up beside us so I could get a good look. Freddy sat in the passenger seat, nose crooked and bleeding. He had the window down and in his hand was a big-ass long-barrel revolver. It was so big it looked fake. Like a cartoon of a gun. He took aim, and that's when I mashed the pedal. I edged them out, but he fired anyway and put a round through the driver window. The glass spiderwebbed and the bullet went straight through the dash, wrecking the speedometer.

"These boys ain't fuckin' around," I said.

"No shit," Roy said. He looked sober as a nun, fingers clutching the oh-Jesus handle for dear life. "What kind of gun was that, anyhow? They huntin' Bigfoot?" The night air rushed into the cab through the busted window and I almost couldn't hear anything but the sound of the highway.

Up ahead was Moseley Dixon Road, the straightest road outside Macon. If I could surprise them on the turn, we'd be a mile away before they backtracked. I weaved from shoulder to shoulder, trying not to give away my next move.

Another gunshot.

Glass pelted the dash.

I took a final sweep across the highway, cut the gas, and dropped the shifter into third. I wheeled hard onto Moseley Dixon, and the right side of the car lifted like you'd see in some Steve McQueen film before it slammed back down. Tommy screamed like a child. The car pitched left, pitched right. It swerved all over the road. For a minute, I thought we were headed into the pines. Once I put my foot into it, we straightened out and launched down the road like a DC-9 racing down the tarmac.

I checked the rearview. The rear window had partially blown, but there were no signs of headlights on the road.

"They missed the turn," I said. "We lost them."

But Tommy kept screaming.

I flicked the dome light.

There was blood on the dash. Blood on the headliner.

Blood everywhere.

Beth hung forward in her seat, hair dangling. When Roy touched her shoulder, she fell back and slid slantwise against the seat like the broken minute-hand of a clock. Her face looked like something you'd see at a butcher store counter. Like all her features had been violently rearranged.

Tommy screamed and screamed.

The headstone read Elizabeth Jones Reed, and it lay beside the plots of her kin in Rose Hill Cemetery on the banks of the Ocmulgee River. The burial was supposed to be private, but word had gotten out and it looked like all of Macon had turned up to put her in the ground.

Everyone but Roy.

I thought it was chicken shit that he didn't show. I felt guilty about what happened too, but I went anyway. I stayed late and watched her casket sink into the hole. The thought occurred to me that a big oak casket might be the only thing in the world to contain all that wild red hair.

I checked on Roy every week or two. Then maybe a month would pass without talking. When he got his one-hundred-day chip, I found him a job at an auto parts store on the westside. It looked like he'd gotten his act together. All the energy he'd put into booze and dope went into his gun collection. Handguns, rifles, shotguns. Some exotics. Like he was preparing for the end of the world. It concerned me some, but in central Georgia, everybody knew somebody with an arsenal in their closet.

A year after the funeral, I got an urgent call from Roy. He wanted to meet at The Sandtrap Lounge on the northside of town and wouldn't take no for an answer. We hadn't spoken in a few months. It was just plain hard to be friends anymore. All we had to talk about was Beth, and I was still a mess over it. I hadn't slept a full night since that big caliber slug took away all Beth's laughs I'd ever hear again.

Roy told me to meet him behind the bar just before midnight, and when I rolled through, I found him cross-legged on the loading ramp, smoking. A sheet of cigarette smoke drifted in the flood lamps over the bay door like night fog.

I cut the engine, cranked the window.

"Hey buddy," I said. The whole vibe felt ominous, and my instinct was to keep it friendly. "What's up?"

Roy flicked his smoke and it pinwheeled into the dark. "Well, it ain't really my news to share," he said. When he said it, another man came around the building, wearing a dirty apron, hair tied in a big ponytail. It took me a minute to place him.

"That you, Tommy?" I said.

"Hey Hal," Tommy said. He didn't look good. Face sunken

and gaunt. Haunted eyes. "Haven't seen you since you-know-when."

I got out of the car, leaned against the fender with my arms folded, trying to make sense of it. "You fellas all right?"

"Tell him, Tommy."

"They're here," Tommy said. "I been runnin' the bar every Thursday and Friday night for a few months now. They come most Fridays, the three of them. They're here now."

"Are you talkin' about—?"

Roy beat him to it. "If you're thinkin' about the motherfuckers that killed Beth, then you'd be correct. Tommy followed them home one night, didn't you, Tommy?"

"Sure did."

"Tell Hal what you saw."

"They got a place out in Dry Branch. All of them livin' together up a rock road."

"It's true," said Roy. "I checked it out last week. Verified with my own eyes."

It was good news for sure, but I didn't understand the secrecy. "If you got them figured, why'd you bring me here? Why not turn them in?"

"There's more," said Roy. He lit another cigarette and spat. "Tommy says they're workin' with the DA. That's why the sheriff won't investigate. That's why they ain't been arrested."

"I don't know it for sure," Tommy said. "But I seen that Freddy guy talkin' to some suits in a car right over there. I think maybe he's an informant or somethin' like it."

Roy watched me, eyes like steel bearings.

Then it hit me.

"You're gonna fuck those boys up and you want my help," I said.

"If we don't do it, who will?" Roy went to the roll-up door and cracked it open just enough to slide out a long black duffle. "Tommy says he won't do it, so it's up to you and me, buddy. Let's do it for Beth."

"Is that what I think it is?" I said.

Roy dragged the duffle the rest of the way down the ramp and rested it at my feet. "You thought I was gettin' ready for the end of the world," he said. "Nuh-huh. I was gettin' ready for *this*."

I ran the zipper halfway up the duffle and looked inside.

He'd brought his arsenal.

Roy's idea was to let Kenny's gang get good and drunk at The Sandtrap—Tommy would make sure of it—then set up an ambush at their place out in Dry Branch. It would look like a gangland-style hit. I wasn't convinced. When Roy climbed into the passenger seat of my car, I aimed to talk him out of it. But the last time he sat there, we were taking fire from those speed freaks and they'd turned Beth's pretty face inside out. Knowing they wouldn't get hooked for it made me a little crazy. Roy had never been right about anything in his life, but this time he'd come close enough to straddle the line.

Close enough to pull me across.

If not us, who?

We sped down the highway past fruit orchards, hickory groves, and all-night truck stops. Brick churches with marquees that read "FREE TRIP TO HEAVEN, DETAILS INSIDE." A mile past the Dry Branch post office, Roy had me turn off the highway and it wasn't long before I cut the lights and drove up a narrow rock road that took us into the pines.

"This is the place," said Roy.

I stopped the car and we got out, circled to the trunk.

Roy unzipped the duffle and handed me a Mossberg pump-action shotgun. He took an identical one for himself. "They had a sale at the gun shop, Hal. You got six rounds loaded up, and that makes a dozen between us."

"What if we end up in a shoot-out?"

"Just keep workin' that trigger, sparky. I got a few tricks in case we get surprised."

"I don't like surprises, Roy."

"You and me both."

We stood in the pines, smoking and waiting. The Plymouth blocked the driveway so they'd either have to get out on foot or back down the rock road. Either way, we'd set the trap.

"Hey, Roy?" I said.

"What, buddy?" He'd leaned the shotgun against a pine tree and was tucking a handgun into the back of his pants.

"I'm not sure Beth would have wanted this."

Roy fished for another cigarette and put it between his lips without lighting it. "I guess we'll never know," he said.

"Well. Thing is, she was kind of a hippy."

"You mean peace and love and Joni Mitchell and all that?"

"She liked Joni Mitchell but that's not what I meant."

"Then you got to be specific."

"She didn't like guns. Wouldn't watch violent movies."

"Well."

"Well, I'm wonderin' who we're really doin' this for."

"We're doin' this for Beth, no doubt."

"What I'm also sayin' is, it's not too late to go home."

Roy took the unlit cigarette out of his mouth and settled it back in the pack. He pointed his chin down the driveway. "I'd say it's a little too late now."

I looked.

Headlights painted the trees, and the growl of a Chevy Nova came trundling up the way. We pressed deeper into the pines so we wouldn't be seen from the road. The Chevy didn't stop; it ran right up into the back of my Plymouth like they never saw it was there. One of the headlights winked off in the collision, and I heard shouting from inside the car. The driver door opened, and a big man with a bald head and ponytail emerged from the driver seat. He slipped on the rocks and caught himself on the open door, clearly drunk.

Roy set the Mossberg on his shoulder and marched forward.

I wasn't far behind.

They never saw us coming.

Roy fired. The bald man toppled into the dirt, and the one good headlight filled with a bloody fog. I started on the windows. What came next was pure carnage. The shots, the glass, the click and slide of the pumps bringing forth the next volley. When we'd emptied the shotguns, not a single window was intact. Even the side mirrors hung shattered from the doors. Thin white smoke curled from the windshield like spirits winding their way to the hereafter.

Roy circled the Chevy, inspecting the interior for movement. Bloody figures slumped and silent. He peered over the bald man with a speculative look, as if he knew some way to confirm death by sight alone.

"The good guys win," said Roy. "Let's get this thing off the road and go home." He reached into the car and cranked the steering wheel, and we pushed the Chevy into the pines. It coasted a few yards before high-centering on a fallen log.

I slung the empty shotgun over my shoulder and Roy found the unsmoked cigarette and set it in his lips, lit it. I didn't know what to say or what to do next. The quiet forest felt peculiar after what we'd done. Night bugs pulsing in the outer dark. The sad chant of a whippoorwill.

Then, another sound.

The groan of a car door.

A figure scampered toward us, strobing through the Chevy's lone headlamp.

Like some ghoul let loose from his tomb.

Roy pulled his pistol, but he was already on me, trying to take me to the ground.

The tattoos, the fucked-up nose.

It was Freddy. *He must have been playing dead.*

I shoved him off, but he surprised me with a hard punch to the gut. When I doubled over, he grappled me, taking me down to the rock road. He was fast. One hand on my throat, the other blocking my punches. He squeezed tighter.

"Looks like he's evened up the score, Hal," Roy shouted. There was an amused quality to his voice. "What a rematch!"

I connected with a punch to the ribs, but he clearly had more fight in him than I did. I swung again, weaker this time. My vision tunneled, a vignette of Freddy's blood-soiled face shrieking in the moonlight.

A gunshot.

Freddy's arms darted into the air in some trick of the nervous system, and he went limp and toppled over me. Blood geysered from the top of his head. I pushed him off, gasping.

"What took you so long?" I said, wiping the gore from my face.

"It was a fair fight, up until that last bit." He returned the pistol to his waistband and gave me a hand up. We each took one of Freddy's legs and dragged him off the driveway.

We did a sweep of the area, collecting shell casings and cigarette butts.

"About time we get outta here," I said, edging over to the Plymouth. The chrome bumper was wrecked, taillights shattered, orange shards mixing with the gravel. "Before someone calls in the shots."

"Hold up," said Roy. He stood with one hand in the air, the other reaching behind his back, listening.

"Now what?"

"Hush up." He fixed on the Chevy.

The door creaked. Another form tumbled into the pine needles.

"Goddamn," said Roy. "How many motherfuckers fit in a Chevy Nova?"

Roy went to the duffle and removed a Maglite, handed me a fresh revolver. We went slowly through the pines, weapons drawn. The form crawled in the shadows, groaning and sobbing. Roy trained his Maglite, and something glinted from the figure's bloody hand.

Not a gun. Not a knife.

We stopped, both of us knowing at the same time.

A badge.

An ID.

He was identifying himself.

I turned back. I didn't want to have anything to do with it anymore. As far as I was concerned, it was over.

Roy called after me. "You gonna make me do it?"

I stopped. "You don't gotta do nothin'."

"What if he crawls to the main road?"

"Look at him. He won't make it that far."

"How do you know?"

"Shit, Roy." A wave of panic rose within me. My hands shook with it. "It's gone too far. This wasn't part of the plan."

"You knew they were workin' with the DA."

"Is that who he is?"

Roy kneeled over the figure, and when he stood again, he had the badge in his hand, turning it over. He whistled. "Looks like Tommy was almost right. They weren't workin' with the DA, though. This old boy is *DEA*."

"That's all I needed to hear," I said. "For the last time, we're outta here." I climbed into the Plymouth and fired the ignition. I called Roy, but he didn't come. I saw him squatting over the DEA agent, their forms yellowed and backlit in the Chevy's headlight. I called again but he still didn't come. When I yelled his name a third time, Roy stood, fingers splayed at his sides as if finding his balance. He hustled across the driveway and got in.

We were a few miles up the highway when Roy broke the silence. It would be the last thing either of us ever said to each other.

"He ain't makin' it to the main road," said Roy. "In case you were wonderin'."

I looked him over, gave a silent nod.

I thought I'd feel relief.

A sense that justice was served.

Maybe the cold satisfaction of vengeance.

But my only thought was that Beth wouldn't have wanted it this way.

I pulled an eight-track from beneath the seat and plugged it into the console. The moon cast a silver spotlight over the hickory groves, and the highway reeled on toward Macon. The bell-like ring of Joni Mitchell's voice crooning about angel's hair and ice cream castles.

I tilted the rearview and got an eyeful of my bruised and blood-stained face.

No, Beth wouldn't have wanted this.

But there was no taking it back.

BORN A RAMBLIN' MAN

Michel Lee Garrett

One summer during his misspent youth, Raymond Reynolds found himself leaving Nashville, Tennessee and wondering if he should head on down to New Orleans.

It was one night on this southward ramble, passing through some nameless patch of country lost to time, that Ray stumbled into a vagrant's oasis: a roadside plaza boasting diesel pumps, a liquor store, a slasher flick motel, and a so-called gentlemen's club named Filthy Billy's. He didn't care to find out how accurate that name was.

Instead, he wasted the last of his cash on a bottom-shelf bottle of something brown and sat behind a dumpster waiting for a southbound tractor-trailer. Until then he was content to drink and pluck away at his guitar, his lone souvenir from his misadventures in Nashville—one that he had, um, "liberated," Ray might've described it, from its previous owners.

He was liver-deep into his bottle when a southbound big rig finally rumbled into the empty lot. He quieted his guitar. A driver emerged and stood smoking, an ogre's frame silhouetted by brake lights. Ray expected him to head to the strip club, but instead he lit a second cigarette and continued waiting in the darkness.

Before long, a second truck pulled in off the highway, circled the lot, and parked beside the first. The ogre opened his trailer. A new figure, tall and narrow like a dead tree, exited the second rig. They stood conspiring. Ray pushed back the wide brim of his flat-top hat and began creeping forward through the shadows. Snatches of conversation reached his ears.

"That ain't what we agreed," the ogre rumbled.

"Ain't no different," croaked the narrow man. "Hell, it ain't even that far."

Ray sidled the length of the trailer and knelt behind the open doors, waiting for his moment.

"It ain't about how far. It's about risk and reward."

"It's good money, and they're already packaged for transport. No trouble for you at all. Just a point A and a point B that needs gettin' to, and you know he don't like to be kept waiting."

Ray peered around the doors. The two men turned their backs and approached the second truck. *Here goes!* The rambler clambered like a rat up into the belly of the trailer. Several dozen boxes of fireworks filled the inside. He curled up behind a stack of red, white, and blue bottle rockets. *Goddamn, is it really almost the Fourth of July?* And then a second question: *How long has it been since I been home…?*

Ray swayed where he sat for a long time, but the ogre did not return. Before he knew it, he'd slipped into a drunken sleep. He dreamt of burgers grilling over open flames, drooling on the trailer floor.

When he woke, it was to the sound of a woman screaming. Ray jolted upright, face slathered in saliva, still half-drunk, and the other half already hungover. He poked his head out from behind his rockets.

His blood chilled in his veins.

Two young women were locked in a cage inside the trailer. One couldn't be more than sixteen, wearing a Nashville Christian School uniform, unconscious on the floor. The other was older only by a couple years, hard-eyed and dressed in denim and leather, shaking her cage bars and screaming herself raw.

"Anyone! Help! *Help!* Get us the fuck out of here!"

Goddammit. Ray sucked his teeth. *Should've picked a differ-*

ent truck...

The girl continued screaming. The truck lurched suddenly to the right, throwing Ray off his feet, then braked hard, sending boxes tumbling down. Ray found himself buried in fireworks, groaning. The girl's screaming hushed.

"Wait. Is someone...?"

Ray held his tongue. The ogre ripped the trailer doors open—three hundred pounds of hulking muscle in overalls, roaring with fury. The girl turned to him, hellfire in her eyes.

"You! Piece of shit!" she shrieked. "Make you feel big and strong, kidnappin' little girls? If there's *anyone here,* if *anyone* can hear me, please—"

The ogre unlocked the cage and threw her to the floor. "Shut your fucking mouth!" He drove a boot into her stomach. "No trouble, he promised me! Twelve hours you were supposed to be under! And here you are, screaming like a goddamn banshee!"

Slapping and yelping filled the trailer. Ray winced.

"You don't understand." The girl spat blood. "I'll *kill* you, you motherfu—"

The driver pulled a Smith & Wesson from his overalls and pressed the barrel to her temple. "No, sweetheart. *You* don't understand. I'll kill *you*, I swear to *god*, if you dare open your mouth *one more fuckin' time*. You understand?"

The girl didn't answer, staring up at him through newly blackened eyes. He moved his finger to the trigger.

"I said, you *understand*?"

"Yeah," she seethed. "I understand."

"Then keep your dickhole closed 'til someone pays to open it." He shoved her back into the cage. "Next time I have to come back here," he said, relocking it, "I'm putting a bullet between your pretty eyes."

The ogre thundered out, slamming the trailer closed. In the reformed darkness, the girl's rage melted into tears. Ray sat there, buried in boxes with his pounding head, wondering what to do. The girl caught her sobs in her throat and forced them back down.

"I know you're here," she said, sniffing back tears. "I heard you."

Ray bit his lip. Could've been the engine groaning, right? Maybe he could just keep his mouth shut, stay hidden, and take the first chance to slip away.

"Nothing?" she said. "Just gonna sit here, ignoring this? Or..." Her tone sharpened. "You with *them*? Supposed to keep an eye on us, make sure we can't get out?"

Again Ray said nothing, part of him *still* wondering if he could get away with hiding quietly—a vagabond Jonah ignoring the storm raging around the ship he'd stowed away aboard. He thought about something his dad used to tell him.

"All you ever do is make *one* decision in life, over and over," the old man said. "Just the one. Ain't sayin' I always made it right. Far from it. But everything you do, you can choose to help folks or to not. The rest is jus' details."

And the devil, as they say, truly is in the details, ain't he?

Laughter punctured his silence. "Okay, wait," she said. "I get it now. You just wanna hang out and *watch*, right? This how you get your kicks, you disgusting animal? You gutless pervert? *You sick fuck*?"

"Woahwoahwoah, that ain't fair," Ray finally protested. "Y-You're making all sorts of assumptions, and..."

"*A'int fair?!* Listen, shitheel, all I know is I got promised good money dancing at Filthy Billy's, and next thing I know I'm locked in a cage being fuckin' *kidnapped*, and you think *you're* bein' treated unfairly?"

"...Fair 'nuff."

"So?"

"So...?"

"*Who the fuck are you*? Why are you here?"

"Oh, I'm just, uh...a ramblin' man, y'know? All I wanted was a free ride."

"You, me, and everybody else. How'd that turn out for ya?"

"Well, I'm *here*."

"Wouldya look at that, me too. Lemme guess: now you're thinkin' you *clearly* made a big mistake and want off this truck, *asap*, am I right?"

"Hey, I'm not a sap!"

"My god. Listen. Dumbass? Are you gonna help me outta here, please? Like… now?"

One choice. That's really all you get in life? Ray sighed. *Might as well make it better than the old man did.*

"Yeah, I reckon my dumb ass is gonna try. Pretty sure I'm about the last person you want in your corner."

"You're higher on my list than our chauffeur. What's your name?"

"Ray."

"Joan. Charmed, I'm sure—you know how to pick a lock?"

"Oh sure," he grumbled, emerging from beneath his fireworks. "No 'nice to meet ya, Ray,' nothin' like that?"

"It ain't 'nice to meet ya!' This is all *terrible*! How goddamn dumb *are* you?"

"Um… fairly."

In spite of herself, she chuckled. "Least you realize it."

"The only one more dangerous than the fool who don't realize it," Ray stumbled toward her, "is the fool who do."

"And which are you?"

"…wha?"

She sighed. "Nevermind. Just get me out."

Ray knelt in front of the cage, trying to eyeball the mechanisms inside the lock. He produced his old swiss army knife and lighter, then struck the flame to better inspect the lock.

"The fuck are you *doing*?" Joan yelled.

"Keep your voice down! I'm *trying* to get you out?"

"The light! The fireworks everywhere!"

"I'm serious, if Shrek comes back here again there is *nothing* I can do, so *shut,* please, the fuck, *up*!"

Which was the exact moment the other victim in the cage

roused blearily back to consciousness, briefly processed her surroundings, and immediately began screaming in blood-curdling terror.

"No, no, no! Fuck! Shhhh!" Ray tried his best to look reassuring. "I'm here to help you get out! Everything's fine!"

Joan bypassed Ray's attempts at subtlety, gagging the younger girl from behind.

"Listen now," she snapped. "I already tried screaming. It ain't gonna work. If the bastard drivin' hears you, he's gonna come back here 'n' kill us both."

Tears welled in the teenager's hazel eyes.

"Hey now," Joan continued. "Listen! It ain't all bad. We're gettin' out of this. Way I see it, we got the upper hand here. You and I ain't even supposed to be *awake* yet, and we got a secret weapon—Mr. Stowaway here, who the driver knows nothin' about."

"And I, just to be clear," Ray offered, "am definitely not some pervert who's only here because he likes to watch, okay?"

The girl made muffled noises of protest, her terror renewed.

Joan looked at Ray like he was an idiot. "Why would you say that?"

"'Cause it's…true…?"

"When you say it like that, it sounds like you *definitely are*."

"Wha!? But you had said!? And I didn't want her to think—"

The younger girl resumed sobbing.

"Please," she moaned. "I'll be quiet…"

Joan sighed and released her. She curled into a ball and sobbed softly into her knees. Joan and Ray both looked to each other. He pointed to her. She pointed to him. Ray turned back to the younger girl, frowning doubtfully.

"So, uh," he ventured, "what's your name?"

Sobbing was the only answer.

"I'm Ray. That's Joan."

Still, nothing returned but crying.

"She was right," he continued. "We're gettin' out of this.

You'll be safe 'n' sound in your own bed 'fore you know it."

The sobbing continued.

Ray sighed. "Look, I ain't good at bein' comforting, okay? One time, had this girlfriend, right? And her cat, Mr. Socks, he was all black with white feet, looked like he was wearing socks, got out and ran away. And *my* dumb ass tells her at least she don't have to scoop up cat shit and clean up hairballs no more. *Not* the right answer, turns out."

"Did..." The girl's voice sounded like it might break at any moment. "Did she find him?"

Ray blinked. "Yep," he lied. "Came back the next day. Safe 'n' sound."

Joan laughed. Ray glared at her.

The younger girl smiled. Her breathing steadied and slowed. "Mr. Socks," she laughed. "It's a cute name."

"What's yours?"

"Kayleigh," she said.

"Great, we all know each other," snapped Joan. "Now how're we goin' to get out?"

"I *was* gonna pick your lock," Ray said, "but *someone* started hollerin' at me."

Joan stuck her hand through the bars. "Give it here."

"Wha?"

"The knife! I'll pick it my damn self," she grumbled. "What kind of thief can't pick a lock by feel?"

Ray handed it over. She worked one of the attachments into the lock, digging like a miner searching for gold.

"Never said I was a *thief*, by the way. Said I was a *rambler*."

"Never met one who wasn't the other."

"Pleased to meet you?"

"Oh yeah?" She pointed to his guitar—rich mahogany, the neck inlaid with silver roses for fret markers, and the pickguard adorned with an image of sunrise breaking over a mountain ridge. "Pretty nice guitar. Where'd you buy it?"

"Um... okay, thing about *that*, is..."

"Exactly. What I thought."

"Wait! This might sound crazy, but does it *really* count as 'stealing' if it's from the *goddamn Nashville Mafia*? Right? There's gotta be, like, a Robin Hood rule or something..."

"You're *so* full of shit," Joan laughed.

"I'm serious!"

"*Suuuuure.*" Components clicked inside the lock. She pushed the door open. "You're a regular criminal fuckin' mastermind. Just look how quick you got that lock open!"

Ray pouted while Joan exited the cage. Kayleigh stayed behind, kneeling with her eyes closed.

"...and even though I walk through the shadow of the valley of death, I shall fear no evil..."

Ray looked to Joan, who looked back to him. Ray pointed to himself, then to Joan, then finally to Kayleigh. Joan sighed and rolled her eyes.

"Hey dummy," she said.

Ray regretted letting her handle it.

Kayleigh looked up to Joan with trembling eyes.

"Prayer ain't gonna help you now."

She gasped. "How could you say that? It was General Robert E. Lee who said prayer is our most *powerful* weapon!"

"Probably why he lost."

"What I think she's *trying* to say," Ray intervened, "i-i-is, um, like the Bible says? God helps those who help *themselves*. And we need to get to helpin' ourselves offa this truck, 'cause we ain't got much time."

Joan scowled. "How you figure?"

"Feller the driver was talkin' to said he didn't have far to go."

"Wait y'all," said Kayleigh.

"Ain't no time for fuckin' prayer!" snapped Joan.

"No, don't you hear? It's...quieter."

The steady whine of the wheels had softened. The truck had slowed, and the hum of the highway had been replaced by the crunching of gravel.

Joan grimaced. "Shit."

"What?"

"We're nearly there."

Kayleigh gasped, gazing upward. "Your rod and your staff! They comfort me!"

"Ain't no time for—"

"You prepare a table before me in the presence of my enemies!"

"Nevermind. What about you, Robin Hood? You got a plan?"

Ray bit his lip, furiously searching for a way out and fidgeting with his lighter. *Wait.* He looked at the lighter, then to the closest box of bottle rockets.

"Fuckin' *duh*," Ray said. "The rockets!"

"You realize they got guns?"

"Said yourself, we got the element of surprise!"

"Think that's enough?"

"It ain't all," Kayleigh said, stepping up beside them. "We also have—"

Joan cut her off. "Are you about to say prayer?"

Kayleigh blushed. "N-No."

"No?"

"I was gonna say '*faith*,' actually..."

"Hell, I'll take faith," Ray said. "If you got any this might work, hold onto it. We're gonna need it."

The truck shuddered to a stop.

"Wherever they was takin' us..." Joan said.

"We're here." Ray took a deep breath. "Back behind the boxes, grab some'a the rockets, let's *go*..."

They waited, breath baited, for their captors to come.

Joan's knee bounced like a rubber ball. "Hey." She turned to Kayleigh. "Now, don't you say a goddamn word, but, um..." Her voice softened. "Maybe finish that prayer you were saying?"

Kayleigh smiled and placed her hand on Joan's anxious knee. Joan placed her own hand overtop. "Even though I walk through the valley of the shadow of death, I will fear no evil," Kayleigh whispered. Joan bowed her head.

Ray had never been a praying man. He removed his hat anyway.

"For you are with me—your rod and your staff, they comfort me..."

A door slammed closed. Muffled voices murmured outside.

"You prepare a table for me in the presence of my enemies. You anoint my head with oil, and my cup overfloweth..."

Footsteps approached. The voices had reached outside the trailer doors.

"Surely goodness and mercy will follow me all the days of my life," Kayleigh prayed. "And I will dwell in the house of the Lord forever. Amen."

"Amen," Joan said.

"Amen," Ray mumbled.

The handles turned and the trailer doors opened. The ogre entered, joined by a new figure in a tailored suit, designer shades, and Rolex watch.

"Bit of a spitfire," the ogre was saying. "Might have to remind her of her manners."

The buyer smiled. "I don't mind breaking 'em in. Part of the fun."

Ray, Joan, and Kayleigh each readied their bottle rockets, taking aim. Ray flicked his lighter. It didn't catch.

"Part of *your* fun, maybe," the ogre said. "Made *my* job more difficult. About an extra fifteen percent's worth, I'd say."

"Wait a minute." The buyer moved his sunglasses down, revealing bloodshot blue eyes. "Where the fuck are they?"

"Where..." The ogre turned to the cage and grew fury-red in the face. "Those fucking cunts!"

Ray thought they were out of time, but the buyer bought them another couple seconds. From inside his jacket, he produced a pearl-handled 9mm H&K and pointed it at the ogre's chest. Ray flicked the lighter again. Still nothing.

"I don't take kindly to bein' fucked with!"

"I ain't fuckin' with you!"

"Then *where* is my *goddamn merchandise*?!"

Joan leaned into Ray's ear. "So," she whispered, "you gonna get it up?"

"I swear," he said, desperately flicking, "this has never happened to me before..."

The lighter finally sparked to life.

"There's no way they got off," the driver said. "They're still in here!"

The ogre began fe-fi-fo-fumming his way toward the back of the trailer. Ray brought the flame from fuse to fuse with shaking hands. The wires glowed red as the fire ate its way toward the rockets.

"When I find you," roared the ogre, "I'm gonna—"

"Wait a second," said the buyer. "You hear that?"

The driver stopped, mere feet away. The hissing of fuses filled the quiet truck. The ogre swallowed hard.

"Get back! They—"

Light, sound, and color screamed through the truck as the rockets burst to life, sparks and fire following like comet tails. One surged right into the ogre's sternum, where it burst like a grenade. The beast stumbled backward, beard burning.

Ray dropped his lighter and led the charge: "Thundercats *hooooo*!"

He grabbed Kayleigh's wrist with one hand and his guitar with the other, charging forward into the chaos. Rockets whistling and popping around him, he brought his boot up into the ogre's crotch, hard enough to send him to the floor. But between them and freedom still stood the buyer. Imposingly tall, head shaved to a polished dome, beard trimmed to cling to his jawline—and pointing his pistol squarely at Ray's chest.

"You got something of mine," he said, gesturing to Kayleigh. "Ain't no one ever told you stealing was wrong?"

Ray didn't answer. Kayleigh's grip tightened around his hand.

"Tell you what. I'm a generous man. You hand her over, and I won't put a hole through your belly." He laughed—a sound like cars crashing. "I'd call that a pretty good deal. Better than you deserve."

Ray gulped, hoping for a miracle. *Wait a second...Where's Joan?*

He glanced back just in time to see her, still at the rear of the truck, lighting another rocket. Ray ducked, yanking Kayleigh down with him.

The rocket ignited and whistled over their heads, burning forward toward the buyer's face. The reflection in his glasses grew brighter, his eyes widening behind their lenses. "Oh *shi—*" It exploded inches from his nose, leaving him screaming on the floor and clutching his hands to his face.

"Jesus Christ, I'm fucking blind!"

Ray put his boot over the buyer's wrist and yanked away his gun. "I'd call that a pretty good deal," he said. "Better than you deserve."

"I'll kill you...!" He swung at Ray, in the wrong direction.

Ray left him there, still screaming, and jumped from the trailer. They were in some warehouse, rusted machinery lining sheet metal walls. Joan ran to catch up, quieting the buyer with a hard kick to the temple. She jumped down beside Ray but Kayleigh lingered inside, still kneeling with her head bowed over the blind man.

"Ain't no time for...!" But Joan's words caught in her throat as Kayleigh turned back to them, shaking the buyer's car keys.

"Thought we'd need a ride out of here," she said, climbing down.

"Thought the Bible said something about not stealing," Ray said.

Kayleigh blushed. "M-Men do not despise a thief if he steals to satisfy his hunger when he's starving!"

Joan nodded. "Proverbs 6:30."

The younger girl gasped. "How did...?"

Joan took the stolen keys. "Maybe we're more alike than either of us would like to admit."

"Hey!" Ray pointed to a luxury SUV parked at the other end of the warehouse. "Maybe we should make like a banana and, uh, *get the fuck outta here*?"

They sprinted toward their escape vehicle. The ogre, his beard singed off and blistered chest flesh visible behind his charred overalls, stumbled out of the truck. He raised his handgun, firing wildly. The SUV's back window imploded, showering them with broken glass as they piled inside.

"Hit it!" Ray hollered, watching the ogre take closer aim.

Joan cranked the keys and slammed the gas. Gunfire screamed, taking out the passenger-side mirror as their tires squealed against the warehouse floor. Bullets flying past them, they sped through the open warehouse doors into the light of day.

Only minutes later, they were back on the highway, the entire ordeal behind them. Ray looked down at the pearl-handled pistol in his hand, wondering if he could pawn it for liquor money. Instead, he wiped away his prints, rolled down the window, and flung it into the underbrush.

"Thank you, God," Kayleigh said, eyes closed and hands clasped, "for—"

A terrific explosion interrupted her, shaking the earth beneath their tires. In their rearview mirror, a volcano of fireworks erupted. Each of them looked at the others. No one said anything.

Kayleigh cleared her throat. "Thank you, God, who are so good and merciful, for your protection and your guidance today..."

Joan rolled her eyes, but with a small smile. She turned to Ray. "So, what's next?"

"You can let me off anywhere," he shrugged. "I ain't picky."

"What?"

"I prefer if you'd *stop*, but I can always tuck and roll..."

"No, you idiot, I—"

Kayleigh stopped praying. "You're... leaving? Just like that?"

Ray looked back and forth between them. Kayleigh stared at him, earnest and expectant. Joan had turned away, watching the road with a sour scowl.

"Well…yeah? I mean, what else would we even…?"

"I don't kn… I just…." Kayleigh sniffled. "Figured we'd at least find a police station, that you'd stick around until my parents came?"

"Yeah…no. I don't really *do* cops." Ray's cheeks burned. "I just…" He sighed. "I'm just doing what I do, okay?"

"What's that?" Kayleigh asked.

"*Leaving*," Joan spat.

"Well…it's time," Ray shrugged. "I hope you'll understand."

The look on Kayleigh's face assured him that she did not. Tears rolled down her cheeks. Joan rested her hand on Kayleigh's, still not looking at Ray.

"I'll pray for you," Kayleigh said.

"I won't," Joan said.

Ray chuckled. "I wouldn't either."

Joan pulled over but didn't bother to stop. Ray opened his door and looked back to them, tried to think of something to say, couldn't, then jumped without saying goodbye.

He fucked up the roll, landed hard, and stood up holding a throbbing shoulder. The SUV vanished into the horizon like the sun into the ocean. A nameless sadness burned deep inside his gut.

"Wait! Fuck!"

He'd forgotten his guitar in the backseat.

ENCORE: EAT A PEACH

"There ain't no revolution, only evolution, but every time
I'm in Georgia I eat a peach for peace."
—Duane Allman

ONE WAY OUT

Bill Baber

You ever had one of those nights where the bourbon went down real smooth and easy and somewhere along the way you just know that something really bad might happen, but you don't care because everything about the night is just so damn good? Might be a pretty girl or a good fight. Might be a band or the crowd at a wild and crazy bar. Could be a lot of things. You're having so much fun nothing else matters except for the magic the night brings.

Yeah, it was one of those nights and nothing bad happened—at least not that night—but that's sure as hell when it started.

Saturday nights in Gainesville were all the same. The bars were packed. Gainesville wasn't a small town, but it sure wasn't a city. It was known as the Poultry Capital of the World and just about a quarter of the population worked in chicken processing plants. Some distinction. Thank God I didn't.

If you processed chickens all week, about the only thing you had to look forward to was tying one on when Saturday night rolled around. Except in the fall, which meant football and just another excuse to get smashed.

So, I was passing this warm, humid Saturday night in May at the Mule Camp Tavern, sipping a good quantity of Kentucky's finest. Bud Miller and the Tallboys were cranking out some down and dirty blues. As you might expect, if you spent all week plucking chickens then getting drunk, a brawl or two broke out. That sums up Saturday nights in Gainesville. And that's as far as I thought that night would go. I might find a fight or maybe one would find me.

I had started feeling pretty tight. Just drunk enough to have an edge. The band was on a break and I felt a tap on my shoulder. I turned, ready to swing and instead looked right into the beautiful brown eyes of Donna Ann Say.

"Don't I know you?" she asked.

"Well darlin'," I replied. "I know who you are, and I know we went to high school together, but I don't recollect we ever knew each other."

She looked a little hurt by my response.

We had run in different circles. She was a cheerleader and dated Darrell Hodges all through school. He was the star quarterback on the football team. After they won the state championship his junior year, he committed to the University of Georgia, which I guess fulfilled his lifelong dream to be a Bulldog. After graduation, he left for Athens. He was thrust right into the starting lineup. They started the season 5-0, and Darrell seemed destined for the pros until a 325-pound defensive end from Bama blitzed and got him from the blindside. He was taken off the field on a cart, everything that could be torn in a knee was. He never played again.

Darrell came home to Gainesville, Donna Ann got pregnant, and he went to work on the processing line at Fiedale Farms. Donna Ann was six months along when she lost the baby. There were rumors that he was a mean drunk and beat her up and that might have caused it. Everybody did know that he was a gash hound who chased tail all over the county like a dog hunts a bone. Because of his football notoriety, it wasn't long before Darrell was made a foreman, overseeing a line of chicken pluckers. The old boy was a long way from the NFL.

My high school years were different. I hung out with a bunch of gear heads. We wore leather jackets and motorcycle boots, smoked Camels, and drank beer most nights of the week. We raced motorcycles and old muscle cars. I could tear an engine apart and put it back together, but I'll be damned if I could diagram a sentence or make any sense out of algebra. Dropped out at the start of my senior year and enlisted in the Navy. Iraq was happening at the time and figured I was safe since sailors didn't do the desert.

I wasn't the kind of guy girls like Donna Ann showed much interest in—at least not then.

I had learned diesel mechanics in the service, and with all the rigs hauling chickens from Gainesville, I had no trouble landing a good-paying job. A few years later opened my own shop. Business was good, I started saving my dough, thinking about going west and permanently leaving Gainesville in the rearview.

Donna Ann asked me to dance. I was drunk enough not to consider the repercussions. Word was Darrell carried a gun, that he was crazy jealous and had shot at a couple of boys he thought might have been tempted by his wife. We danced to an old Elmore James tune. Lord, the girl could shake it. I started to have nasty visions, forgetting the first rule of my official code of conduct—stay away from married poon.

The next song was a slow and sexy thing Bobby Blue Bland had done. She kind of melted into my arms.

"Let's go somewhere quiet and have a drink," she said when the song ended. I was sniffing pretty hard at whatever bait she was trolling with. The scent of her perfume and a peek at a black bra strap sliding down her shoulder from under her sleeveless top had me ready to bite.

We went to a little lounge down the street. A gin and tonic for her, more bourbon for me.

"Tell me what's on your mind," I said. "Ten years ago, you wouldn't have looked twice at me."

"I was lookin', sugar, every time Darrell couldn't see me do it."

"You been waitin' all this time for me?' Ain't sure I believe that, darlin'. You think whatever problems you have are going to get fixed if you go steppin' out?"

"I don't know," she replied. "But I aim to find out. Darrell doesn't satisfy me. I need a man that does."

"What don't you just leave him then?"

"I'm afraid he might kill me if I did."

"What do you think he's gonna do if he catches you screwin' around—and to the man you're messin' around with?"

"He won't catch me." She put her hand on my thigh. "Darrell isn't that bright. I'm smarter than him. Besides, he's chasin' it around half the state of Georgia. Lies to me about working overtime. His paycheck isn't any bigger. He's screwin' half the woman chicken pluckers down at that plant."

"So, you're lookin' for a revenge fuck?"

"That's not a very nice way to put it," she said. "I saw you in that bar and I always thought you might be the kind of guy I could have some fun with. I was just too dumb to know it way back when."

She leaned in closer, ran her hand a little further up my leg. Damn near to my crotch. Ran her long, red nails against my leg.

"You up for it or not? This town is full of horny men on Saturday night. I ain't here to waste my time."

Any judgement I might have used was drowned at the bottom of a glass of ninety proof.

"Follow me home and park in the back. Don't want the neighbors getting suspicious."

I did as I was told. She let me in the back door and without a word led me upstairs.

She shoved me on the bed. The one she shared with Darrell. Within moments, she had me inside of her. Even as she was rocking my world, I was looking around the room. There was a single window. Just one way out if Darrell came home. I wondered how far down it was.

After we finished, we lay there for a minute before she said I should go.

She also said we should do it again. A little voice in my head said "don't ever come back. Be glad you're getting out of here alive." I never thought I would be a back-door man—but that was the door I walked out of. I looked up at the window; it wasn't that far down and there was lawn underneath it. But I told myself I would never leave that way because I wouldn't be back.

That didn't last long. On Sunday, all I could do was think about her. Damn, the girl was fine. Monday I was back at work and had something to occupy my mind. I had a Cummins Diesel torn apart, and just prior to quitting time, she walked into the shop. Darrell worked the four to midnight shift at the chicken plant. I washed my hands and did her on the desk in my small office. She called the next day saying Darrell was at work and wondering if I wanted to drop by. I was drawn like a moth to a flame.

We got together a couple of times a week for a while. I knew I was playing with fire and that I should call it off. But I couldn't. Donna Ann had her hooks in me. I guess one of the neighbors said something to Darrell that made him suspicious. It was an early Monday evening. She had tried to cover the bruises with makeup to no avail. It pissed me off that the asshole had beat this beautiful woman. She deserved something better, and I couldn't help but wonder if it might be me.

I had gotten in the habit of opening that bedroom window in case I needed to beat it out of there quick. It was quiet in their bedroom, but I heard a slight squeak as the front door slowly opened. I pulled on my pants, grabbed the rest of my stuff, and eased out the window. I held on to the ledge and dropped to the ground.

I decided that was it. The bastard could have shot us both. Donna Ann was awfully fun in bed and I dug her, but she wasn't worth dying over.

She was at my shop the next day, sporting fresh bruises. Again, I felt anger.

***

"Why the hell do you stay?" I asked.

"I don't want to, but I have no money. Nowhere to go."

I held her. She softly cried.

"I've got a quarter-million-dollar insurance policy on him. If he was out of the way, we could go to Mexico. Or Costa Rica. Just the two of us."

It was an age-old story. How many saps had fallen for it? Somehow, I did.

We discussed different plans, trying to come up with something foolproof. I had an idea that we might get away with.

Two nights later, I was at their house when he came home. He had closed a bar after getting off at midnight. I had hidden in a closet and snuck up behind him and clubbed him behind the ear with a .45 as he sat at the kitchen table with a bottle of beer and a shot of whiskey. He was out colder than a Wyoming winter night, dropping to the floor like a buck shot with a .30-06. I choked him until he no longer had a pulse, wrapped him in a blanket, and started out the back door.

There were no signs of life in the alley behind the house. I hoisted his body into the trunk of my Chevy and drove to the shop. She followed in his car. I had just finished rebuilding a Peterbilt cab. I transferred the body and drove to a rural road behind the chicken plant. We left his car a quarter mile down the road and rolled Darrell's body onto the pavement. I backed up, got up to fifty, and ran right over the sucker. Went down the road and did it again, this time at sixty-five. There wasn't much left.

I dropped the semi at the shop and drove Donna Ann home. She gave me a quick peck and before she got out said, "After tonight, we shouldn't see each other for a while. Don't want to make it look suspicious. I'll let you know when the insurance settlement comes in."

The story was in the paper. Even made the Atlanta news. The headline said, "Ex-Football Star Dies In Horrific Accident." The story said his blood alcohol content was over twice the legal limit. The theory was that he had gotten out of his car to take a leak and got hit by a semi-truck. End of story. There was no investigation.

Three months passed without a word from Donna Ann. I drove by her house one day after work. There was a for sale sign and another underneath it that read “under contract.” I walked up to the front porch, looked in a window knowing what I would see. The place was empty. Donna Ann and her quarter of a million were long gone.

For me, there had always only been one way out. But that girl had other plans. In the end, they just never included me. I should have known better. Should have never had to go out that back door. More importantly, I should have known when to lay off the bourbon.

She had said she was smarter than Darrell. Turns out, she was smarter than me as well. I should have known that too. Most of all, I should have stuck to my personal code and never become a back-door man. Guess I should have looked for a fight that Saturday night; it would have been a whole lot less trouble.

WHIPPING POST
Bobby Mathews

Sunny had her hand in Eric's lap when I dropped into the other side of the sticky vinyl booth, her arm moving slow and rhythmic, inevitable. She stopped when she saw it was me, the muscles in her shoulders and upper arms taut with anger. No shame, though. She was caught; she knew it, and she was pissed. Eric was an afterthought. He was so glassy-eyed from getting his joint greased that it took him a full thirty seconds to pull himself together. I coulda shot them both right then.

Maybe I should have.

The saloon wasn't nothing but a neon smear. Miller Time and Bud Light, PBR in cold longneck bottles. Smoke so thick you could almost stand on it, the juke playing low-down hurting cheating songs and the sound of billiard balls clicking hard and falling home. The ceiling was brown with tobacco stains and the paint on the walls had been unevenly applied so that it bubbled up and peeled away from the sheetrock. Framed Alabama jerseys hung askew on the walls alongside posters for the Allman Brothers and Molly Hatchet and the Drive-By Truckers. Schooners of cheap draft beer stood half-drunk in front of Sunny and Eric, and the liquid sloshed from where I banged the table with my hip when I sat down. The well whiskey was just like the juke, low-down and mean, and I ordered a double shot of it when the waitress hustled past.

"What are you doing here?" Sunny said. Her hands were

empty now. Eric fixed himself while she reached for the paper napkin dispenser that sat on the table between us. Sunny wiped her hands, wadded the napkin into a ball, and threw it at me. I swatted it away, trying not to think about what she'd wiped on it. "Aren't you supposed to be at your mother's?"

"That's all you got to say? You empty the bank account, you wreck the car. You think I'm that stupid?"

Sunny flashed her teeth at me. She was long and lean, predatory. A cheetah ready to pounce.

"You really want me to answer that?" She asked.

I ignored her.

"You're out with him?" I pointed a thumb at Eric. "With him?"

"Hey," Eric said, and sat up straighter. "Come on, man. None of us expected this. It just, you know, it happened."

The waitress dropped off my double shot and I pounded it down, the alcohol burning away my indecision and leaving me with nothing but a good clean hate. It tasted like all of the shit that I'd taken from Sunny over the past four years, all the times she told me that she was going out with the girls and instead was face down and ass up with some stranger at the Skyway Inn or the Rodeway or the Trailhead Motor Lodge, rooms where you pay by the hour and the walls look like something Pollock might have painted if you look at 'em under a black light.

I shook my head to clear it, stared Eric down with a bulldog gaze. He tried to hold my eyes but finally looked away. Muttered "Sorry" under his breath, but I knew that was a lie because I knew what Sunny was like. Every moment with her was enthralling. When it had been my turn with her, everything felt new and fresh, like soft-bladed grass in the spring and I would have done anything at all to prolong those sweet and happy moments when we were together and nothing else could ever matter.

"Shut your mouth," I told him. "You'll live longer."

***

I met her when I was twenty-seven. That's a great age to meet the woman of your dreams unless your first date is on the same day your grandfather dies. I got the news as I was leaving to pick Sunny up that first time, and I didn't know what to do. My grandfather had been an anchor in my life, a sharecropping farmer who chewed Red Man tobacco and drank warm Schlitz beer when granny wouldn't let him bring alcohol into their house. He had always been there for me, and I had thought in my naive young brain that in some way he always would. But then he was gone and I was unmoored.

I rang Sunny's bell and she answered the door in a yellow backless sundress that made me believe there could be a God. She took one look at my face and knew something was wrong. She did the only thing she knew that would fix it. The sundress puddled itself on the floor and spread out like the dying light of day, and we went to her bed and stayed there for three days. We left the apartment to buy wine or weed, had Chinese food delivered, and the rest of the time we spent naked.

By the time my grandfather's funeral came around, I knew her body like it was a road map to buried treasure. I had traveled the curve of her back and tasted the tiny red blossom of a dilated vein or a broken capillary between her shoulder blades, read the braille of her breasts, and drank from the chalice of her navel. She wasn't perfect but she was perfect to me. She was mine and I was hers and I knew with the certainty of a fool that I would never want anything else and that we would be intertwined like this forever.

Ronnie Locke was the first one of my friends to tell me that Sunny was cheating on me, and I punched him in the mouth so hard that it broke three of his teeth and two of my knuckles. There was no way, no way in hell, that she was cheating on me. She was with me every night except for the nights I was in class trying to finish my degree. I had ten credits to go and economics was kicking my ass so bad that I needed a night off. I stopped off at a supermarket and bought some flowers, a bright spray of yellow and pink and purple that I knew Sunny would love.

I knew something was wrong when I opened the door. The sounds from the bedroom were guttural, moans and panting gasps and strangled cries. I rushed in, worried that Sunny had somehow hurt herself and found her astride some guy I had never seen before, hips bucking hard and grinding down on him the same way that she had been with me just that morning. The flowers fell to the floor and scattered like ashes from an urn. My heart dropped in my chest and I screamed. I had heard people say that they felt their heart breaking and now I knew what they meant. I felt as though I'd been bound, struck hard over and over with something brutally sharp, my heart carved from my chest. But I couldn't move. I couldn't do anything but scream and wait for the next blow to land and pray that it would strike me dead.

The guy rolled away from me to the far side of the bed. He fell on his ass and scrambled around for his pants. He said something, words that were lost in the raging waves of blood pounding in my ears. I don't even remember what he looked like. The only way he mattered was as an obstacle between Sunny and me. Then he was out the door and gone, and it was just us—just Sunny and me again—and my soul re-entered my body.

I trembled when she touched me, and I held her while she cried and said she was sorry. And I believed her when she said that it would never happen again.

Sunny and I had different definitions of *never*. Over the next two years we fell into a pattern where she would find some new guy, grow infatuated, and begin sleeping with him. But it wasn't enough that she cheated. She wanted me to know, wanted to see me choke down her shit and take her back. She wanted to see my heart break, wanted to see my soul take another beating. It became a contest.

"I don't deserve you," she told me one night after I had taken her to a Shakespeare festival. Hamlet, We were drunk on the bard's words and a little high, kicking through the grass of a little park and looking up at the stars winking down on us from an impossibly clear sky. There was no one around. I had my fingers in the waistband of her skirt, my need to touch her, to possess her, overwhelming after the last time I had found her with another man. In bed she had become impassive. I could beat myself against her body like a ship against a rocky shore, hull breaking and everything good and safe spilling out into an angry sea.

She never denied me pleasure but took none of her own, and I considered that a bigger betrayal than any affair that she could ever have. Whenever she left the apartment, I followed at a distance, fearful of what I would find.

One night she drove to the Sun Inn by herself and got a room. I watched from the parking lot next door as she pulled her Jeep into the slot in front of Room 147 and parked. My phone rang on the seat next to me, and it was Sunny.

"Hey," I said when I answered her call. My voice wasn't shaking at all. "What's up, babe?"

"Not much," Sunny said. "I was just about to go into the gym. Wanted to let you know I'm about to hit my Zumba class and won't be able to answer the phone for a bit."

"Oh," I said. "OK."

A late-model Acura with windows tinted so dark they could have doubled as a Republican' heart pulled into the space next to Sunny's car, and a tall, thick-bodied man about my age got out. I knew him. Of course I knew him. Patrick and I had known each other since kindergarten, maybe even before that, a couple of goofy kids trying to learn how to swim at a YMCA summer camp. He played guitar and had substance abuse issues that I heard he'd overcome. I had always liked him and now I hated him.

I ended the call with Sunny, pushing myself to a dead run across the Sun Inn's cracked and buckled parking lot. Got there just before Patrick knocked, my face right up in his. We stared at one another without saying anything, and I knew what he knew. Sunny was his new drug, the thing that got him high. She did the same thing for me. Being in her presence was like blasting into orbit. Being without her could give a man the DTs. Patrick's hand hovered at the door until he dropped it to his side and turned away from me, shoulders slumped. He went back to his car, opened the door, and nodded at me. When he pulled away, I turned to the motel room and mashed my thumb over the peephole on the door to room 147.

My knock was soft, almost timid. Sunny opened the door wide and she was beautifully, wonderfully naked. Her jaw dropped open and her hands came up to ward me offand my arms went around her, the sound of my sobs cut off by her mouth. I bore her back into the room and down onto the bed.

Later, when we were done and the near-perfect darkness of the room had settled over us like a blanket, Sunny said "I'm sorry," and I knew she was sorry while at the same time knowing that she wasn't sorry. If I hadn't followed her, if I hadn't seen Patrick, she would have been as happy under his thick rutting body as she had been beneath me. I understood that it would happen again and again, that I was Sisyphus and she was the stone. And in my secret heart I thought that I could accept my fate, that being with her like this made all of the cheating and all of the pain worth it. I could survive being tied to this whipping post of a woman. I could endure until she loved and needed me the same way I loved and needed her.

The worst lies are the ones we tell ourselves.

I don't know when I started carrying the gun. Sometime in the last year. The comfortable weight of it in my pocket was a balm to my soul. And now as I sat across from Sunny and Eric in this derelict bar, I kept one hand in my jacket so that I could rest my fingers against the hard cold steel of the trigger. That Taurus .38 revolver with the stainless-steel plating was my only anchor, the tenuous thread that connected me to whatever was left of the real world. With my other hand I waved down the server for another double shot. Pounded that one just like I did the first.

The rotgut tasted like hate, but I didn't know if it was hate for her or for me. Maybe it was hate for the world and for everything that had brought me here to a place where there was nothing but hurt and pain and blame. I don't know. Beat a dog and it still loves you with that kind of shaking whimpering crying love that breaks your heart. But you beat a dog long enough and one day it's gonna snap.

I had finally snapped. Across the booth Sunny had registered that there was something different about me this time, and she was trying to get back into her contrite polite sweet young Southern woman act. But I knew it was an act, had known that for years, and I was determined that I wasn't going to fall for it again.

"I'm sorry," Sunny said, but it all sounded rote. The rest of the words didn't matter. I closed her off in my mind. All that was left now was how many times she had made a fool of me. That was the part I couldn't take anymore. Eric looked from Sunny to me and back again, like a spectator watching a tennis match.

"I can't take it anymore," I told her. "You go off with somebody. I chase after you. I don't know what you get from it."

Sunny didn't say anything. She was studying the way the bubbles popped at the surface of her beer. Eric had an arm around Sunny. Protective. Possessive. As if there was anything he could do to keep Sunny somewhere that she didn't want to be.

"I want you to know that I see you," I told her then. "You're a goddamn succubus. You used me up and now that you're done you spit me out. I know what you are."

"Took you long enough," Sunny said. She didn't look up. She couldn't bring herself to meet my eyes anymore.

"Look, man—" Eric started in again, and I took my hand off of the gun just long enough to slap him hard across the face. His hands flew to his cheek, fingertips hovering over the bright red welt I left there. My hand went back to the gun. I almost pulled it then.

"You got something else to say, you can say it to me outside," I said. "Bring the cheating whore bitch with you."

I was feeling bold and inflated, full of anger and blood and bile. I stood up from the vinyl bench, hearing it squeak. I put a twenty down on the table to cover my bill and marched out the door.

The air in the parking lot smelled like soot and burned oil and baking asphalt, but the moon was bright and flat and hard looking down on us puny humans with neither resentment or judgment. I leaned against the wrecked front bumper of my car, the one that Sunny used to leave me that morning. I thought about Gary Cooper in High Noon, and John Wayne as Rooster Cogburn. A man's got to do what a man's got to do and all of that bullshit. When Eric hit the door, Sunny was right behind him.

He stood a few feet away from me, fingers curling and straightening like he couldn't wait to get his claws on me. Sunny stood off to the side a little ways behind him. I pulled the gun and brought it up.

Look what you made me do you bitch look what you made me do you roundheel slut look what you made me do look what you made—

ABOUT THE CONTRIBUTORS

ART TAYLOR is the author of *The Boy Detective & The Summer of '74 and Other Tales of Suspense* and *On the Road with Del & Louise: A Novel in Stories*. His story "English 398: Fiction Workshop," originally published in Ellery Queen's Mystery Magazine, won the 2019 Edgar Award for Best Short Story. His short fiction has also won the Agatha, Anthony, Derringer, and Macavity Awards. He is an associate professor of English at George Mason University. ArtTaylorWriter.com.

BILL BABER's writing has appeared on numerous sites across the web and in print anthologies-most notably from Shotgun Honey, Dead Guns Press, Close to the Bone and Authors on the Air Press- and has garnered Derringer Award and Best of the Net nominations. He lives with his wife and a spoiled dog in Buckeye, AZ. On the edge of the desert and sometimes just on the edge.

BOBBY MATHEWS is a writer and journalist in suburban Birmingham, Alabama. His checkered past includes stints as a bartender, paralegal, roustabout, and reporter. His short fiction has appeared in Rock & a Hard Place, The Dark City, Shotgun Honey, All Due Respect, Yellow Mama, and several other publications. He is the author of two novels, *Living the Gimmick* and *Magic City Blues,* forthcoming in 2022 and 2023 respectively from Shotgun Honey.

BRIAN PANOWICH is an award-winning author and father. His novel, *Bull Mountain*, won the ITW Award for Best Debut Novel, as well as the Pat Conroy Award for Best Mystery. The book was also nominated for the Barry Award, the Anthony Award, the Georgia Townsend Book Prize, and was a finalist for the 2016 LA Times Book Prize. His second novel, *Like Lions*, won him Georgia Author of the Year, while his latest, *Hard Cash Valley*, was released in April 2020 to critical and commercial acclaim. Brian's short stories appear in numerous publications including *Best American Mystery Stories 2020*. He also maintains a popular monthly opinion column in *Augusta Magazine*.

BRODIE LOWE was awarded the 2020 Elizabeth Boatwright Coker Fellowship in Fiction. He was a semi-finalist for the 2020 Nancy Zafris Short-Story Fellowship and a finalist of both *The Broad River Review*'s Ron Rash Award in Fiction and Still: The Journal's Literary Contest in Fiction. His stories have appeared in *The Broad River Review*, *Mystery Tribune*, *Nebo: A Literary Journal*, *Antithesis Journal*, *Eastern Iowa Review*, *The Mark Literary Review*, *The Windhover*, and elsewhere.

CHRISTOPHER SWANN is a novelist and high school English teacher who earned his Ph.D. in creative writing from Georgia State University. In 2018, Chris was a Townsend Prize finalist, a finalist for a Georgia Author of the Year award, and longlisted for the Southern Book Prize with his first novel, *Shadow of the Lions*. His second novel, *Never Turn Back*, was published in 2020. He lives with his wife and two sons in Atlanta, where he is the English department chair at Holy Innocents' Episcopal School.

CURTIS IPPOLITO is the author of *Burying the Newspaper Man*, a crime novel from Red Dog Press. His short fiction has been published with *Shotgun Honey*, *Mystery Tribune*, *Bristol Noir*, Yellow Mama, Ghost Parachute, and others. He lives with his wife in San Diego, California.

C.W. BLACKWELL was born and raised in Northern California, where he still lives with his wife and two sons. He has been a gas station attendant, an auto mechanic, and a crime analyst. His passion is to blend poetic narratives and pulp dialogue to create evocative genre fiction. His recent work has appeared in *Pulp Modern*, *Shotgun Honey*, *Switchblade Magazine*, and *Rock and a Hard Place Magazine*.

JAMES D.F. HANNAH is the Shamus Award-winning author of the Henry Malone novels, as well as the novel *The Righteous Path*. His novel *Behind the Wall of Sleep* was named Best Paperback Original P.I. novel of 2019. His fiction has appeared in *Rock and a Hard Place*, *Crossed Genres*, *Shotgun Honey*, *The Anthology of Appalachian Writers*, and *Only the Good Die Young: Crime Fiction Inspired by the Songs of Billy Joel*. Born in southern West Virginia and raised in eastern Kentucky, Hannah was an award-winning journalist and columnist before moving into governmental public relations. He lives with entirely too many cats in Louisville, Kentucky. He occasionally updates his website at JamesDFHannah.com.

J.B. STEVENS lives in the Southeastern United States with his wife and daughter. His short story collection *A Therapeutic Death* is being released in October 2021, his poetry chapbook *All the Violent Memories* was released in March 2021—both from Close to The Bone publishing. He won *Mystery Tribune*'s inaugural micro-fiction contest and was a finalist for the Killer Nashville Claymore award. His writing has been featured in *The Dead Mule School of Southern Literature*, *Points in Case*, *Criminal Element*, and numerous other publications. He is a veteran of the Iraq war where he earned a Bronze Star. Prior to the war, he was an undefeated Mixed Martial Arts Fighter. J.B. graduated from The Citadel.

A Kentucky transplant, **JERRY BLOOMFIELD** now lives on the east coast of Canada. His work has appeared in *Beat To a Pulp*, *Protectors 2: Heroes*, and *Waiting To Be Forgotten*. Look for him on Twitter at @JerryBloomfield.

JESSICA LAINE writes contemporary crime fiction and horror with a Latinx twist. She has written stories for the Anthony-nominated crime fiction anthologies *Murder-A-Go-Go's*, and *Pa'Que Tu Lo Sepas*. Jessica is a past winner of the Sisters in Crime Eleanor Taylor Bland award and the Mystery Writers of America-Midwest Hugh Holton award. She tweets @msjessicalaine. Learn more at JessicaLaineBooks.com.

JOEY R. POOLE is a writer from South Carolina who would gladly sell his soul to be able to play slide half as well as Duane Allman. *I Have Always Been Here Before*, his debut collection featuring a dozen stories rooted in grit lit and glancing in the directions of horror and science fiction, was published in 2020 by Cowboy Jamboree Press. He is currently working on and seeking representation for a new project, tentatively titled *The Maze Campbell Stories*, a hardboiled detective novel set on the moon.

JOSEPH S. WALKER is a college instructor living in Bloomington, Indiana. He is a member of the Mystery Writers of America, the Short Mystery Fiction Society, Sisters in Crime, and the Private Eye Writers of America. His stories have appeared in *Alfred Hitchcock Mystery Magazine*, *Ellery Queen Mystery Magazine*, *Mystery Weekly*, *Hoosier Noir*, *Tough*, and a number of other magazines and anthologies. In 2019 he won the Al Blanchard Award and the Bill Crider Prize for Short Fiction. Follow him on Twitter @JSWalkerAuthor and visit his website at jsw47408.wixsite.com/website.

MARK WESTMORELAND is a Georgia native living in Oklahoma with his wife and two dogs. He's a part time writer, full time Dawg fan, and bourbon enthusiast. He is the author of *A Violent Gospel*, his debut novel from Shotgun Honey. You can find him hanging out on Twitter @ItsMarkYall.

MICHAEL FARRIS SMITH is the author of six novels, including *Nick* and *Blackwood.* His books have appeared on Best of the Year lists with *Esquire*, *Southern Living*, *Book Riot*, and numerous others, and have been named Indie Next List, Barnes & Noble Discover, and Amazon Best of the Month selections. He has been a finalist for the Southern Book Prize, the Gold Dagger Award in the UK, and the Grand Prix des Lectrices in France, and his essays have appeared with *The New York Times*, *Bitter Southerner*, *Garden & Gun*, and more. He lives in Oxford, Mississippi, with his wife and daughters.

MICHEL LEE GARRETT is a small-town noir author and Pennsyltucky poet. She has investigated courthouse corruption as a journalist, directed communications for a U.S. Senate campaign, and played in a handful of shitty punk bands. Her fiction about recurring protagonist Raymond Reynolds—a country-singing alcoholic vagabond turned hometown pothead reporter—has been published by Flame Tree Press, Close to the Bone Publishing, and Shotgun Honey. She lives in Central Pennsylvania with her partner and their daughters. Follow her on Twitter @MichelMartinGarrett.

N.B. TURNER is a writer living in Virginia, trying to mine stories from his time growing up along the Great Lakes. He hopes one day to write a story with a happy ending, but the best he's done so far is emotionally ambiguous. His work has appeared in *Hoosier Noir*, *Shotgun Honey*, and *Rock And a Hard Place Magazine.* You can follow him on Twitter at @NathanTurner15.

NIKKI DOLSON is the author of the novel *All Things Violent* and the story collection *Love and Other Criminal Behavior*. Her stories have appeared or are forthcoming in *Vautrin*, *Tri-Quarterly*, *Tough* and other publications. Her fiction has been nominated for a Derringer and noted as Distinguished in *The Best American Short Stories 2016*.

ROB PIERCE wrote the novels *Blood By Choice*, *Tommy Shakes*, *Uncle Dust*, and *With The Right Enemies*, the novella *Vern in the Heat*, and the short story collection *The Things I Love Will Kill Me Yet*. All books are available at AllDue-Respect.com, as well as via the usual slumlords. He lives and will probably die in Oakland, California.

RAQUEL V. REYES was raised in oppositional cultures. Her early childhood was not unlike an *I Love Lucy* rerun with a heavy-accented, handsome Cuban father and a red-headed Southern mother whose smile brightened the room. A short story fan all her life, Raquel's stories are in several anthologies, including *Mystery Most Theatrical* and *In the Midnight Hour*. Her Caribbean Kitchen Mystery series is published with Crooked Lane. Raquel's soul food is croquetas with a Jupiña chaser. She lives in Miami, where she watches the waters for mermaids and leviathan. Find her @LatinaSleuths and at LatinaSleuths.com.

S.A. COSBY is an award-winning author from southeastern Virginia. His novels include *My Darkest Prayer* and *Blacktop Wasteland*. When he isn't writing he is an avid chess player, hiker, and lover of fine and not so fine whiskey. He also sings "Whipping Post" badly in the car whenever it comes on the radio.

On the following pages are a few
more great titles from the
Down & Out Books publishing family.

For a complete list of books and to
sign up for our newsletter,
go to DownAndOutBooks.com.

Moonlight Weeps
A Dick Moonlight PI Thriller
Vincent Zandri

Down & Out Books
August 2021
978-1-64396-226-9

Moonlight should be grateful for his current job. But when it becomes clear the cash-starved brain surgeon he's been hired to drive around is protecting his son from a rape conviction, Moonlight becomes disgusted.

When the charges turn into a case of "reckless murder," Moonlight's the only one trying to keep the kid from the electric chair. Then Moonlight and his unwilling assistant, a fat Elvis impersonator, stumble into a much bigger plot and are soon dodging Hollywood obsessed drug-running Russian thugs, corrupt government officials, and the specter of Moonlight's recently deceased girlfriend.

Northern eX
A Vince McNulty Thriller
Colin Campbell

Down & Out Books
August 2021
978-1-64396-214-6

Once a cop always a cop.

Ex vice squad cop Vince McNulty copes with life outside the force by visiting the Northern X massage parlours he used to police. Until a return to his old stomping ground prompts a change of fortunes. Several girls have gone missing. All young masseuses. All from parlours that McNulty has visited.

When one of them turns up dead everything points to a regular customer being involved. And McNulty is top of the list.

Dead-End Jobs
A Hitman Anthology
Andy Rausch, Editor

All Due Respect, an imprint of
Down & Out Books
June 2021
978-1-64396-212-2

A collection of eighteen short stories about contract killers by some of the hottest crime writers in the business.

"An incredible collection of powerful and haunting stories that exist in that shadowy realm between tragedy, nihilism and noir." —S.A. Cosby, author of *Blacktop Wasteland*

Blood Like Rain
A Big Island Mystery
Albert Tucher

Shotgun Honey, an imprint of
Down & Out Books
August 2021
978-1-64396-192-7

Detective Errol Coutinho of the Hawaii County Police faces the most difficult case of his career, when his wife's best friend is murdered.

Eleanor Swieczak's current boyfriend is a man without a past, but Eleanor's own history turns up other suspects, and someone is trying to put Coutinho among them. And what do a legendary marijuana dealer, a rightwing militia, and the coldest murder case in Hawaii history have to do with the case?

Must blood fall like rain before Coutinho finds out?

Made in the USA
Coppell, TX
18 October 2021

64236236R00166